Death on
the Menu

Also available by Lucy Burdette

Key West Food Critic Mysteries

An Appetite for Murder

Death in Four Courses

Topped Chef

Murder with Ganache

Death with All the Trimmings

Fatal Reservations

Killer Takeout

Death on the Menu

A KEY WEST FOOD CRITIC MYSTERY

Lucy Burdette

CROOKED
LANE

NEW YORK

PUBLISHER'S NOTE: The recipes contained in this book are to be followed exactly as written. The publisher is not responsible for your specific health or allergy needs that may require medical supervision. The publisher is not responsible for any adverse reaction to the recipes contained in this book.

Published in the United States by Crooked Lane Books, an imprint of The Quick Brown Fox & Company LLC.

Crooked Lane Books and its logo are trademarks of The Quick Brown Fox & Company LLC.

Library of Congress Catalog-in-Publication data available upon request.

ISBN (hardcover): 978-1-68331-746-3
ISBN (ePub): 978-1-68331-747-0
ISBN (ePDF): 978-1-68331-748-7

Cover illustration by Griesbach/Martucci
Book design by Jennifer Canzone

Printed in the United States.

www.crookedlanebooks.com

Crooked Lane Books
34 West 27th St., 10th Floor
New York, NY 10001

First Edition: August 2018

10 9 8 7 6 5 4 3 2 1

For immigrants everywhere, who dare to leave what they know and love in search of a better life

One day in Cuba,
I met a lady
Who made the best coffee
And Cuban toast.
She told me fantastic stories
And showed me how to make
A real café con leche.
I will never forget
The Cuban Coffee Queen.

—From the menu of the Cuban Coffee Queen,
Key West, Florida

Chapter One

This frozen daiquiri, so well beaten as it is, looks like the sea where the wave falls away from the bow of a ship when she is doing thirty knots.
—Ernest Hemingway, *Islands in the Stream*

Some days you can take the temperature of our island's anxiety by reading the column in the *Key West Citizen* called "Citizens Voice." Those phoned-in snippets of opinion can veer into the red zone on any number of topics—leaf blowers, the homeless, traffic, how the city handled the latest hurricane, a new amphitheater at the waterfront.

But the comments and rants and worries about this weekend's Havana/Key West conference sounded even more hysterical than usual. For one, none of us seemed to understand its true purpose. Were we celebrating our shared connections with Ernest Hemingway, who'd lived in both cities? Were we discussing environmental issues? Making music together? Or was there some unspoken political agenda about which most of us residents were being kept ignorant? Even my police officer pal, Steve Torrence, and my detective boyfriend, Nathan Bransford, didn't seem clear on the agenda. Or, more likely, they weren't able or willing to share it with me.

Rumors had circulated that both Raúl Castro and Jimmy Buffett were scheduled for brief appearances at the Harry S. Truman Little White House, where the conference would be headquartered. This would gum up traffic on the island and leave us open to all manner of visiting nut jobs.

I believed the Jimmy Buffett scuttlebutt because Parrot Heads, Buffett's super-fans, had been pouring into town over the past few days dressed in Hawaiian shirts and parrot hats. Since it wasn't the season for their annual convention, I suspected they'd gotten some insider information about Jimmy's schedule.

But Castro in Key West? That seemed downright preposterous. On the other hand, it would definitely up the ante for the weekend, as protestors who felt the United States should have no contacts with a repressive Communist country clashed with people who believed this kind of event would help the Cuban people find a voice in the free world. The comments in the paper had been coming fast and furious and ugly, reminding me of a full pot of potatoes boiling too hard. If someone didn't turn down the heat, there'd be a huge mess on the stove.

Why did this matter to me—Hayley Snow, food critic for the style magazine *Key Zest*—aside from the sheer entertainment provided by the wacky comments in the *Citizen*? Because my mother had somehow wormed her way into landing the catering gig for the three-day event—a huge coup for her fledgling business—and had asked for my help. The fact that she had been chosen to cater the weekend of joint Key West and Havana discussions and events was beyond miraculous. Since so many weddings and other special events occurred during our island's high season, many experienced and accomplished chefs vied for plum catering gigs. We were neither experienced nor accomplished, not in the way the bigger local chefs were. Nor were we Cuban. But hopefully my mother had deflected any possible complaints about that by hiring two women of Cuban descent who happened to be amazing cooks.

In the days leading up to the event, Miss Gloria, my octogenarian roommate, and I had been pressed into service as Mom's trusty sous-chefs. We were already flattened by the first day of food prep. After enjoying a glass of wine on the deck of our houseboat, we planned for an early night.

The evening felt wintry by Key West standards—temperatures in the sixties and a wind blowing from the south that caused our boat to rock with a steady motion. We had fleece blankets wrapped around us, purring cats on our laps—my tiger-striped Evinrude and her black Sparky—and a plate of nibbles stashed on the little table between our chaise lounges. We'd already scarfed down the jalapeño poppers. The pink shrimp still sat on the plate in a red pool of spicy cocktail sauce. It was hard to work up an appetite for the little buggers when we'd been shucking skins and digging out those disgusting veins all afternoon—and still stank of the sea even after our showers.

The sun had set half an hour ago, brushing a tinge of rose on the bank of clouds that hung over our houseboat neighborhood. I could hear the clink of silverware on plates and the soft drone of the nightly PBS news from a boat up the dock—probably Miss Gloria's best friend, Mrs. Dubisson. My friend Connie's baby babbled "ma, ma, ma, ma" a little farther down. And on the boat next door, Mrs. Renhart murmured terms of endearment to her three elderly animals, one Schnauzer and two felines.

Miss Gloria and I shared a grin. We had heaven right here on earth, and we knew it.

"I hope we like the new neighbors," she said for the umpteenth time. She ran her hands through her white hair so it stood up in elfin peaks and pointed an arthritis-crooked finger at the FOR SALE sign on the houseboat to the other side of us.

"We've got to hope for the best," I said, squeezing her birdlike hand and trying not to think about the group of college kids who'd taken a tour of the place over the weekend, beers in hand and voices thundering.

"This place is too cool," one of them had boomed.

"It's lit!" answered another.

"I think that means they love it," Miss Gloria had said, her face drooping all sad and worried.

My boyfriend, Nathan, thinks Houseboat Row resembles a trailer park, only floating. "Why do you want to live somewhere where everyone knows your business?" he keeps asking.

"We love that," I've told him more than once. "They're our friends. Miss Gloria has known some of these people for over twenty years."

I have to assume he's thinking about our future life together, though we've touched on that only in what other folks might think are the vaguest terms. Last fall, we witnessed my mother and her Sam taking wedding vows during a hurricane when we all believed we were goners. Nathan and I came out of that close call pretty sure we would end up together. Though we haven't gotten specific, he knows—I think—how much I love weddings, but am anxious about marriage. And I know, with him having been married before and then divorced, that he's even more uneasy about both.

But he doesn't seem to grasp that Miss Gloria couldn't stay here if I moved out, that I'm the bulwark of friendship that stands between her and a move to assisted living in the frozen north. Her sons wouldn't be able to stomach her living alone. Honestly, I'd give up marrying Nathan before I'd abandon my friend.

As I got up to pour one more slosh of wine in our glasses, a text message buzzed in.

Miss Gloria glanced at my cell's screen. "It's Prince Charming," she said with an impish snicker. I snatched up the phone.

Parking lot in five?

The usual terseness of Nathan Bransford. I can never tell until I see him whether he wants to give me a good-night kiss (be still my beating heart) or give me one of his professional warnings, using my full name for emphasis: *Hayley Snow, stay out of trouble.* Or, *Hayley Snow, let me know if you see anything fishy going on.* Or, *Hayley Snow, for god's sake, don't try to handle anything yourself.* Besides being my boyfriend these days, he's also a detective with the Key West Police Department. And he takes his work very, very seriously. To be fair, I have had a tendency to act before thinking things through. Smallish things, like dashing into a restaurant where a crazy person was holding a gun on people I knew and loved. But what was I supposed to do, leave them there to be mowed down?

I shrugged off the fleece blanket, clutched my sweater around my shoulders, and hopped from our boat to the dock. Miss Gloria's wind chimes tinkled in response. I trotted down the finger to the parking lot, eager to catch a glimpse of Nathan's broad-shouldered form waiting for me. His police vehicle idled by the laundry room, and he was pacing outside. I ran toward him and folded myself into his waiting hug, followed by a kiss that set me tingling from head to toe.

Then I took a step away so that the spotlight by the laundry lit his face. Over the two years I'd known him, I'd never seen him appear more worried. His eyes were a murky hazel, like the shallow water off Smathers Beach on a cloudy day just before a storm hits. His dimples were pressed flat from the tension in his jaw. He hadn't come only for a good-night kiss.

"What is it?" I asked. "What's wrong?"

I tucked my fingers into fists so my hands wouldn't shake. He'd looked something like this the day he'd had to call the parents of a visiting college coed, dead from an overdose during spring break. Sometimes Key West visitors have more fun than their brains or bodies can handle. And the police are always on the front lines to clean up the mess. Plus, my detective is not so good at what my psychologist friend, Eric Altman, would call "processing his feelings." He pushes them down so hard they sometimes leak out in unpredictable ways.

"Hayley Snow," he said, with more of his usual abruptness,

"I'd like you and your mother to step aside from the catering responsibilities during the Cuban/American conference."

My mouth opened and closed, opened and closed. "But we've talked about this a hundred times. We're going to be so careful—"

But he cut me off. "There are going to be protests. It could get violent and ugly."

"We knew that going in. Everyone says there's going to be tons of security. You said that yourself."

He crossed his beefy forearms over his abdomen and glowered.

But I barreled on. "I read an article yesterday about protecting concerts and other kinds of events. Your guys are supposed to be over there already, looking for people who don't seem to belong, taking pictures of things a tourist wouldn't be interested in, stuff like that. And I'm sure they are. We'll help too. We'll notice things and report them—"

He interrupted again. "It's impossible to protect every soft target on this island. You and your people are exactly that. You have no idea . . ."

"And you don't know what you're asking," I said, feeling my face heating up to a red that probably matched the glints in my hair. "We've bought thousands of dollars' worth of perishable ingredients, and we're deep into the prep work. You can't turn hundreds of shelled Key West pink shrimp back over to the boat captain—even if you have already cleaned out those hideous veins." I chuckled, but he didn't crack a smile.

"I want you to be safe," he said, reaching for my upper arms and gently squeezing with the big square hands I loved so much. "We've gotten wind of a possible negative event during the weekend."

I took a little gulp of air. Everyone in the country had been on edge lately—it was hard not to think of what might be coming next. Or who. "What does that mean, 'a possible negative event'? Can you give me a hint?"

He let go. "You know I can't tell you the details."

So unsatisfying. It was impossible to tell whether he'd really heard something concrete or whether he was merely continuing the argument we'd been having since my mother got the contract. He believed that the risks of working the conference outweighed the benefits of staying out of it and, therefore, staying safe. I didn't agree.

Studying the contours of his face, I determined it was most likely more of the same. "But we've hired extra help—skilled people who turned down other work and are depending on this income. And besides that, this gig is hugely important for Mom's career. She's been slip-sliding down a chute of Key West culinary ignominy." I was going for a laugh with that description, even though it was also painfully true. But I didn't get even a chuckle.

"I'm failing to see how any of that matters compared to the possibility of being blown to smithereens."

His face was red now, too. And I was getting enveloped in the familiar creeping stubbornness that he brought out in me the same way an impending trip to the vet affected my cat Evinrude.

"Is that what your source said, that the place will be blown to smithereens? How reliable is this information? Good gravy, there will be loads of security, and they know what they're doing, right? In my mind, the Little White House is probably the safest place to be on the island. No one wants a disaster with all the VIPs visiting."

"So you're saying no. Again." His voice had dropped lower, almost to a growl. "You're saying you won't do this for me, a move that could very well save your life, and your mother's? And Miss Gloria's?"

A low blow, because he knew darn well that I adored both my mother and my roommate and would do absolutely anything to save them. I sucked in a big breath, trying to slow my heartbeat enough so my reply would sound thoughtful, not defensive. "Of course, we appreciate the notice. And I promise we will be on the lookout for fishy activity and report it immediately to the proper authorities—"

He turned on his heel and stomped back to his car, his shoulders rigid.

Such an infuriating man.

It isn't that easy being involved with a pigheaded law enforcement type, especially if you're a hot-blooded redhead who hates backing down almost more than he does. Sometimes my bull-headed nature clashes with his in an ugly way. Though, on the other hand, all that fire makes for sparks in a good way, too.

I swore to myself that I wouldn't do anything impulsive or dumb this weekend. I'd call him instantly if I noticed any trouble. Though I didn't expect it. After all, I'd had my cards read two days earlier by Lorenzo, my tarot-card-reading buddy. And he hadn't said a word about danger.

Chapter Two

*Her knives were so sharp they severed the flesh of an onion
or a chicken as softly and cleanly as a wish.*
　　　　　　　—Michelle Wildgen, *Bread and Butter*

As the first streaks of light seeped through the slats of my
blinds the next morning, Evinrude began pacing back
and forth across my chest, patting my cheek with each pass
and rumbling his loudest purr. "I'm coming, you little dick-
ens," I said as I rolled out of bed.

In our little galley kitchen where both Evinrude and
Sparky waited, the coffee maker was hissing and spitting at
the end of its preprogrammed run cycle. I topped off the cat
bowl with kibble and refreshed their water, wishing desperately I had time to sit with a cup of coffee on the deck, watching the marina wake up. Instead, I filled a travel mug adorned
with the Cuban Coffee Queen logo from my favorite coffee
shop on the island and drove my scooter to the industrial
kitchen on North Roosevelt Boulevard, where my mother

does food prep for her big events. Mom and her new husband, Sam, had begun to wrestle the vats of food and containers of equipment into the back of her van, and they both looked plum-faced and flustered.

"Thank god you're here, Hayley," she said. "I was beginning to think you'd forgotten."

I kissed her on the cheek, rolled my eyes at Sam, and took the handle of the heaviest cooler from her.

"Bill Averyt texted me this morning—he says get there early. The protesters are already starting to gather, and passing through security took longer than he expected," she said.

Bill was Eric's husband, a regular tour guide at the Little White House, and one of the planners for this weekend's events. And unflappable. If he was anxious, we should be too.

By the time we'd loaded the remaining stuff into their vehicle, I was drenched in sweat. I hopped back on my scooter and followed Mom and Sam in the van, south on U.S. 1 toward the White House. The Truman Little White House sits on a grassy lawn within a gated community of homes and condos at the tip of the island called the Truman Annex, formerly owned by the U.S. Navy. On normal days, the gates leading into the Truman Annex are left open at the Southard Street entrance and the guard's booth inside the gates sits empty. This was obviously not a normal day—the gates were closed tight as the Stock Island jail and two men with monstrous guns stood guard. Even considering Nathan's warning last night, and the fact that we'd been required to submit our personal information months in advance to be vetted for working the weekend, I hadn't expected a lockdown. I also hadn't expected a cluster of silent women wearing white and carrying placards to be frowning at us from the sidewalk.

We stopped in front of the gates, and one of the armed men approached the driver's side of my mother's van. Sam rolled down the window.

"State your business," the man said.

Sam explained about the catering.

"I need to see your identification."

Sam handed over their licenses and added that I was part of their entourage. The guard collected my license, too. After he'd slipped through an opening in the metal gates and disappeared into the booth, a second man dressed in camouflage fatigues with a major-league gun draped across his chest came over to the van. He was accompanied by a German shepherd who looked all business, with alert ears and a still tail. Sam hopped out and opened the back doors so the animal could sniff our equipment and supplies. The dog circled around me, his eyes dark and his bearing severe. I resisted the temptation to cluck my tongue and hold my hand out so he could enjoy the many scents of Houseboat Row, as I would have with any other animal. The team finished their work as the first man returned from the gatehouse with our licenses and two parking stickers. The gates swung slowly open.

The watching women in white glared some more and held up posters with old photos on them. The one nearest to us read, simply, CUBA SERA LIBRE. *Cuba will be free.* Before the brouhaha in the papers leading up to this weekend, I'd had a vague understanding that some Cuban-Americans were unhappy with the idea of opening up relations between the two countries. They'd lost property and the shape of their former lives when they or their relatives had fled the country. But why were these women so angry? And who were the faces on the posters? The intersection of that moment you think you have a handle on something with the moment you realize you have no freaking idea can be chilling.

As we drove from Emma Street to the Little White House, I counted at least twenty black SUVs and five Key West police cars, including our friend Lieutenant Steve Torrence's vehicle. He was deep in conversation with a man dressed in all black and didn't respond to my mother's enthusiastic wave. Though I was certain he'd seen her. He'd married her and Sam (in a closet, during a hurricane) and was one of my favorite friends. So I waved, and got the same response—nothing. Yet one more sign that this weekend would not be normal.

At the Little White House, the red, white, and blue semicircular buntings hanging below the second-floor louvered shutters flapped gently in the breeze. Lighting specialists were stringing enormous white globes between the gumbo limbo trees, and a banner welcoming the Cuban guests hung by the front entrance.

¡La Bienvenida a los Distinguidos Invitados!
Welcome, distinguished guests!

Sam circled around to the front of the building, facing the Harbor Place condominiums. He stopped the van near the row of flags that commemorated Colin Powell's peace talks with the presidents of Armenia and Azerbaijan, and I parked behind them.

Although Harry Truman himself had used this property as a working getaway from the stresses of Washington, DC, while he was president, these days it served as a tourist attraction and a popular venue for weddings and parties. Most often, the parties took place out on the lawn and caterers brought their own rolling kitchens and grills in trucks and vans. But this time, considering the density and importance of the Cuban/American conference, my mother and company had been given permission to use not only the lawn but the small kitchen inside the Little White House as well.

On an ordinary winter day, with several cruise ships docked in the harbor, a steady stream of tourists filed in and out of the Little White House to gawk at the historically correct furnishings and hear about Mr. Truman's tenure. Bill had told me that tours were canceled for the weekend so that special displays could be set up and guests could be treated to private showings of the house and its treasures.

"And for reasons of security," he had added.

A little ominously, I thought, realizing again that this weekend was a much bigger deal than I'd imagined. I'd been so busy proving my point to Nathan about how I could handle myself that the rarity of the event hadn't sunk in. I hoped my mother wasn't starting to feel the uneasiness mount as I was. One anxious Snow woman per event was enough. Two could start a blizzard.

As I lugged a huge cooler of shrimp toward the little kitchen at the back of the house, I spotted Bill talking with a small group at the spot where the tours usually began. Wearing his official navy-blue polo shirt but long pants instead of his normal khaki shorts, he had about ten people gathered around him on the white benches just off the living room. The men wore Cuban guayaberas, untucked dress shirts with narrow pleats and big pockets; the two women wore dresses and high heels. The taller of the two turned to look at me— she had beautiful black curly hair and tan skin, and she broke into a dazzling smile. I couldn't help grinning back. Bill gestured to the jalousied booth where a Secret Service person would have been posted during Truman's visits, the final line of defense between the public and the president. I paused to take a breath and eavesdrop on what he was telling them.

"In those days," he said, "this house was on Navy property, so visitors would have already been through several layers of vetting. As you have." He waved at the metal gates in the distance that led out toward Mallory Square. These too were always open for the public during the daytime, but not today. He tipped his chin at me in greeting and ushered his guests inside.

Irena, one of my mother's assistants for the weekend, emerged from the back door and saw me struggling up the sidewalk with the load of seafood. "Let me help with that," she said. She grabbed one of the cooler's handles and we carried it into the kitchen.

"*Gracias*," I said, wiping my forehead with my sleeve. "*Es pesado.*" Meaning, "It's heavy."

Months ago, after my mother had gotten word that she'd been awarded the contract for this weekend, I'd started taking Spanish lessons from an adorable Puerto Rican–American man at the Key West library. Not that I had become fluent, by any means; I wouldn't have been able to conduct a political negotiation in Spanish, for example, or a police investigation for that matter—a fact I was tempted to file away and share with Nathan later. He would be greatly relieved. Not. But I had managed to learn a few phrases and words that I thought might come in handy when the Cuban visitors arrived. I was definitely stronger at understanding the language than making myself understood.

"When are you going to share your aunt's flan recipe?" I asked Irena, knowing the answer before she said it. Because I'd craved that magical, creamy custard drenched in caramel every day since the time I'd first tasted it, and begged her for the recipe at least a dozen times.

"*Un tesoro de la familia,*" she said with a wide grin. "It's a family treasure. My cousin would kill me." She pointed to the plump woman with a twist of dark hair pinned to her head and dressed in a spotless white apron who waited by the sink. "And her mother would kill her." She took my elbow and steered me closer to her cousin.

"You remember, my cousin, Maria?"

"*Hola,*" I said, shaking hands with her. "*Mucho gusto.*" I vaguely remembered her from a party my mother had helped cater during the Key West Literary Seminar.

Irena herself was unforgettable—willowy with a glossy fat braid the color of black cherries. Besides being drop-dead gorgeous, she was famous for making the best *café con leche* on the whole island. She wouldn't share this recipe either, but she would share the product. On the counter sat the Breville coffee machine that she would use to make espresso after dinner and *café con leche* in the morning. Maria was the architect of today's flan. My mother had been thrilled to score them both. She was always willing to pay a little extra to get these cheerful and industrious workers when they were available. And I imagined they, in turn, must be excited to be part of a historic weekend involving the homeland of their Cuban ancestors.

Mom and Sam appeared at the back door. "What's first, Señora Janet?" Irena asked.

"We four will get started in the kitchen while Sam and Gabriel unload the boxes and start setting up tables." She nodded to a swarthy man with a blocky shape who looked so much like Maria that he had to be her older brother, a carpenter who'd been pressed into service this weekend. He gave her a smile and a bow and shook Sam's hand, and then they began to unpack the food my mother had rolled to the kitchen in a red wagon. She explained the flow of the night's event.

"They decided to launch the weekend tonight with two themes they hope will be noncontroversial: Ernest Hemingway and Diana Nyad," she said. "Both managed to bridge the divide between the countries."

"A funny couple," Sam said with a big smile, hoisting a box of supplies onto the counter next to the espresso maker. "And since Hemingway's been dead for decades, it would be even funnier if you managed to get both of them to show up."

Mom grabbed a spatula that was lying on the counter and swatted his behind. "Be serious!" she said. "The touchier discussions on trade and possibly even immigration will come tomorrow, so the organizers thought Hemingway and his double legacy in Havana and Key West would get things off to a friendly start. Irena and I have planned a menu including Mr. Hemingway's favorite cocktails, followed by an appetizer of avocados stuffed with Key West pink shrimp salad, *ropa vieja* with white rice and black beans for the main course, and ta da, Maria's mother's famous flan with mango sherbet on the side for dessert." She opened the refrigerator, where the shelves were filled with trays of shimmering custard.

She hugged Maria, then straightened her apron and continued. "Hayley and Miss Gloria and I cooked and prepared the shrimp yesterday. Today we make the shrimp salad. And cut up the veggies and the beef so Irena and Maria can start the stew. We need to get on that pronto as it likes a long simmer. After that, the appetizers."

"What about Diana Nyad?" I asked. "What's her role tonight?"

"She'll be speaking briefly." She was grinning like a monkey now—Diana was her role model for persistence and dreaming big. Though they'd never met, Mom credited Diana for giving her the nerve to start her own business. Another thing my detective hadn't understood when he'd asked us to bow out of this gig—my mother was absolutely glowing. This weekend was the culmination of a year's hard work, scrapping for little jobs and completing them with more flair than they might have called for. If she flopped, no one else was going to give her a big break. No one. This weekend meant *everything* to her.

Bill poked his head into the kitchen from the door leading to the old living room. "I couldn't help overhearing, and that menu sounds sensational," he said. "You've got my mouth watering even though I had an enormous breakfast. If I hang around and wash dishes later, can I nab a taste?"

Mom grinned again. "Of course. We'll save you a whole plate. No dishwashing necessary."

"How did your bigwigs like the tour?" I asked.

He heaved an enormous sigh. "The Havana mayor and Commissioner Turner Markham got into a small shouting match about the U.S. 'wet foot, dry foot' policy."

"What was the argument?" I asked. "That law was ended ages ago." The policy, discontinued during the Obama era, had allowed Cuban people who managed to get one foot on U.S. soil to stay in the country. Cubans were allotted special immigrant status if they made it to the United States without getting intercepted by the Coast Guard, bypassing the wait that migrants from other countries had to abide by. The Cuban government had seen this both as a slap in their face and an invitation to their citizens to attempt the dangerous crossing over the Straits of Florida in makeshift boats.

"That doesn't mean the outrage is over," Bill said. "Historical scars can be more painful than recent trauma." He shrugged and straightened his gold metal glasses. "Anyway, then I showed them the display cases for the Hemingway treasures borrowed from his homes here in town and outside Havana. That led to arguments over whether the items would be safe if they were mingled, and who knows what else. They overwhelmed my high school Spanish. I was afraid things would disintegrate further into who was really at fault with the Bay of Pigs and the Cuban Missile Crisis."

"Maybe you need to borrow one of our ladies to help translate," Mom said.

Bill nodded his thanks. "Luckily, I was able to direct them to Truman's card table and get them arguing over poker hands instead. Then I explained how President Truman liked to start his day with a shot of bourbon, so there was no reason we shouldn't have an early tasting before we break for lunch." He picked up four fifths of golden liquid from those lined up on the counter, one Havana Club from Cuba and the other three from local Key West distilleries. "Rum instead of bourbon as a nod to more connections between us."

"Clever man," I said, hoping the Cuban visitors wouldn't take offense at the heavier weighting of local offerings. We were in Key West after all, but it sounded as if everyone was starting the conference poised to be offended.

"Once they're properly lubricated, I'll take them upstairs to see the bedrooms, hope they get sleepy by the power of suggestion, and then suggest we all adjourn for a siesta," Bill added as he started back to the living room. "I have a feeling it's going to be a long weekend."

He froze as heated voices reverberated from the other room. "I hope I'm not too late," he muttered, pushing through the swinging door with the rum bottles in hand.

My mother and I exchanged worried glances. Sam put a hand on her shoulder, smiled, and patted her. "Everybody's jumpy. Let them sort it out," he said. "We need to focus on the food."

He and Mom had been married less than three months and he still wore the mantle of an adoring newlywed. Or, more likely, as lovely as he was, he'd always feel protective of her. He insisted that a hurricane marriage was enough adventure for a lifetime. Why did Sam's protectiveness feel endearing, whereas Nathan's warnings to me emphatically did not? I was sure my psychologist friend Eric would steer me to look inside for answers. And I should, and I would, but not right now. I wasn't ready to explore that question in any more detail, even in the privacy of my own head. What if I discovered the whole relationship was a disaster and I'd lose this man I'd grown to love? What if I had to start over? What if I had some kind of warped internal radar that steered me right into the path of relationships doomed to fail? Aren't some things better left unknown?

Focus, Hayley, I told myself sternly.

"I'm just going to nip in and see if Bill needs help," I said as I pushed through the door leading from the storage area next to the kitchen out to the living room. I hated to see Bill enter the fray alone. And I was plain curious, too, I had to admit.

Chapter Three

Ms. Puig believes those emotions can even affect the food. "A dish that has been cooked under tension and in a bad mood will certainly taste different," she said.
—Raphael Minder, "Stressed by Success, a Top Restaurant Turns to Therapy," *The New York Times*, February 28, 2017

S tepping into this living room was like sliding back into the 1940s, decorated as it was with fashionable antique furniture that might have come out of my grandmother's home, right down to the faint smell of must. This was exactly what the renovation begun in 1988 had been aiming for. Well, maybe not the must.

I edged through the living room, past the piano where Harry Truman once played, and peered into his favorite room, the bar. Several of the guests were leaning against the carved wooden bar that had enough dings in it to conjure up the ghosts of Truman and his cronies. Shot glasses sat on an etched silver tray, some empty, some still full of rum. But Turner Markham and the Havana mayor crowded around the display case, yelling in a combination of angry English and Spanish, the police officers at the ready.

I recognized Rusty Hodgdon from the Hemingway Home in town and Dana Sebek, the owner of a local dive shop, both hovering a few feet away, looking concerned. I wondered how these people had been chosen to attend the conference, which was giving them unprecedented access to the Havana dignitaries. Was it familiarity with the issues? Money greasing palms? Or something else entirely? I ducked through the dining room to get closer, and Bill backed away from the arguing men to stand next to me.

"What's up?" I whispered.

"I mentioned that we were planning to take them out to Stock Island tomorrow morning to do a quick tour of the Cuban chugs at the botanical gardens. The Havana mayor went ballistic." He tipped his chin at a handsome, dark-skinned man, wearing a neat mustache and a perfectly pressed white shirt. His face, however, was taut with rage.

Many Cubans had attempted crossing the Straits of Florida in these homemade boats or chugs to risk a chance at a better life. Key West residents found the ingenuity and doggedness of these immigrants astonishing, and about a dozen rafts had been transported to the botanical gardens for display. The Cubans' transportation ranged from old fishing boats to structures made out of oil drums and foam to windsurfers, the last having been tried by three desperate men. One of them had made it alive. Now this policy was history, but wounds obviously still lingered.

"I knew this weekend could be touchy, but half of what we've planned seems offensive to the Cuban visitors. And the Key West people are equally hotheaded." He sighed, inclining his head in the direction of our most famously opinionated commissioner, Turner Markham. He owned a fair slice of real estate and businesses on the island and didn't hesitate to advocate decisions that appeared to directly benefit him. At some points it felt impossible to distinguish what was in Key West's interests from what lined his coffers. Locals laid bets on how long he'd last in city commission meetings before losing his temper. At one particularly contentious public meeting, the city attorney had come to the session dressed as a sports referee.

"I better wade back in there and apply more rum to the troubled waters," Bill said.

I returned to the kitchen, where Tito Rodriguez's version of "Cuando, Cuando" was blasting from the speaker on the counter. Sam was down on one knee in front of my mother, singing into an oversized spoon. "When, when, when," he crooned into the utensil. She had an enormous goofy smile on her face, and the other women were giggling with delight.

Mom turned off the music. "What'd you find out?"

I summarized the fracas involving the chugs.

"They didn't say anything about canceling the conference, did they?" Sam asked as he got to his feet. "It's not that bad, is it?"

"I don't think so."

"Then I suggest we keep our attention on preparing an outrageously amazing dinner," my mother said, clapping her hands together. "Sometimes food soothes impossible situations. Remember Connie's wedding?"

She was right, as usual. In my mother's family, lovingly prepared food meant comfort and care and even hope. A warm snickerdoodle cookie, for instance—maybe with a little chai spice added in for mystery—was a declaration of heartfelt affection. Great meals hadn't been able to save my mother's marriage to my father because he didn't speak her language. For him, food was fuel—the dinner table merely a quick stop at the human gas station. But food had saved my friend's wedding. My best pal Connie, who lives on the water near Miss Gloria's boat with her husband and baby, had had the worst constellation of prickly relatives ever show up for her celebration—both my relations and hers. But the food (including, all modesty aside, my contribution of lime cupcakes with lime cream cheese frosting) was incredible. And by the end of the weekend, almost everyone was on speaking terms.

There was probably a good compromise for the visit to see the chugs—such as making it optional. I chuckled to myself. Even if it wasn't that easy, no one had asked for my help. Nor would they—my expertise was food, not politics.

I dumped a box of firm green peppers into the sink, washed them one by one, and then began to carve them into strips. Next to me, Sam was chopping a mound of onions, his eyes streaming with tears as he reprised more sad love songs in broken Spanish. When the onions and peppers were done, Maria scraped them into the olive oil sizzling in a large pot on the stove and Sam and I began to cut the beef.

"This looks like very nice meat," he said to my mother. "How are we doing with the budget?"

It wasn't out of line for him to ask—when they'd first met, she'd just finished running her fledgling catering business in New Jersey into the ground. She couldn't bear scrimping on the quality of her ingredients—everything she ordered had to be top of the line. So, in the end, the outgo of money had been larger than the inflow, the enterprise had cost her a fortune, and she'd regretfully closed it down.

This time around, she had her finger on the pulse of every expense. "I'm all over it," she said. "I got a great deal from Jimmy Weekly at Fausto's." Our local market, our local butcher, and another local city commissioner, all in one funny Key West package.

Once the beef mixture was bubbling in two enormous pots on the six-burner Imperial stove, scenting the air with cumin and garlic, Mom hurried outside to help Sam and Gabriel set up tables. I cleaned the white Formica counters and swept the black-and-white tile floor. Irena and Maria sat at the small kitchen table chopping the prepared shrimp into bite-size pieces and mixing them with mayo, lime juice, fresh dill, pimientos, and slivered almonds. Closer to dinnertime, we would halve and stuff the ripe avocados; if done too early, the fruit would turn an unappetizing brown.

I poured myself a glass of water and sat down to help mince the fresh fronds of dill, then moved on to slicing the pimientos and stuffed green olives that would be added later to the stew. Irena talked softly in Spanish to her cousin, who looked distressed.

"Boyfriend troubles?" I asked Irena, taking a guess, always a reasonable guess in my life. Maria was not only cute; she could also cook like an angel. I imagined she was swamped with prospects. Not all of them desirable.

Irena shook her head and pinched her lips. *Okay, I got it. None of my business.* I nodded and kept chopping, trying my hardest to understand the fast chatter but without much success. When the women lapsed into silence, I looked at Maria and winked. "Throw me a bone, and tell me what ingredients go into that flan."

She grinned, and the smile reached her eyes this time. "*Leche,*" she said. "*Y huevos.*"

I planted my hands on my hips in exaggerated outrage. "Eggs and milk? That's all you can give me? That could lead to an omelet or French toast or even plain old scrambled eggs."

The women laughed, and Maria said something in Spanish. "Maybe when you get married, she'll share it," Irena translated.

"Or how about you two make me Cuban flan instead of wedding cake?" I asked as I got up to clear the dirty plates and cutlery from the table. "Don't worry, that's not happening anytime soon. So you'll have lots of time to think this over."

When the kitchen was tidy and the other women had started working on the hors d'oeuvres, I stashed our rinsed, empty coolers in the storeroom off the kitchen. The shelves were lined with cans of paint and boxes of other supplies for touching up the Little White House as needed. In the long pantry hallway at the other side of the kitchen, the white tablecloths that we'd use for this evening's dinner hung on hangers. A favorite local florist, Gourmet Nibbles and Baskets, had constructed gorgeous arrangements of flowers and tropical greenery, all chosen to represent the flora of both Havana and Key West. The brilliant crowning touch was the fleet of small boats in which the foliage was planted, with red birds of paradise representing sails. On the stern of each boat, someone had painted the name of Hemingway's beloved craft: *Pilar*. Only the biggest sticklers for detail might complain that the *Pilar* had been a motorboat—no sails involved.

With my part of the early preparations finished, I took a tiny bite of shrimp out to Barkley, the Little White House cat, named after Harry Truman's vice president, Alben Barkley, in spite of her sex. A few other feral cats sometimes made their homes under the building, but handsome brown Barkley was the one and only official mascot. She wound through my legs and mewed her thanks, and then I began to help Gabriel ferry the arrangements out to the tables.

"*Muy hermosas*," I said, pointing to the flowers.

"Very pretty," he agreed shyly.

After we put all the flowers out, I paused for a minute to wipe the perspiration off my forehead. Gabriel didn't even look winded. "I would have known you were Maria's brother anywhere," I said. "I'm Hayley." I reached out to shake his hand, which was firm and somewhat calloused—not unexpected, as he worked with his hands. He had dark skin and dark hair and eyes and didn't stand much more than three or four inches taller than me. A sturdy man who appeared solid and reliable. "I don't suppose you have her flan recipe and would be willing to share it?"

He threw his head back and laughed. Which I took as a no. Then he nodded and smiled and trotted back to the house to take a heavy load of glassware from Maria while I joined my mother on the other side of the house.

She and Sam had set up tall cocktail tables on the west lawn of the house and the large round tables for dinner in the most protected area near the Harbor Place garage. Perhaps the garage was not the most scenic backdrop for dinner, but it would allow the security detail to keep a close eye on our guests and repel the potential intrusions of curiosity seekers.

My ex-boyfriend Chad, whom I'd followed here from New Jersey three years ago before getting shucked out of his life like an undersized oyster, lived in this condominium complex. He and the other residents were probably chafing at the inconvenience of the special security measures. He had not been one to look on the bright side. I could imagine him grousing that the security was more stringent than a few minor-league Cuban dignitaries warranted.

When everything seemed to be in place—the birds of paradise sailing gracefully in the center of each table, sound system tested, bar stocked, more foliage arranged on the stage—I touched base with my mother.

"Okay to run home to change clothes and pick up Miss Gloria?" My octogenarian roommate had wanted desperately to work the entire weekend. Mom had persuaded her to compromise: rest during the day and come for the excitement of the opening party.

"Of course, honey," she said. "I think the place looks beautiful, don't you?"

I nodded my agreement. "Magical."

She kissed me on the cheek. "Don't forget, clean white shirts and black pants even for you two. No sequined leaping dolphins. No sweatshirts. No red high-tops." The dolphins and sweats were Miss Gloria's uniform, the high-tops all mine.

"It's going to be perfect," I said, hugging her shoulders. "You've thought of everything. What could possibly go wrong?"

Suddenly, two Key West police officers with radios crackling ran past the back door, headed to the front of the building.

Chapter Four

*All good secrets have a taste before you tell them, and if
we'd taken a moment to swish this one around in our
mouths, we might have noticed the sourness of an unripe
secret, plucked too soon, stolen and passed around before
its season.*

—Brit Bennett, *The Mothers*

I heard shouting from the living room of the Little White
House. I went back through the kitchen and the pantry
and into the dining room, trying to puzzle out what was happening. The Havana mayor and our fiery Key West commissioner were going at it again, this time in heated Spanish. I
wished my teacher were here to translate. Seeing no one to
stop me, I skirted past the large dining table and peered into
the entry hall.

The Cuban visitors, the Key West dignitaries, and the two
officers I'd seen run by the kitchen were gathered around a
display case in the living room next to the desk where Harry
Truman had worked on his visits to the island. Most of the

shouting was happening in Spanish, way too fast and furious for my limited comprehension. I did catch the words *Hemingway*, *Nobel*, and *la catastrophe*, which even a beginner student of Spanish could safely assume meant catastrophe.

I edged a little closer, circling around Harry Truman's blue velvet couch, which, like the other items in the Little White House, had been restored to exactly the way it had looked when Truman was in residence. Bob Wolz, the director of the Little White House Foundation, stood next to one of the Cuban visitors, who was shaking a furious finger at our city commissioner. Bill hung a few yards behind them.

I inched up behind Bill. "What's going on?"

He looked grim. "I'm not sure exactly, but it appears something valuable is missing. Something on loan from the Cuban people."

He'd told me earlier in the week that he worried about this most—what if something went wrong with one of the priceless artifacts on loan from Hemingway's life in Havana? Any cautious progress we'd made in normalizing relations between the two countries could be destroyed in an instant.

A second posse of uniformed Key West policemen, including my friend Lieutenant Torrence, burst in from the entrance next to the former Secret Service booth.

"Let's all stand down a moment," Torrence said, once he'd had a few seconds to assess the situation. "We can certainly get to the bottom of this, but shouting at one another will not help."

A man standing in the gaggle translated the lieutenant's words into Spanish. And some of the rage and tension in the air seemed to leak away. I felt a breath of relief—Torrence was a wizard at defusing difficult situations. Unlike my own Detective Bransford, whose native impatience tended to spike at inconvenient moments and who was much better at interrogating than peacemaking.

"Now one at a time," said Torrence, "tell me what's going on here." He pointed to the man closest to the glass case, and that unleashed another torrent of Spanish.

"*Despacio y con claridad, por favor,*" said Torrence. "Explain what happened slowly and clearly, please."

The babble of voices continued, but eventually it all seemed to boil down to the following: the Nobel prize gold medal that Hemingway had won for his masterpiece novel, *The Old Man and The Sea*, was missing from the case. I retreated into the kitchen, feeling sick to my stomach. Every one of us was frazzled and exhausted, and there was still tons of work to do tonight and lots more to come in the remaining days and hours of the weekend. Even if my mother's food and service were spectacular, the lost medal could be all most guests remembered. And the press would have a field day with this news.

The others stopped what they were working on and gathered around to hear my report. "Hemingway's Nobel prize medal has gone missing. I'm sure the cops will start to interview people separately to see if they noticed anyone near the display case. The Cuban visitors are enraged, and I can't say I blame them. It's not left the country since Hemingway gave it to them."

My mother moaned softly.

"I suspect they'll be in here next asking us the same questions," Sam said.

Irena jumped right in, sounding defensive. "We haven't left the kitchen or the grounds since we got here. None of us other than you even went into the main part of the house. Wasn't the case locked?"

"I assume so. Bill and Bob Wolz are in charge, and they're both meticulous planners. Besides, the medal wasn't the only valuable item in the case. The Hemingway Home here on the island loaned some valuable artifacts, too. The owners will have a fit when /they hear about this." I started to pull my phone out of my pocket, then instantly stuffed it back in. Who did I think I was going to call? Certainly not Nathan. He'd hear about it anyway, but to have me calling him so early in the conference, sounding worried, would only give him more ammunition for his argument that we should withdraw. And why would it be my business anyway, when the place was crawling with security?

Bill came into the kitchen, looking depressed, and confirmed what I'd told the others. "Bob is trying to convince the cops and our Cuban visitors that the medal was misplaced or overlooked in the unpacking and therefore maybe never made it into the case."

"But you gave a tour this morning. Doesn't anyone remember seeing it earlier?" Sam asked.

"I have no idea," Bill said, his shoulders slumping. "You know eyewitness reports are notoriously unreliable. Bob's going up to the attic to search through the packing materials. We saved every piece of paper and every single Styrofoam peanut. We fully expect that's where we'll find it. He's convinced everyone else this is what happened."

But this sounded like magical thinking to me, and I suspected that Bill agreed—I could read it all over his face. He was a lousy liar. He was a guy who played by the rules. And I could have sworn I personally had had a glimpse of the gold medal in that cabinet when I was lurking in the living room earlier.

"You'll help me figure this out, right?" he asked, his eyes begging.

Chapter Five

Franklin barbecue doesn't have to be so humane. Employees could probably stand on the roof pouring hot lard over customers' heads without driving too many people away. Once you start thinking about how much brisket you want, it's hard to leave.

—Pete Wells, "Celebrating the Sweet Science of Brisket," *The New York Times*, March 15, 2017

Before zipping up the island to Houseboat Row, I decided to check in at the office. As the food critic for *Key Zest* style magazine, I was responsible for restaurant reviews, along with the occasional feature on island activities. This week, I had promised to review local Cuban cuisine and also write a piece on the influence of Cuba on our island. I sighed. Nothing like biting off more than I could chew to impress the boss.

Although impressing Palamina was definitely less stressful than during the period I'd been dating the other boss, Wally, while working for him. I would have to be careful what I said about the morning so as not to give Wally the idea I planned to get involved with helping Bill find the missing medal. He would remind me that I was a food critic, not an investigative reporter. This was partly why Wally and I had always been a bad idea. Nathan might try to discourage me from running into danger, but he never questioned my passion. Oh boy, did he ever understand passion.

Wally and me, on the other hand, had had as many sparks between us as a fizzled campfire surrounded by disappointed Girl Scouts with cold s'mores. It was a case of two people who liked each other fine, so why shouldn't something more work? In other words, a disaster right off the blocks. Even so, these days he looked a little wistful when I mentioned plans with Nathan. But the chemistry hadn't been there with us, and both of us had figured this out—eventually. Sometimes it takes a good rap on the head when you're as stubborn as I am.

I parked my scooter in the lot behind Preferred Properties Realty and dashed up the stairs to the second floor *Key Zest* office. My pal Danielle was working at the computer in the reception area, if you could call this tiny space anything more than a bulge in the hallway. On the near corner of her desk, she had arranged a plate of assorted doughnuts from the Glazed Donuts shop next to Tropic Cinema. Honestly, no one other than me was usually tempted by them, except for the occasional visitor. She'd gotten in the habit of delivering the leftovers to the police department at the end of the day—insurance, she called it, for my shenanigans. I suspected she was sweet on one of the men in blue polyester. ("And polyester in the tropics? Really?" my friend Torrence often wondered. "What knucklehead further up the food chain made that ridiculous decision?")

"I was hoping you'd show up," Danielle said, waving at the plate of treats. "How's everything going at the Little White House?"

"Very exciting and a ton of work," I said, biting into a pillowy glazed and rolling my eyes in appropriate ecstasy. "As heavy as the security is, you would think we were getting ready for a conference of world leaders. Have you ever seen the gates at Southard Street closed and locked?"

Danielle shook her head. She was younger than me but had been born and raised on this island. Conchs, the true locals called themselves. Not to be confused with freshwater conchs, aka people who had lived in Key West for more than seven years. Miss Gloria, for example, was the freshwater variety, despite her fondness for referring to herself as a barnacle.

Wally and Palamina, my two bosses, came out of their office to join the chat.

"How's the conference so far?" Wally asked.

"Nothing official has started," I said. "But they're already squabbling." I explained the fight between Mayor Diaz and Turner Markham over the placement of prized objects in the display cases and the planned tour of Cuban chugs. I was considering whether to tell them about the possibly missing medal when Palamina spoke up.

"I'm a little surprised Markham is at the helm on this one," she said. "For the sake of appearance, shouldn't it be our mayor?"

"That's a good point. I was so engrossed in the moment, I didn't think to question that. Maybe he's coming tonight?"

"Keep an eye on it," said Wally. "Sometimes the mayor sends a commissioner when the controversy that might be generated is not something he wants to take on."

"Will do," I said, feeling a little bit as though I'd already missed the story's hook. *Buried the lede*, as Palamina would have put it. "Anyway, the food is going to be amazing, and we are all over the moon about Diana Nyad."

"Will you still have time to do your Cuban color pieces?" Palamina asked.

"I'm not on KP duty tomorrow morning," I said, "so my plan is to grab a quick early lunch at El Siboney. Their food is pretty straightforward, so it won't take a lot of time to write up. And I possibly can nip by Frita's Cuban Burgers," I added, sensing a lack of enthusiasm from Palamina about a review of one single Cuban restaurant when my roundtable articles comparing several eateries were clearly more popular. "I shouldn't have any problem with the Cuban influence on Key West culture bit, as both of my mother's hired sous-chefs have roots in Cuba." I grinned, hoping I exuded confidence. Out loud, the schedule did sound grueling. And on top of that, I now seemed to be in charge of nosing around for the scent of town politics.

"You'll let us know if it's too much?" Palamina tapped one flake of loose doughnut glaze on the plate with her forefinger and touched it to her tongue as I swallowed the last incredible bit of my doughnut. Which totally explained why she was tiny enough to wear leggings and shape-hugging tops, while I . . . was not.

"You look worried," said Wally. "It's too much, isn't it?"

"No, I swear I'm fine with the work. I am a little worried,

but that's because of what happened just before I left." I broke down and spilled the news about the missing gold medal, and how I'd been grilled before I was allowed to leave, and how all that was making the weekend feel even more fraught with potential minefields. "We're hoping it will magically be back in place for the evening's festivities."

"It's a super big deal that Cuba allowed that gold medal out of the country," Wally said. "Did you know that it's been secreted away in a convent near Santiago de Cuba in the south of the country? Hemingway wanted to give it to the people of Cuba to honor the setting of his prizewinning novel, but he didn't want Batista getting hold of it. So he gave it to the Catholic Church for safekeeping. Hardly anyone has seen it since then, never mind it visiting a strange country."

"No wonder Bill was in despair at first and the Cuban dignitaries were enraged," I said. My anxiety was shooting higher and higher talking to Wally. I needed to get back over there and support my mother. "I'm pretty sure they'll find it in time for tonight's party. I'll keep you posted."

I grabbed my backpack and helmet and trotted out to my scooter. The day felt a little warmer than yesterday, and less breezy—perfect for a dinner al fresco. Assuming the whole thing was still on. I buzzed over to U.S. 1, then up the island to the busy corner where Houseboat Row floated. The boats facing the highway caught more noise and tourist gawking than Miss Gloria's location, which always felt too good to be true. But the familiar form of my realtor friend Cory Held in our parking lot made me think that our luck might be running thin.

I parked my scooter, pulled it onto its stand, and waved her down. "Another showing?" I asked.

She nodded. "Everything in this town is selling briskly. Once that hurricane rolled over us last fall with hardly any structural damage, people have the idea we're invincible. That kind of thinking may not be smart on the customer end, but it sure is good for business."

I was almost afraid to ask. But more afraid not to. "And the boat next door?"

"Lots of interest, but nothing firm. You know I'll let you know, as soon as I can. And I'm reminding all prospective buyers that it's a family neighborhood, not a party boat."

"We appreciate that," I said as I hopped onto the finger leading to the boats. Miss Gloria was perched on her lounge chair on our tiny deck, dressed in a collared white shirt and black sweat pants with sporty satin stripes running down the length of her hips and legs. Where did she even find these things? She had left a shoebox on my chaise. The cats were tucked under her arms, depositing gray and black fur, I was sure. She looked adorable—and glum.

"Did she tell you anything?" She pointed at Cory's receding car.

"Nothing happening yet. We'll hope for the best."

"Why was she here by herself?" she asked. "What kind of showing doesn't involve a buyer? That's what I can't figure out."

"We have no control over it, not a whit," I said, kissing the top of her head, her white hair warm from the afternoon sun. "I'm going to wash my face and change clothes and then

I'll be ready." Both cats trotted into the houseboat after me. "Didn't she feed you?" I asked, ruffling the gorgeous gray "M" on Evinrude's head and then wiggling my fingers at Sparky. He pounced and I gave them each a trio of tuna-flavored cat treats. "More to come later," I promised.

"I bought something for you," Miss Gloria said when I came back outside in my own white shirt and black cropped pants.

Quivering with delight and excitement, she pointed to the shoebox. I opened it up. A pair of sneakers carpeted in black sequins was nestled in the pink tissue paper. Now I noticed she had the same shoes on, only in her china-doll size.

"I know your mother said no sequined dolphins, but she didn't ban sequins altogether. And these I couldn't resist—Zappos had a big sale. And don't they look comfy?"

"They're perfect," I said, slipping them on and tying them quickly. I executed a little hop-step to watch them glint in the sun. "Don't forget your helmet and your driver's license. They're triple-checking everyone at the Southard Street gate."

Chapter Six

If you can't stand the heat, get out of the kitchen.
—Harry S. Truman

We scooted down the island and came to a standstill on Southard Street a block from the entrance to the Truman Annex. The small group of protesting women in white clothing had mushroomed to quadruple its size, joined by more people carrying signs.

KEY WEST, DON'T CODDLE THE CUBAN GOVERNMENT! shouted one sign.

DON'T SUPPORT OPPRESSION! proclaimed another.

On the other side of the street, I read THANK YOU KEY WEST FOR OPENING DOORS! The two sets of protesters were exchanging chants, shouting across the road. "*¡Cuba para todos!*" and "*¡Cuba sera libre!*" drowned out by "Let Cuba join the world!" and "Set my people free!"

A few of the anti-conference protesters surged toward us. I could feel Ms. Gloria tensing up on her seat behind me. She gripped my midsection and began to breathe faster. But then several Key West police officers materialized and pushed the people away from the gate. We submitted to another examination by the businesslike police dog and his handler and were waved inside. I spotted our friend Lieutenant Torrence parked along Emma Street. I veered over to check in.

"I've never seen security like this," I said, shouting over the rough idle of the bike.

"Geez," Miss Gloria added, "you'd think I was the Queen of England."

Torrence laughed, but his eyes were serious. "It's something, isn't it?" he said, revealing nothing.

Which made me even more curious, because he was usually more willing to share news about our island, or at least hint. "This isn't about Diana Nyad, is it? Are you expecting some kind of trouble with the protest?"

"Have a great night," he said with a strained grin, and waved us on.

I parked my scooter in a tiny space behind an adjoining brick building, and we hustled across the private drive to the Little White House grounds. A man dressed in a dark suit and wearing an earpiece stopped us at the flags. He checked our licenses again, then marked us off on a list of names. The woman stationed with him searched through my backpack and Miss Gloria's fanny pack and then asked us to stand with arms and legs open while she waved a metal-detecting wand.

"Geez Louise," said Miss Gloria, once we'd put ourselves back together. "Who's hot stuff tonight?"

The lawn around the Little White House was already a beehive of activity. The party had begun early. A few guests were milling around the cocktail tables, drinks in hand. Bartenders in white shirts with black bow ties were busy mixing mojitos, rum and Cokes, and daiquiris, and distributing wine and beer to the less adventurous guests. As we passed the first of three bars, I could smell crushed mint leaves and lime zest.

"Mojitos, my favorite," I said, imagining how pleasant it would be to attend the party rather than work the crowd. On the other hand, we had an inside track to all the excitement. And I'd already had the chance to see the tensions between some of the attendees that would never be shown in public. For a curious cat like me, our vantage point was unbeatable. Miss Gloria was vibrating with excitement as well. One mojito and she would have been looking for a Barcalounger. Or maybe, knowing her, dancing on the tables.

"Who could be coming who would rate this kind of security?" I asked.

"President Obama," Miss Gloria said with a wide grin.

She was a major fan of the past president and, even more so, his wife. She craved seeing one of them in person—the way that toast yearned for jam, that hot biscuits called for butter, that peach pie pined for vanilla ice cream. His appearance here seemed unlikely, although not impossible. Harry Truman aside, the Little White House has hosted plenty of political celebrities over the years, including Jimmy Carter, Bill and Hillary Clinton, and John F. Kennedy. Since Mr. Obama had played a major role in thawing frosty relations between the United States and Cuba during his last years in office, it seemed possible that he'd want to be involved in how the relationship between the two countries might unfold.

But wouldn't the security challenges be insurmountable?

The band began to warm up on the stage, delivering blasts from a trio of glorious trumpeters wearing fedoras and crooning from a sexy Cuban man in a white suit and cowboy hat. I felt as though I'd been dropped into the Buena Vista Social Club in old Havana. Miss Gloria swished her hips in a rhythm I hadn't known she possessed.

We trotted into the kitchen where my mother, looking frazzled, arranged platters of hors d'oeuvres for us to ferry out to the guests. She handed me a plate of skewered chorizo and cheddar cubes glazed with guava jelly and gave Miss Gloria a plate of ham *croquetas*, freshly turned out of the hot oil that Irena managed on the stove.

"Circulate!" she instructed us as she slipped a stack of cocktail napkins engraved with a line drawing of the Little White House into our fingers. "And then come for more. On your way back, please check the veggie-and-cheese table and make sure everything looks neat and appetizing?"

My first stop was the trio of men I'd seen arguing over the chugs earlier that afternoon: Havana mayor Diaz, Turner Markham, and Bob Wolz. They were standing a bit back from the party crowd. Though dressed for a party—Bob with a bow tie, Markham in a stunning rose-colored silk shirt, and Diaz in another crisp, white guayabera—they clearly weren't absorbing the happy vibes, nor reflecting any out. Bob made a face that looked to me like an SOS, meaning they needed a little cheerful hospitality—maybe even an intervention.

"*Hola*!" I said, flashing my brightest smile. "*Bienvenidos a* Key West!" I described the delicacies on my tray, but only Bob reached for a skewer and a napkin. The other two remained standing stiffly with arms crossed over their chests.

"Have a wonderful evening," I said brightly, which had no salutary effect at all. I moved on to the next set of guests. By the time my tray had been emptied three times, the party was in full swing, the hum of the crowd growing louder and more joyous.

Once the lawn was buzzing with guests and conversation, Bob bounded up the few steps to the stage, and the band quit playing. I paused for a moment with my empty tray. "We are thrilled beyond words to be hosting this first-ever conference between Havana and Key West," he said. "Harry Truman would be so proud." The crowd applauded. "Please enjoy the music and the hors d'oeuvres and we'll be back to you with our program shortly."

The singer, a slender, dark-haired man, jumped off the stage, reached for my hand, and pulled me out to the dance floor. Salsa and rumba were definitely not my thing, but he was so graceful that I felt like I was floating through the steps. I wished Nathan were watching—it wouldn't hurt to have him see me twirling with another man, my sequined feet spar-kling. Commissioner Markham was dancing too—with a young blonde woman who looked half his age. He was an excellent dancer, making the footwork look effortless and his partner sexy and smooth.

As I dipped and whirled, I saw Sam gesturing furiously from the White House. I thanked my partner and excused myself, picked up the empty tray I'd abandoned on a cocktail table, and ran to the kitchen. My mother's hair had escaped her headband and frizzed to an auburn halo. And she looked as if she might burst into tears at any moment.

"I'm so sorry," I said. Was the stress of the evening to come too much for her? "He grabbed me and I got caught up in the moment. I won't go anywhere near the dance floor the rest of the night."

"It's not that," she said. "Everyone is so tense. The gold medal hasn't turned up and poor Bill is sick about it, inventing ideas about where it might be and reassuring the Cuban dignitaries. Or trying anyway. Meanwhile, Maria's brother is a no-show. She's beside herself with worry." She pointed to a back corner of the storage area, where Maria was crouched on a short stool, weeping. "Irena has no idea why he isn't here, or so they say." She lowered her voice. "She looks like she knows something terrible, doesn't she? But whatever the reason, I have no one to wait on Maria's tables or take Gabriel's place bussing."

Irena came up to us, wringing her hands.

"What on earth is going on?" I asked.

"It's only a matter of time before they pin the theft of that medal on Gabriel," she said. "Maria is convinced of it."

"Why would she think that?" I asked.

She held out her hands. "Because he isn't here, for one. And for two, he has dark skin—"

I started to protest. I'd gotten into my share of rhubarbs with the local authorities, but my experience with the Key West police had always been fair in the end.

Irena cut in. "You don't have any idea what it's like, do you?"

I had to admit that I didn't. I had been thinking of this weekend as a happy celebration of Cuba–U.S. relations, and I was beginning to realize how complicated the truth might be.

"I can take an extra table or two, no worries," I said. "Lucky thing you decided to serve the stew and rice family style. After dinner, we'll put our heads together and find Gabriel."

I spent the next forty-five minutes at a dead run, serving the individual shrimp-stuffed avocados to each guest, ferrying bowls of *ropa vieja* to the tables, filling bread baskets, clearing dirty dishes. The little kitchen had begun to look like a combat zone. Finally the diners were finished eating and Bob took his place at the microphone to invite guests to turn their attention to the area around the stage.

"We have some very special guests tonight. First, it is my greatest pleasure to introduce you to Diana Nyad, the only athlete to have completed the swim from Havana to Key West— without a shark cage!"

A trim and athletic woman with short blonde hair bounded up the steps, and the audience rose to its feet in a thunderous ovation. Once the clapping died down, she described how thrilled she'd been about being able to make a physical connection between the two countries.

"Spectators saw two arms in the water—one swimmer. But my effort was possible only because of amazing teamwork. One of my teammates is here with me tonight." She introduced her trainer, Bonnie, and then told a story about her early days when she'd been competing for a spot on the U.S. Olympic swimming team. "A friend advised me not to leave one fingernail of effort out in the pool. Then, no matter what happened, win or lose, I would have no regrets.

"This is how I see the work to rebuild the relationship between Cuba and the United States," she said. "It may not be easy; we must put forward all the energy we have to make this happen in order to discard the conflicts of the past and help the people of both countries benefit. But I've touched the land in Havana and Key West, and the people in both cities have touched my heart. We can do this, together." She picked up a cornet from a music stand and played "Charge," then exited the stage to vigorous applause.

As she went off, Jimmy Buffett appeared onstage and began to sing "Havana Daydreamin'," and the guests went wild again. Some of them donned crazy hats featuring stuffed parrots and fish and even beer bottles, and began to dance with choreographed motions that went with his song. The conference organizers had certainly held nothing back. I would have liked to stay and gawk, but remembering my mother's stress level, I hurried into the kitchen to pick up a tray of glorious flan.

As I rounded the corner with the dessert, former president Obama sprang onto the stage, looking more relaxed than he'd ever appeared while in office. Beside me, I heard Miss Gloria gasp.

"Diana," he said, pointing into the audience, "come back up here, please. I want to give you a hug."

She returned to the stage and he hugged her. Then he took her by the hands and nodded to the band. They swung into a fast rhythm and Jimmy Buffett began to croon "Volcano." I stood by my mother and Miss Gloria, all of us mesmerized and eyes brimming with tears, as they spun around the stage. We'd seen this president cut loose occasionally while he was in the White House, but tonight he looked so much at ease. Like a man who'd had a ten-ton weight lifted off his shoulders.

"I don't know . . ." sang Jimmy.

After this song wound down, Mr. Obama posed for photos with Diana and Jimmy, and then stepped up to the microphone. "It's a pleasure and an honor to be here tonight, on the same lawn where one of my heroes, Harry Truman, took working vacations during his terms in office. He was a man who inherited the leadership of a dazed country in mourning and guided us through a period of chaos and grief with great common sense, humility, and humor. Had I visited this island and the beautiful grounds of this Little White House earlier in my career and seen how charming they are, I would have spent more time here."

The audience broke into applause. To my right, Bob and Bill grinned with delight.

"Thank you," Mr. Obama said. "Thanks so much. I was asked to speak tonight because of my historical connection with Cuba. My team and I were thrilled to be able to assist in opening up relations with our sister country."

He continued to talk about the hope he felt for a resurrection of the relationship between the countries. As he wrapped up his remarks proclaiming optimism for the future, I heard popping noises and then a terrible scream. Shouts erupted from the Little White House for the second time today. My heart thudded wildly and my hands broke into a slippery sweat. I looked around for my mother—right beside me, thank goodness—and for Miss Gloria. I felt a surge of relief, seeing that Sam had his arm around her shoulders and was guiding her to a folding chair near the building's restrooms.

"Everybody on the ground, now!" shouted two Secret Service agents.

"Now!" repeated Lieutenant Torrence, who had materialized feet from us.

I dropped to my knees, bobbling the tray of flan I'd been carrying. The custard slid off the plate and smashed into the grass, spraying caramel across my face and into my mother's hair. And all over our city commissioner's gorgeous pink silk shirt. Instead of the happy tinkle of silverware on china and the amazing, cheerful music of Jimmy Buffett, the grounds had fallen silent. The only noise left was a whisper of palms as a breeze drifted through them, and then barked commands from the direction of the White House kitchen.

"No way," my mother said from her place next to me in the dirt near the sidewalk. "This amazing night can't be ending with a disaster."

Chapter Seven

Any fool can make a sauce but you can't fake the crust.
—Adam Gopnik, *The Most Beautiful Room
in New York*

"Don't panic," I muttered, although inside that's exactly what I was doing. We hear about shootings and other terrorist incidents every day, but who thinks it could happen to them? I craned my neck from side to side to try to see what was happening. Within seconds, the former president and the other celebrities had been whisked off the stage into waiting vehicles. The cars sped off, and security guards and police began swarming the building. Two German shepherds and their handlers wove among the flattened guests, sniffing.

Some long minutes later, the authorities cleared us to get to our feet. I brushed the dirt off my face and knees and tried to sop up the worst of the caramel sauce as it trickled down my chin and chest. Following Sam's lead, I hurried among the tables, assisting guests who were struggling to get up. Sam

53

and my mother instructed the bartenders to move around the diners, offering more wine. We raced back to the staging area outside the kitchen to pick up undamaged flan and deliver the dessert. As I wound through the tables with a large tray, Bob climbed the steps to the stage and took the microphone in hand.

"Sorry about the interruption, folks." He looked sheepish and unhappy but tried to cover it with a smile. "One of our bartenders came across a defective bottle of prosecco, and that unfortunately, made the popping noise you heard. And that startled one of our waitresses. Hence the yelling."

There was some laughter from the guests, but underneath that, a murmur of complaints and disbelief. And I had to agree—how could a bottle of fizzy Italian champagne make a sound that would cause someone to scream as though they were being murdered? And besides, his face was lined with anxiety—the longer he stood on the stage, the sicker with worry he seemed. He breathed in deeply.

"Unfortunately, there has been an incident with someone inside the building who was frightened by the noise. Rescue workers are with him now. Meanwhile, authorities will most likely need to talk with many of you, so please sit tight for the moment," he added. "The caterers are in the process of serving the most amazing flan you might find anywhere, outside of Cuba, of course. Please enjoy that while you wait." He patted his forehead with a white hanky. "A quick note for conference participants: tomorrow morning, meetings will be taking place at our new city hall on White Street rather than here on the Little White House grounds. Following those sessions, we will gather at the Sunset Key boat dock on the Margaritaville Westin pier at noon for our short trip to have lunch on the island."

A babble of questions rose up from the guests, but Bob descended heavily from the stage without answering.

"What in the world is going on?" I whispered to my mother, who seemed ready to cry or burst into a thousand pieces. "The police wouldn't ask to talk to bystanders if someone had a heart attack."

"Not clear yet," said Sam, his mouth set hard and his hand resting protectively on my mother's back. "Something to do with Maria. For sure, she won't be available to help clean up; that's all we've heard."

As I delivered the last tray of flan to one of the tables, I saw Lieutenant Torrence deep in conversation with Mayor Diaz. Diaz, who'd worn a sour expression since the gold medal incident this morning, had grown increasingly furious. I hoped my friend's Spanish would be up to the task. I hustled around my section as well as what would have been Maria's, picking up empty plates and listening to the conversations.

"This flan is astonishing," said a redheaded woman at one of my tables. "What are the chances you could get me this recipe?"

"Not a whisker," I said. "And I've tried everything outside of kidnapping the chef."

Shortly after my mother and Sam were taken inside, though it seemed like hours later, my turn came to talk with the authorities. As I was ushered into the building, I felt relieved to have the chance to go into the kitchen and find out what had really happened. Maria sat at the kitchen table sobbing hysterically, smudges of blood on her face and hands. Police and other security formed a circle around her, trying to calm her enough to answer some questions.

"Oh my god, what happened?" I asked my mother, who had retreated against the windows in the hall.

"I can't even believe it," she whispered. She pointed in the direction of the storage area where I had placed the empty coolers earlier. "She found her brother in that closet. He'd been stabbed in the chest, and there was blood everywhere." Mom looked dazed and frozen.

"Why isn't anyone doing anything? Where in the world are the paramedics?" I asked, feeling a rising tide of panic.

"They've already been in with him," Sam said grimly. "It's too late to do any good. Obviously, this is a crime scene now."

I clapped a hand to my mouth and took a step back. "Dead?" Nathan had warned me about a possible negative event, but never in a million years had I imagined something like this. Or maybe I just hadn't wanted to consider a possibility like this. "What can I do? How can we help?"

Sam tipped his chin at Irena, who had her hand on Maria's shoulder, shushing and calming her as though she were the mother and Maria a desperate baby. And having about that much effect too, which is to say, none. "Nothing to do right now."

Steve Torrence came up behind us, his face fierce. "We need to talk with each of you again, one at a time, to find out what you heard and saw. So please remain in the area until we finish the interviews. Likely, we will need to talk to you again tomorrow as well."

"Did the president get away all right?" my mother asked, a sorrowful hitch in her voice.

"He's fine," said Torrence. "Jimmy Buffett too. Hayley, can you come with me please?"

He nodded at me and I followed him to the other side of the kitchen and then down the opposite hallway, where a chair had been set up to face the police. Nathan was waiting, along with a woman detective I had met several years ago when my stepbrother disappeared into a spring break crowd. They both looked deadly serious. Behind them stood a man dressed in black, wearing an FBI jacket.

"Take a seat, please," the woman said.

I held a hand up to my boyfriend, my lips beginning to quiver. "I know, I'm sorry, I should have listened. But you can see there is no way we could have canceled this evening. Not with all those big stars coming. And it's a terribly important subject—I'm only now beginning to realize how different the points of view are and to understand some of the history—"

I could tell from the horrified look on Nathan's face that I was frothing-at-the-mouth babbling. But I couldn't seem to stop. "I guess the more immediate question is why in the world would someone want to kill Gabriel? He has nothing to do with any of this; he was just working for the caterers."

I collapsed onto the folding chair and began to hyperventilate.

"Mom needed some extra muscle and he was available, and, oh god, poor Maria—"

"Hayley, stop talking for a minute," Nathan said quietly. He squatted down next to me and took my hand, stroking it from wrist to fingertips. "Take a deep breath, sweetheart. Finding the killer is our job now, isn't it? You don't need to worry; we'll find out the answer. We've got all kinds of professionals here. Good ones."

I closed my eyes for a moment and tried to take in a couple of deep yoga breaths, feeling his warm hand on mine and noticing the scent of his perspiration. This night had been a horrible and tragic shock for everyone, not just me. I needed to pull myself together.

Once I'd stopped shaking, I opened my eyes again. "Okay. Sorry. I'm ready now. Sorry." Nathan stood up and indicated to the others that the interview could proceed.

"Start at the beginning," said the lady cop. "When did you notice anything off about this party?"

I reported how the protesters and the heavy security had set everyone on edge right from the get-go. And then I described the fighting—squabbling really—between Commissioner Markham and the Havana mayor. "Of course, once the gold medal disappeared, we were all on tenterhooks. Maria"—I pointed down the hall, where we could still hear the sobbing woman—"was sure her brother would be blamed."

"What was the reason for that assumption?" asked Nathan.

"Do you want facts or speculation?" I asked.

My detective sighed. "Definitely facts, if you happen to have any, and might as well hear the speculation now as later."

I bit my lip and tried to concentrate above the injured animal sounds Maria was making in the kitchen. But I could feel her terror and sorrow swirling, winding me tighter and tighter.

"Things could be worse, right? At least you have a closed crime scene. And a list of all the attendees. The problem will be going through all the names and trying to figure out who in the world had a connection to Gabriel or Maria. Or Irena, for that matter, since Gabriel was her cousin. Or maybe it wasn't personal at all. He could have happened upon someone doing something bad and simply been horribly unlucky. My gosh, there must be Secret Service agents everywhere, even on the condo roofs, right? Surely . . ." My words were coming out faster and faster and my breath, too, whistling like the wind in a set of bagpipes that couldn't quite get going.

Nathan reached across the space between us and took my shaking hand again. "Hayley, sweetheart, we don't need you to run the investigation, remember? We've got the FBI here and the Secret Service and most of the Key West Police Department. We only need you to tell us what you saw and heard, okay?"

I nodded, looking down at my small hand in his big one, grateful beyond words for his kindness.

"Breathe with me first," he said, inhaling a big gulp of cumin-scented air and letting it out slowly.

I followed his lead, whooshed out some air, shuddered, and found myself a tiny bit calmer.

"Can you handle one more thing?" he asked, his voice soft.

But I got the underlying meaning. They needed me. "Sure," I said. "Anything."

"Do you recognize this knife?"

Chapter Eight

*A kitchen has high temperature and a lot of people work-
ing at high speed, very close to each other—and with a
knife in their hand, Ms. Puig said. Such a place certainly
can create tensions.*
*—Raphael Minder, "Stressed by Success, a Top
Restaurant Turns to Therapy," The New York Times,
February 28, 2017*

We finishing cleaning up from the dinner after the
interviews had been completed and the last guests
had filtered off the grounds. It was well past midnight when
we powwowed in the kitchen. Concerned about her cousin's
reactions to the attack, Irena had gotten permission to follow
Maria in the ambulance to the hospital. I was grateful to
Turner Markham, who had lobbied to allow her to leave early.
He'd shifted into overdrive after Gabriel was discovered, like
a gracious host at a party gone terribly wrong.

Maria had grabbed my forearm on her way out, gripping

roughly like a drowning woman. She tried to speak, but she was sobbing too hard to get the words out.

"Hayley, please," said Irena, moving forward to circle an arm around her cousin's shoulders. "Can you help us find out who murdered Gabriel? My cousin doesn't believe anyone will tell the truth. She doesn't believe the police care either."

I nodded reluctantly. "Given how many important people were here, no one's going to tell me much of anything. I'll try, though. I'll keep my eyes open." I watched her hurry down the steps after her cousin and the paramedics who supported her, then turned back to the kitchen.

My mother looked exhausted, as did Sam, though he also looked exhausted with the satisfaction of a job well done. Miss Gloria was sound asleep in a chair in the storage hallway where the interviews had been conducted. Her chin was tucked into her chest and she snored softly. Someone had folded clean dishtowels around her shoulders and over her lap to keep her warm.

Sam hovered around my mother, attempting to cheer her up. "I think the beef dish was a huge hit," said Sam, rubbing his belly and grinning. "Did you see how little was left over? And the flan was to die for, just as you said it would be."

But he was trying too hard, sensing as we all did how horrifying the end of the night had been: my mother's best and sharpest kitchen knife found plunged into the chest of her worker's brother. No wonder the whole evening felt like a flop. Who would have an appetite for Cuban food or Cuban history after such a night? Who would remember anything but the brutal murder? And who would ever hire my mother again after such a debacle? Finally, I wondered, briefly and selfishly, whether I could ever taste flan again without thinking of this exhausting and terrifying night.

"Did Nathan explain anything to you about what they think happened?" my mother asked. "Those people interviewing me wouldn't answer a single question."

I mustered a smile. "The last thing he's going to do is leak insider information about a murder—to me especially. The last thing he wants is me inserting my finely honed interview and observational skills into the mix."

Sam snorted with laughter, but Mom looked on the edge of tears.

"Do you think the conference is ruined?" she asked. "Can they possibly continue on as though nothing has happened?"

"In some ways, it's not a bad idea to keep going," I said. "Because if one of the attendees is the murderer, it holds him here longer so the cops can do their work. Or notice if anyone leaves early, or otherwise acts suspicious."

"Him," Sam said. "You think it's a him?"

"Gabriel was very strong," I said, thinking of the dead man's stocky shape and muscular arms and thighs. He'd carried more tables, more chairs, more boxes of heavy plates and cutlery than anyone else while we were setting up earlier in the day. "A lightweight wouldn't have been capable of tussling with him and using the knife like that." I shuddered. "I know I couldn't have done it."

"Even if I could have, I can't imagine doing such a thing. Maybe he was taken by surprise." Sam shook his head and looked around the tidy kitchen. "Looks like we're in good shape here. Let's get home and get rested for tomorrow."

"I feel terrible for Bill, though." We'd all watched him slump out to his scooter, on his face an amalgam of disbelief and disappointment. He and Bob had put so much work and heart into planning this conference—and it had been such a coup to convince the others to hold the biggest events here at the Little White House. I glanced at the time on my phone. "I'm going to run by their place and make sure he's okay, if that works for you. He may not be up, but I can drive by."

My mother nodded. "We have to drop some things off at the commercial kitchen, so we will take Miss Gloria on our way."

"So what's the plan for tomorrow?"

"Thank goodness they are herding the muckety-mucks over to Sunset Key for a fancy lunch at Latitudes. We'll take care of the pastries and the coffee for the morning meetings at the town hall. Feel free to check in, but I think we can manage it." She looked at Sam, who nodded with encouragement. "But we'll need you for the cocktail party at the Hemingway Home tomorrow night. Assuming they're still having it."

"They won't cancel it," Sam said, though the doubt showed on his face, too.

Mom frowned, knitting her brows together. "And if you can possibly come by the kitchen in the afternoon. Oh lordy, we have all those hors d'oeuvres to make. And who knows which of my workers will come. Certainly not Maria. And the way Irena looked, we shouldn't expect her either."

She was starting to wind herself up, which I recognized

perfectly, since in this emotional arena, I was her carbon copy. I felt my insides churn in sympathetic but useless harmony.

"We'll deal with it," said Sam. He widened his eyes and made a shooing motion to me. "You go on along home. Check on Bill and we'll see you tomorrow afternoon."

I gathered my things and went out into the night, which had turned quite cool. The closest we might come to the Key West version of winter—I might even see locals in hats and mittens around town tomorrow. I hopped onto my scooter, fastened the helmet strap under my chin, and motored out of the Truman Annex, past all the large single-family homes that had been designed to look as though they'd been here for a hundred years. Several officers still waited at the guardhouse, but one waved me through the gates without asking me to pull over. Several blocks later, I drove into the Bahama Village neighborhood where Bill and Eric lived.

I passed La Creperie, a small restaurant where tourists often crowded to inhale delicate buckwheat pancakes stuffed with cheese and bacon or fruit and Nutella and mainline café au lait in an attempt to recover from celebrations the night before. I could almost smell the lingering scent of butter and chocolate. The building looked like a survivor from the nineteenth century. But, as Bill had told me, it was only ten years old, like the homes in the Truman Annex—a bit of faux Old Town. Its neighbors on opposite corners, on the other hand, were genuine relics—Blue Heaven restaurant, the former bordello where Hemingway coached boxing, and Johnson's Grocery, run by descendants of the late Bishop Albert Kee. Kee had been a resident of this neighborhood, a preacher, and a self-proclaimed ambassador of the island, who could often be seen by the Southernmost Point, selling pink conch shells and teaching tourists how to blow them.

Bill and Eric lived in a cute conch-style house in the thick of Bahama Village, a neighborhood formerly confined to descendants of the Bahamas. The contrast with the Truman Annex could hardly have been greater. This was not a place where many snowbirds or tourists landed; some of the houses were perfectly manicured, but others lacked the well-kept sheen of the Truman Annex, and a few were truly ramshackle.

Eric and Bill's front porch, with its tropical houseplants and brightly colored cushions, promised leisurely mornings of coffee and afternoons of wine. But the real treasure lay in the backyard, where the kitchen opened to an eating porch and, steps past that, a beautiful tropical garden. The lights were still on in the house, so I went in the side entrance to the back garden. I was greeted inside the gate by a vibrating blur of white fluff, their new dog, Chester, followed by their more reserved Yorkie/Maltese mix, Barkley (also named after Truman's vice president.) If the dogs hadn't gone to bed, the guys would be up too.

"Hello?" I called out, keeping my voice low, as the neighbors were close enough to reach out and take a cup of sugar. "Mind if I come in for a minute?"

Eric welcomed me onto the porch. "Bill just finished filling me in about the disaster at the Little White House. Do you have any news?"

"Nothing." I shook my head. "My so-called inside sources wouldn't tell me anything. Honestly, I don't know that they have any suspects at this point. I don't know if anybody's had to deal with that many people at a crime scene."

Eric said, "It's Key West. Every time a crime is committed, isn't there a crowd around? You must remember the death at the zombie bike ride!"

I wasn't likely to forget that—I had been right behind the victim when she toppled off her bike.

"How is the poor woman whose brother was killed?" Bill asked.

I sighed. "Distraught, as you might expect. She was worried earlier about whether he'd be blamed for the theft of the gold medal. This is a million times worse."

"I don't suppose they made a quick arrest?" Bill asked.

I could only shake my head.

"Do they think this murder was related to the gold medal?" Eric asked, sneaking an anxious glance at Bill.

"Nathan made it clear that he couldn't share any theories with me. Nor were they terribly interested in mine. I told him what I'd seen and heard, but I wasn't close enough to the kitchen when those pops went off to see much of anything useful."

Still on the couch, Bill looked drained, almost gray, completely done in. "This is so terribly tragic. A man killed right there underneath our noses. If only I'd been there to help him."

"So you could have been stabbed too?" Eric asked.

Bill shrugged. "I feel responsible, you know?" We both nodded. "Absolutely nothing new about the medal?" he asked, almost pleading. "I feel in my gut that the two things are connected."

I dipped my head in agreement. "After the guests and the

police left, we searched the kitchen again," I said. "Except for the part that's still a crime scene. They had an officer stationed there to make sure no one trespassed. I swear we looked in every drawer and cabinet and behind everything on the shelves in the main part of the house, too. Just in case someone hid it away after snatching it up. But we turned up nothing. And who would do such a thing? You could never sell something like that, could you?"

"Honestly, I have no idea. I suppose there's a way to sell anything, if you have the right contacts." Bill ran his fingers through his hair and straightened his glasses.

"Or maybe the gold itself was worth a lot?" Eric asked.

"I know it's nowhere near the equivalent of a human life snuffed out, but you can't imagine the fallout that will come from this," Bill said. "Did you know that this medal has not left their country since Hemingway gave it to them, not once, not ever? It was kept in a convent in El Cobre, a small town outside Santiago de Cuba on the island's southeast coast, for safekeeping. You can't imagine what we had to do to persuade them to loan it. Bob and I swore a hundred times over that we'd treasure it and return it safely. You saw the amount of security at the place—in addition to the people they brought in to protect Obama and Buffett and the Cubans. And after that medal vanished this morning, we checked with every guest and every worker on the grounds. How is this possible?" He dropped his head to his hands. Both of the dogs moved closer to him, nudging his arms and whining.

I exchanged a glance with Eric. I'd never seen Bill quite so down. "Let's think about who might have wanted it."

"Someone with deep connections to a black market that we've never heard of," said Eric. "Because how in the world would you unload something so iconic unless you knew of specific collectors or had buyers who specifically wanted it? A serious Hemingway nut? Or, going a little farther afield, maybe someone with a weird kind of emotional attachment to the prize."

"How about someone who wanted to ruin the conference?" Bill asked. "Because that's essentially what is happening here. First the theft, and now a murder? We're dead in the water."

I went over to the couch to offer support but couldn't think of a thing to say.

He looked up from stroking Barkley, who had climbed onto his lap. "Suppose they were trying to ruin something they thought might come out of the conference."

"Such as?" I asked.

"I don't know, like better relations between Cuba and the U.S.? Someone who holds a grudge against the Cuban government. Someone who refuses to see this as a cultural exchange between cities, who doesn't believe America should be doing business with a repressive regime. But this seems like an odd way to go about staking out your position."

"I have to agree," I said.

"Suppose some kind of financial windfall hangs in the balance, something that could come out of the weekend," Eric suggested.

"OK, who has the most invested in the outcome of the conference?" I asked. "Aside from you, of course." Bill looked up with a horrified expression on his face. I perched on the couch next to him and started to reach for his hand, but he pulled it away. "That came out wrong. No one would ever suspect you."

"But no one sees all the layers of meaning and motivation, not right away," said Eric. "The truth takes time to be revealed. Remember when I was a murder suspect?"

"We couldn't forget," I said.

Eric had been jailed for possibly murdering a man involved in a food writers' conference several years before. It had seemed absurd to me that a gentle, kind psychologist could have killed someone, but he had known something no one else did and had refused to speak up about what he knew. And that had made him look guilty. And the thought of that made me even more worried for Bill. If Eric had gotten caught in that kind of web, anyone could.

"You have to tell the authorities everything," I told him. "Anything you remember. Any theory you come up with. Even if it feels uncomfortable, you'll tell them, right?"

"Right," he said briskly. "You know, I'm beat. I'm going to bed." He pushed the dogs aside and marched into the house.

"I'd better go after him," Eric said. "We'll touch base tomorrow."

* * *

I rode back up the island to Houseboat Row, wondering how I'd ever sleep, as wound up as I was feeling. I texted Lorenzo to see if he was around. He reads tarot cards every night for the tourists who visit the Mallory Square sunset celebration.

Some of his customers are simply tipsy people out for a lark. But many are normally grounded people who feel lost in their lives, basically underadvised. They recognize him as a person who has a deeper connection to the universe than most folks. Someone who might help them find direction. I've gone to him many times myself—and found him to be a wizard.

Once the sun sets and the crowds clear out of Mallory Square, he hauls his card table and accoutrements to a little nook on Duval Street to continue offering his services. According to Lorenzo, drinking and tarot are not a good combination. And drinking prevails on Duval. But like the rest of us who live here, he does what he has to to make a living in paradise.

All of that to say, I figured he'd probably be awake.

ANY CHANCE YOU COULD COME BY THE HOUSEBOAT FOR BREAKFAST TOMORROW? 7:30? BACON AND CHEDDAR SCRAMBLE AND BISCUITS? I NEED HELP.

He texted back almost immediately.

OF COURSE.

I felt a lot calmer after he replied—knowing he was out there in my world and that I'd see him in person in the morning. After pouring a half glass of white wine, I sat out on the deck listening to the sounds of the night—the slapping of water on fiberglass, the tinkle of Mrs. Renhart's wind chimes, harmonizing with ours. And finally, from inside my own boat, the distinctively sweet sound of snoring in triple time, two cats and one old lady.

Chapter Nine

*I can only talk about things I've experienced first-hand.
I'm the kind of person who'd have to get into the pan
with the potatoes in order to give my opinion on French
fries.*

—Nina George, *The Little Paris Bookshop*

I got up early to fry the bacon, slice scallions, and grate
cheese for Lorenzo's eggs. A fresh pot of coffee brewed
while I measured flour and baking powder and a pinch of salt
for the biscuits. I cut a stick of butter into the dry mixture,
added a dollop of milk, and mushed it all into a shaggy dough.
I rolled that out into a rough rectangle and cut it into twelve
biscuits. When the timer on the oven dinged to announce it
had reached the right temperature, I popped the pan into the
oven. What he didn't finish, we could freeze. One of life's
little pleasures was finding a stray biscuit in the freezer when
I most needed it.

Since I needed to eat at El Siboney for the *Key Zest* review,
it would be wise to avoid the temptation of a full breakfast.

Though avoiding temptation was not my strong suit. Or so both my father and Nathan might say. And that thought, coupling the two most prominent men in my life together, brought an uncomfortable zing of recognition. Somehow I'd chosen a boyfriend who resembled my father, even though externally they appeared nothing alike. That wasn't all bad—my father was a good guy and he loved me. However, he was quick to leap to judgment, especially if he thought I was acting foolhardy. Nathan Bransford all over.

And my father had walked out on me and Mom when I was a kid. He'd tried to stay involved in child-rearing, but I hadn't seen him as much as I'd wished. Whether it made fair sense or not, I think I'd concluded that (a) Mom wasn't serious enough for him and (b) I was very much like her, so (c) I'd been left too. And left with a little sliver of doubt about whether my father—or any man—would stick with me through thick and thin. After all, he bailed on my mother, right? Why wouldn't I be next?

When the bacon was crispy, the chopped onions were caramelized, and a mound of shredded cheddar was ready to add to the eggs, I heard the soft "yoo-hoo" of Lorenzo as he trotted down the finger that led to our boat. I pulled the biscuits from the oven and went to greet him. Schnootie, the old Schnauzer on the boat next to ours, burst into a cacophony of hoarse woofs. She could no longer see or hear that well, but when she sensed movement or picked up an unusual scent, she sprang into guardian action.

Lorenzo called out a friendly hello to the dog and Mrs. Renhart, who'd come out to see about the fuss. "It smells divine all the way from the parking lot," he said once inside the cabin. He leaned in to kiss my cheek.

"Grab some coffee, and either sit here while I cook the eggs or go out and enjoy the morning."

He poured himself a steaming cup and added a glug of milk. "I'll keep you company. The loonies were out last night," he said. "It will be a pleasure to talk to someone sane."

I laughed. "Not all parties would agree with that assessment."

He looked tired, dark circles under his eyes and his curly hair in disarray. Which made me feel immediately guilty for dragging him out of bed so early. I imagined that in some ways, his job was like that of a therapist. Or a cop. So many problems were presented over the course of a workday, he couldn't help but absorb some negative energy along the way.

"Don't worry," he added with a little grin. "I know I usually keep vampire hours, but this morning I was up anyway."

"You give me cold chills when you do that," I said. "I knew you could read cards, but I didn't know you could read my mind. If I need to block you out of some secrets, I'm going to have to get one of those lead dental aprons to wear over my head."

"Wouldn't work on me and you." He chuckled and adjusted his tortoiseshell glasses to sit further up on his nose. Evinrude sprang onto the banquette, strutted over to Lorenzo, and began to butt his hand with his head. "I can't read your mind, but I do know you pretty well."

"I'll say." I slid the platter of cheesy eggs onto the table between us, along with the bacon and a plate of biscuits.

"Is Miss Gloria joining us?" he asked.

I gestured at the article from the *Key West Citizen* that she'd taped to the refrigerator. "Even though the event last night went on forever, she's already out walking with Mrs. Dubisson. Ever since she read that column by Leigh and Dan at WeBeFit last week explaining that seniors could extend their life expectancy by walking three times a week, she's been out there every day."

While he ate and I nibbled, I filled him in on the security, the protesters, the missing medal, and the horrendous discovery of the murder at the end of the night.

"A night filled with emotional swings and contrasts," he said.

I nodded. "We were so thrilled about the president and Jimmy Buffett and Diana Nyad—it could hardly have been a more exciting trio. You should have seen Miss Gloria—she was positively vibrating. And then to have it all ruined." I buttered a hot biscuit and slathered on a tablespoon of mango honey. "And even before that, passing the protesters at the gates reminded me that not everyone was happy about this conference."

"People have very strong feelings about Cuba," he said, rubbing Evinrude's jowls as I cleared the table. Sparky made a flying leap, landed on Evinrude's stomach, and began to rabbit-kick him. Lorenzo giggled as he watched them wrestle. "And they tend to forget that the people who are squeezed by all the political posturing are the Cubans themselves."

After the breakfast dishes were cleared and stowed, he brought his cards out from his voluminous pant pocket. "Three cards okay?"

"You're the best friend ever," I said.

He shuffled the deck over and over and then set the stack of cards in front of him with both hands resting on them. He took a deep breath and closed his eyes. If I'd been a new customer sitting with him at his table on Mallory Square, he would have explained that this was a small meditation to clear his mind, to clear the path from the cards—and the energy with which I'd infuse them—to his brain and his heart. Often at that point, the visitors who had chosen to have their cards read as a lark began to sense that his gift was very real.

He asked me to cut the deck into three piles and then choose which one I wanted. This was by far the hardest part of a reading—what if my real cards were in the pile I failed to choose? Did other people actually feel a connection to one of their stacks? I was flying blind, as none of them ever called to me. These kinds of silly thoughts kept me busy while I was waiting for him to deal out my three.

The space between his eyebrows furrowed once the cards lay exposed on Miss Gloria's burnished Formica table: the ten of swords, the two of swords, the two of cups. He rubbed a forefinger across his upper lip and cleared his throat.

I had never seen him take this long to read the meaning of any cards.

"At least it's not the tower," I said brightly.

"It's not the tower," he agreed, "but remember what I told you about the tower–"

"I know, but that card still freaks me out." I hate seeing that card turned up, with its burning structure and people flinging themselves out the windows to their deaths. Lorenzo has assured me that it's not as bad as it appears. It's a card about learning that something we believed to be true is actually false. The true meaning has to do with facing the fact that things need to change. But change is hard, and I'm not famous for gracious transitions.

"The two of cups suggests love and friendship," he said, pointing to my first card, containing figures of a man and a woman facing each other, holding large golden cups. A lion with wings hovered above them. "This relationship is built on passion and strength and a healthy attitude. Do you see the way the man and the woman are gazing into one another's eyes? They have developed a strong understanding, are maybe even considering marriage."

He quirked one eyebrow, waiting for me to comment.

"That's a mystery to me," I said with a grimace, my eyes cast down at the table, studying the card. He knew I was dating Nathan, and unlike some of my other friends, he had yet to reveal his feelings about the relationship. "You wouldn't have guessed that from our interactions over the past couple of days. Don't get me wrong, I'd like to be married. And I think Nathan's my guy. But I don't want to leap into that for the sake of being married. For the sake of the wedding, if you know what I mean?" I looked back up at him and he nodded in agreement. "Right now, the whole idea of marriage kind of wigs me out. Like, I have no idea what makes one relationship work and another one tank."

"You know more than you give yourself credit for," he said as he touched the second card.

This one scared me, featuring as it did a set of swords stabbed into a prone man's back. I shivered, flashing to the horrible sight of Maria stained with her brother's blood. And how shocked she must have been when she found him. I couldn't imagine what she must have seen and how she processed that horror.

"The ten of swords," he said. "This can mean failed plans, loss, and defeat. Although so many swords might suggest that the negative tends to be overdramatized. The background of the card shows more optimism. Though the top is black, underneath the clouds are lifting and the sky is blue. Maybe the storm has passed? Maybe this night is over?"

"I don't like it," I said. "All I can think of is that knife stabbed into Gabriel."

"Was it more than one?" Lorenzo asked, his hands moving to his chest, as if he could feel the pain of that moment. And perhaps he could.

"Only one. But that's all it took," I added. "Maybe this means the investigation will be wrapped up quickly?"

"Maybe," he said. "But remember not to be too literal. I show you what's there in the cards, and you discern the meaning." He reached over to straighten the third card. This one was simpler in design, a large red heart with three swords plunged through it. In the background, there was nothing but gray. Clouds and rain. Even Lorenzo would have trouble brushing the gloom off this one.

"This card can be disquieting," he admitted. "The three of swords. It can mean loss and pain, maybe a death or divorce?"

"I'm not even married yet!"

He barely smiled. "Rain, as you know, brings growth after the storm has finished."

"You're reaching for something positive so I don't come unglued," I said, imagining that maybe I'd left my real cards in one of the other two piles.

"No need for that," he said. "Just keep your eyes open for darkness. I know you like to see the light, but be careful. And anyone could have told you that, based on what you've been through the past twenty-four hours."

"And of course, Nathan did tell me." I sighed and pushed the cards back across the table.

By the time Lorenzo left, I was not only exhausted from the night before but also nervous about his warning, worried about Bill's mental health and my mother's catering business, and fussing about who would take up the slack if Maria and Irena didn't show up for the next catered event. And why would they, with such a painful, violent death in their family?

And all of that was probably covering my own anxiety about the worst of everything: coming so close to another tragic murder.

Chapter Ten

When I need to get away from it all, competing for a table is one of the main things I'm getting away from. That, and meals longer than a filibuster, and hearing that "chef" would like me to eat this particular taste in one bite while rubbing my stomach and patting my head.
—Pete Wells, "So Long, Menus; Hello, Pots and Pans," *The New York Times*, August 19, 2015

The last thing I was interested in doing was eating a meal at the Cuban restaurant and writing the darned thing up. But both Palamina and Wally had been good about allowing me the time off during this high season weekend when our e-zine was most popular, so I wasn't about to let them down. I'd promised them both that I could handle everything—actually, not only promised, but made it sound as though this weekend would be a cakewalk. I'd laid it on thick as chocolate sour cream icing. So I had no choice but to eat fast and write faster.

El Siboney was located in a low-key residential area of

Old Town, and from early morning to late at night, the restaurant filled the neighborhood with the smells of garlic, cumin, and roasted pork. They don't take reservations, so in the busy high season, tourists lined up for dinner starting at five. I was hoping that showing up for an early lunch would help me bypass the wait that I didn't have time for. The outside of the building was unassuming red brick, while the inside had the feel of a diner, with red vinyl tablecloths, yellow beadboard walls, furniture serving function over form, and tons of hot sauce.

I was seated quickly at a two-top, and ordered the traditional roast pork dinner that I hadn't tried before. While I waited, I tried to keep my uneasiness about Lorenzo's cards at bay by drafting the introduction for my Cuban food piece. One ugly, clunky sentence in, I could see this wasn't going to happen.

The tarot reading wasn't my only concern—just the latest in a long line of problems and questions. I was also feeling sad about Gabriel and Maria—who murdered him and why—plus worried sick for Bill, hoping the conference wouldn't be canceled for my mother's sake, and wondering who in the world would've stolen that gold medal. As I gazed into space, mind whirling, a slender woman with long dark hair and a T-shirt reading SUN, RUM, KEY LIME PIE led a group of tourists into the dining room and settled them at a large table against the wall. My friend Analise Smith from Key West Food Tours.

"You'll be eating pork in mojo sauce with onions, served along with traditional Cuban side dishes. Mojo sauce is a classic Cuban marinade made of sour orange, oregano, cumin, garlic, and salt. Keep in mind that this is only the first stop of six," she reminded her patrons, "so make sure you save some room for the rest of the samples. And also, save a little piece of Cuban bread for something I'll show you after lunch. The bread is a particular staple of the Cuban people, and it's made with lard."

Several of the tourists groaned.

"Wait until you taste it," she said with a laugh. "Lard might become your new favorite ingredient." She left them distributing water from a plastic pitcher and slid into the chair across from me.

"What in the world went on last night at the conference?" she asked. "It's all the talk of the island." Analise's mother was Cuban, so she would have had her finger on the pulse of that community.

"It was bad," I said, and told her how Maria's brother had been killed late in the evening, and about the popping noises that had sent the guests diving into the dirt. "We lost several trays of flan, too," I said. "Sounds absurd, doesn't it, that I would even think of that when a man died?"

"Sounds like you're in shock," Analise said.

I felt tears prick my eyes. Though I'd broken down the night before when the police had questioned me, I hadn't allowed myself to truly feel how stressful the night had been since then. I'd tried to wall my reactions off and march forward as though life were normal. And convince myself that even if it wasn't, I could handle whatever was thrown at me. "I think you're right," I said, sniffling and digging in my backpack for a tissue. I finally gave up and wiped my nose on a paper napkin.

"Though lord knows flan can cause a family feud on this island," she added, once I'd composed myself.

I laughed. "I keep wondering if this was about something personal? Was there a personal relationship between Gabriel and some other person at the party that we knew nothing about? Or was the killer someone who disagreed violently with the idea of the conference? But then why kill Gabriel?"

"Plenty of people don't approve of this weekend," Analise admitted. "Not every Cuban-American who lives in Key West or Miami or anywhere in the U.S. feels good about improving the relationship between the countries. If your family lost a lot while fleeing Cuba, then the taste in your mouth could be very bitter."

"Of course," I said.

"The part about Hemingway's gold medal gone missing, is that true?" Analise asked.

"Yes, that's what sent yesterday off to a ghastly start. There were a lot of priceless Hemingway artifacts on display, including the medal he won for *The Old Man and the Sea*. It was stolen right out from under our eyes. Once that happened, the organizers were of course scrambling to locate it, and when they couldn't, explain its absence away. But the Cuban delegation was outraged." I made a face and heaved a big sigh. "We thought that had to be the low point of the evening, but then the murder was discovered at the very time Mr. Obama was onstage."

Her eyes got wide. "Obama? So it's true what I read in the Key West locals Facebook group this morning."

Key West seems to run on the fuel of Facebook gossip, especially in the high winter season.

I nodded. "And Diana Nyad. And Jimmy Buffet. An amazing trifecta. Can you imagine what a coup it was to get them all together on that little patch of lawn?" I sighed again. "To have the night ruined was devastating on so many levels. Do you know Maria?"

"A little," she said. "She's a nice lady and devoted to her mother. Her brother too. I've tasted her magical flan. I believe it's her grandmother's recipe, brought over from the mother country. They guard it as though it was the family jewels."

Just then, an efficient waitress delivered my food. "*Gracias*," I said, inhaling the magical smells that rose from the hot food. "Are you going to the funeral tomorrow?" I asked Analise.

She nodded.

"Can I sit with you? Maybe you can help me translate if the Spanish overwhelms me."

After agreeing to meet outside Our Lady of the Sea at nine forty-five the next morning, Analise returned to her tour group and I to my food. I snapped photos of the dish, then sampled citrusy roast pork, deep-fried plantains, and rice with black beans, trying to think of words that would describe how ordinary ingredients could come together in such a homey and delicious way.

I accepted the check as a text vibrated in from my mother.

I didn't need to hear the tone of voice to realize that she was stressed to the point of hysterical.

IRENA AND MARIA NO GO FOR TODAY. CAN YOU SPARE TIME TO HELP SET UP AT HEMINGWAY HOME?

BE THERE IN 20, I tapped back into my phone.

It wasn't on my calendar, but I felt terrible about the way my mother's first major job was going. And then I realized that if my friend Rusty Hodgdon was on guide duty today, I might be able to learn everything I would ever want to know about that missing gold medal. And more important, even the murder.

Chapter Eleven

He was drinking another of the frozen daiquiris with no sugar in it and as he lifted it, heavy and the glass frost-rimmed, he looked at the clear part below the frappéd top and it reminded him of the sea. The frappéd part of the drink was like the wake of a ship and the clear part was the way the water looked when the bow cut it when you were in shallow water over marl bottom. That was almost the exact color.
—Ernest Hemingway, *Islands in the Stream*

The Hemingway Home and Museum on Whitehead Street is one of the top tourist sites on the island. Hemingway lived in this home during the thirties with his second wife, Pauline. Even with the lines of visitors gawking at the house, the grounds, and the cats, this place still manages to bring my blood pressure down each time I step inside the brick walls that mark the perimeter of the property. Some of my reaction is due simply to the grace of the white painted home with its lime-green shutters and black metal railings, accompanied by a most inviting pool and surrounded with stunning tropical foliage. And some of it is the mob of poly-dactyls who live here, many-toed cats said to be descendants of Hemingway's beloved first cat, Snow White.

Catering at the Hemingway Home takes place from the back gate on a side street so as not to interfere with the guests streaming through the main entrance. Mom's new van was set up next to the gate, and behind that sat a rental truck loaded with chairs and tables. No cooking was allowed on the grounds, so I knew that the food my mother planned to serve would be assembled in her big kitchen, ready for a last-minute finish in the van. I parked my scooter across the street in view of the Key West lighthouse, which Hemingway reportedly used as a target on nights that he was staggering home drunk from Sloppy Joe's bar. Then I headed back around to the side entrance. Mom came trotting toward me from the direction of the cat cemetery, her hair tied back with a green bandana, a fine sheen of sweat on her face, and no makeup. Her face lit up with gratitude when she saw me.

"Thank god you're here. We're so shorthanded. Irena said she could get here by five, but that leaves all the setup to us. If you know anyone who could pitch in with the cleanup tonight, they are hired sight unseen. Sam and some guy named Jorge are working on the tables right now."

"Jorge?"

Mom grimaced and then smiled. "I have no clue where he even found him."

"I'll set up chairs then?"

My mother nodded. I grabbed a dolly, loaded it with white

plastic folding chairs, and then rolled it through the grounds, past the little cat houses where new kittens and the more sensitive cats were housed during big events. Tourists were climbing the steep stairway that led to Hemingway's writing studio, and I heard one of the guides, Rusty Hodgdon, tell them he'd be waiting on the other side to conclude the tour. I raised a finger to let him know I'd like to chat when he was finished.

I carried my load of chairs past the swimming pool to the big lawn where tonight's party would take place. Sam and Jorge had already opened up three round tables and were wrestling the fourth into place. On one of them, two massive cats with extra toes on their front paws sprawled as if they were waiting for the action to begin. I rubbed one yellow-striped belly and scratched under the chin of a handsome gray guy.

"I better not catch you up here after we put the tablecloths on," I said, knowing these cats pretty much did what they wanted no matter who scolded or warned them. My pal Donna Vanderveen, who had formerly worked here as a cat caretaker, had once seen two of the cats licking the icing off the back of a wedding cake. Without a word to the bride or her family, she had shooed them away and repaired the damage.

As I worked, I ruminated about Lorenzo's cards. Maybe he hadn't really been reading *my* cards. Maybe they belonged to our island. After all, Lorenzo believes that cities have astrological signs, exactly as people do. Key West is a Capricorn. Always all about the money: how much, where it will come from, and whose pockets it might line. I reminded myself to look at the "Citizens Voice" in the paper when I got home—this column is often a good snapshot of what folks in town are most worried about. Maybe the vibes he was picking up in my kitchen had come directly from the newspaper, not from me at all. It sounded farfetched, but who knew how the mystery of tarot really worked?

Rusty Hodgdon came over when he'd finished with his group. A big bear of a man with white hair and a beard, he looked like a stand-in for Hemingway himself.

"Any chance you know someone who'd want to earn a few extra bucks this evening during the cleanup?" I asked, figuring he'd probably be at the party anyway. "My mom's kind of desperate after last night's debacle."

"I'm available," he said, and began helping me unfold and arrange the chairs. "I have to be here to take the big guns on a tour of the place." He paused for a moment. "You looked like you had a question back there." He waved in the direction of Hemingway's studio.

"I wanted to ask you about the gold medal. You know, the one that went missing. What's the history there? Until yesterday, I knew nothing about it."

"Oh yeah, the Cuban guests were PO'd about the disappearance," he said. "That's about all anyone could talk about yesterday. Not that I can blame them. Our CEO is plenty nervous about holding tonight's event here. We have a lot of valuable memorabilia and he doesn't want another case of sticky fingers. The security is going to be tight."

"Another case?" I paused for a minute to wipe off the sweat beading on my upper lip. "I don't even know quite how to ask this question, but I'm trying to figure out what the medal might mean to the person who stole it. Was it lifted because of its monetary value? Or could there be some deeper reason?" I wondered if there was any way the medal could be connected to Gabriel's murder. Like, had he seen the theft in action? I wasn't ready to voice this out loud. "I figured you'd know the history of the award and how Mr. Hemingway won it."

We finished unloading the cart of chairs and headed back to the truck to get more.

"Maybe you remember hearing that Hemingway's second wife, Pauline, found a gift given to him by Pablo Picasso in one of her storage boxes long after they'd split up?" Rusty asked as we walked. "It was a statue of a cat. We had it displayed in their bedroom upstairs until 2000, when it was stolen at the end of a tour."

"Yikes! I can't imagine how that guide must have felt," I said.

He shook his head and began to unfold the new stack of chairs. "Awful. And even worse, I think the thief used it as a down payment for a dinghy. He seemed to have no specific connection to the statue at all. He needed fast cash and the guide must have mentioned it was valuable."

"Wow," I said. "That's really nervy! So possibly someone lifted the medal for money, too."

"Maybe. But on the other hand, everything Hemingway did was motivated by competition," Rusty said. "Or informed by it. And I don't mean consciously. That's my theory anyway. He brought out the competitive streak in both the men and the women around him. The women vied among themselves for his attention. And obviously, with four wives, there were a lot of winners and losers."

He gestured at the pool, winking blue and clear in the sunlight. "I'm sure you've heard the story of how Pauline oversaw the building of this expensive swimming pool while Hemingway was out of town. You can bet he was already half in love with his third wife-to-be, Martha, and you can bet that Pauline damn well knew it and was going to make him pay, one way or another."

I grabbed the empty dolly and started to walk back to the rental van for the final load. Rusty followed along, continuing to talk.

"For the men in his life, the competition took a different form, like the size of the fish they caught that day. Or how many drinks they could pound back. Or success in boxing or bullfighting. But he was an enigma because he had a very soft side too." Two young cats, a yellow tiger and a tortoise, darted across the path in front of us. "Who would've guessed such a tough macho guy would be crazy for cats?"

I laughed. "Good point. What about with his writing? Was he competitive there as well?" I'd taken Rusty's guided tours inside the house here on the grounds—he was well versed in Hemingway's literary history. As a writer himself, he was a great admirer of Hemingway's spare style.

"Definitely competitive," Rusty said. "I think he and his peers spurred each other to write harder and better."

"Would there have been someone who might have felt they deserved the medal that year?" I asked.

"Maybe. I'm not aware of anyone in particular," he said. "They certainly wouldn't have been alive to attend yesterday's dinner party." He chuckled and pulled on his beard. "Fun fact: did you know there is a contest for bad imitations of Hemingway's writing?"

I shook my head.

"You should Google it—there are some snippets posted online and they're a hoot. I entered a couple of years ago and got an honorable mention."

"You entered a bad Hemingway contest? Do tell!"

He laughed. "Of course I have it memorized for moments like this. I called it 'A Farewell to Harm,' and it went like so:

He had hired the guide again after one too many women gone wrong. 'You drink too much,' the woman said. 'You stink of beer and fish.'

The man and the guide had been at sea for hours, and reeled in two marlin. Both of them were big as Spanish bulls and that strong too; heaving silver bodies, that glinted in the sunlight and left the man and the guide breathless.

'Let's have a drink,' the fishing guide said, though he knew the man's history. 'One drink won't hurt you.'

'OK, but only if it's rum and beer. And only if you pour the rum slowly so the foam resembles the beach at low tide.'

'Not until five. The tide won't run out until five PM,' the fishing guide said. 'That's when you see the foam.'"

By the end of Rusty's recitation, I was laughing too hard to speak.

One of the other guides gestured to him from the porch. "Got to go," he said. "I have one more tour before I'm off until this evening."

After he'd left to greet his next group of tourists, I thought about my own writing as I loaded the last stack of chairs onto the dolly and delivered them to the yard. My scribbling in no way compared to the prizewinning prose of Mr. Hemingway. But in my own small pond of food critics, I aimed to be the best that I could be at writing restaurant reviews. I wanted to be entertaining while scrupulously fair to the places I visited. I wanted to guide people to choose the best food on the island because they were spending their hard-earned dollars and they deserved to get something delicious in exchange. I dreamed I'd write as well as my idols someday—the *New York Times* food critics Pete Wells, Frank Bruni, Ruth Reichl. But what did any of this have to do with the stolen prize? I couldn't see it clearly yet, but still something was tugging at me, suggesting there was a connection.

Once the chairs and tables were all in place and my mother had assured me that the food was under reasonable control, I ran back home to change clothes and pick up Miss Gloria for the second time in as many days. She had insisted on doing laundry during her so-called rest day, so we both had clean white shirts and pressed black pants. Miss Gloria had added a pin of two dancing cats on her shirt in honor of the polydactyls who would be in attendance.

"Cory Held was here again today," she said, looking glum as she pointed to the houseboat next to ours. "This time with a man who looked suspiciously like a home inspector. She wouldn't say a word about the buyer, just that things have a way of turning out fine on this island." She perched her little hands on her narrow hips. "Now if that isn't the worst sort of clichéd real estate tripe, I don't know what is."

I kissed her on the forehead and went in to take a shower. Because what could I say really? We had no control over our new neighbors. And she had told me that she'd dreaded the Renharts as neighbors when they moved in on the other side, and they'd turned out just fine. Or the missus had, anyway. Mr. Renhart was a terrible grump, prone to political rants and complaints about the elderly animals his wife had adopted. He occasionally trapped us on the dock, but we'd gotten adept at smiling and nodding while shuffling inexorably toward our own houseboat.

Once I'd showered, I grabbed a little container of salty, creamy fish dip from Cole's Peace out of the fridge and smeared it on a couple of pepper crackers. I ate standing at the counter while reading the posts in the "Citizens Voice" column in the *Key West Citizen*. Anyone in our community can call or email in an opinion about life in Key West, and the newspaper prints the comments on page two. Today's "Voice" contained the usual smattering of grievances:

Should we be connecting at all with Cuba when their government's human rights violations are legion? I don't believe this weekend is about a cultural exchange. It's about profit and power. Who is benefiting from this?

Kudos to the staff at the Truman Little White House for what might have been the most spectacular event ever, had it not been for the tragic ending.

Shouldn't we have been using our expensive, top-of-the-line, must-have amphitheater for a show like the party last night on the White House grounds? Isn't that why we spent millions of dollars for something half the citizens of Key West didn't want? Isn't that why we built the "Their Dream, Our Money" showpiece? Or should it be named the Key West Taxpayers Memorial Boondoggle Coliseum?

Why is it that bicyclists on this island feel they don't have to follow the rules of the road? Going up the wrong way on one-way streets, refusing to stop at red lights, weaving among the traffic. Don't they realize that the only people immune from regulations in Key West are chickens, iguanas, and city commissioners?

Our police chief should be embarrassed about the debacle at the White House yesterday. First, a priceless artifact is stolen. And second, a man is murdered under the heaviest security ever seen on this island. Will we ever see anything from our police department aside from boneheaded incompetence?

As usual, most of the comments were anonymous. And negative—although I got a good chuckle from the caller who lumped our city commissioners in with iguanas and chickens.

Both commissioners and police officers in this town have to develop thick skins and a sense of humor or they'll go crazy. I would have loved to learn the identity of the first citizen caller, who talked about profit and power. Because I was getting the sense that Gabriel had been killed for something big, something related to the mixed feelings about the conference. And maybe to the stolen medal. I had no real evidence on which to base this—mostly intuition. Both mine and Lorenzo's.

Would there be a way to find out who that anonymous caller was? Wally would know, if anyone did. He'd worked for the *Citizen* before founding *Key Zest*, and he still had a lot of friends on the staff. I waffled about reaching out.

But this seemed important—figuring out who had murdered Gabriel and whether anyone else was in danger. I'd take that approach rather than telling him I wanted to get my friend Bill and his boss, Bob, off the hook. Before I could overthink it, I dialed Wally's cell and explained my theory that the anonymous comments were possibly connected to the tragedy.

"Listen," he said after an uncomfortable silence. "I was pretty clear that you were to keep your eyes open for political slants but otherwise stay out of this story. Wasn't I? If you have conspiracy theories, you should report them to your police contacts." His voice was level, but the words stung.

I used my snottiest tone to answer back. He deserved snotty. "Fine, I'll stay out of it. If I need information in the future, I'll use my *police contacts*. I'm sure I'll get more from them. In every imaginable way." Then I hung up fast, swallowing the flush of shame I felt after his scolding. And another flush of embarrassment about acting childishly in return. I wished we could find some kind of level ground where we each appreciated the other, unstained by our short romantic past.

I texted Nathan with a breezy check-in, thanking him for his kindness and telling him all was well. Then I mentioned that they might want to follow up on the "Voice" comments in this morning's paper. There would be absolutely no payoff for mentioning Lorenzo. Nathan was the least spiritually tuned-in person I knew, though he would say he had a finely honed woo-woo detection radar.

I forced myself back to questions about the stolen medal.

Supposing that someone could get big, big bucks for that medal, what if poor Gabriel had gotten mixed up with that person? Wouldn't the next logical question be who needed the money?

As the "Citizen's Voice" caller suggested, who stood to benefit most from the conference? Possibly, one of the people included in the small group of VIPs yesterday?

I hated the next question that floated into my brain.

Could there be something bad going on behind the scenes at the Little White House? Bill Averyt would surely know what was happening with the finances.

The question was, would he tell me?

Chapter Twelve

She was not much of a cook, but she married men who could cook. Men, one after another, who beat her, she said, until she looked like a melanzana, *the deep purple color of an eggplant.*
—Victoria Pesce Elliott, "Remembering My Mom's Meatballs," *Miami Herald,* November 24, 2015

Before plunging right into our duties at the Hemingway Home, Miss Gloria and I took a quick swing around the grounds. The crowd seemed subdued, though the lines at the bars were long, with bartenders mixing drinks as fast as the patrons could swallow them—mojitos, Cuba Libres, and Hemingway specials made from rum, grapefruit and lime juices, and a dash of maraschino cherry liquid. I returned to the catering truck and took a tray of mini Cuban sandwiches and black bean burgers garnished with avocado and caramelized onions. Miss Gloria followed me with a tray containing small plastic cups of black bean soup. I kept one eye on her and both ears open for any news about yesterday's tragic events.

Once my tray was almost empty, I carried it to the side of the lawn where my friend Bill was standing with Turner Markham. They appeared to be arguing. As soon as I got within hearing distance of their conversation, I wished I had gone another direction. But they'd seen me, and I thought it would feel more awkward to turn and bolt.

"Why drag them over there and rub their noses in that tawdry history?" Markham was asking. "They're already upset about the problems this weekend with theft and murder, as well they should be."

"Exactly because it's history," Bill said, his posture even straighter than usual. "We are supposed to be talking about historical relations between our island and theirs. The thinking is that once we know where we came from, we can figure out where we go. These chugs were an important, though admittedly fraught, part of our joint history. Eric would say it's like psychotherapy—you don't make progress if you only skate along the surface."

Markham looked stubbornly unconvinced and Bill appeared increasingly annoyed. "We're also doing this because we told them we were planning to," Bill added. "How would it look if we changed the agenda now? We'd look like marionettes, like someone was pulling our strings behind the curtain."

I couldn't help thinking it might also look as though they were responding reasonably to rising tensions at the conference—and fears about the possibility of another tragedy. Or, canceling the chug visit could look like bowing to one side's politics at the price of the other's. It was complicated for sure.

"A lot of things have happened already this weekend that weren't planned," said Markham. "And it seems to me that part of the problem was biting off way more than you could reasonably handle."

"Meaning what?"

"Meaning if you people had kept your focus on the conference itself instead of showing off with fancy speakers and musicians, it might have gone well. And if you had thought to have someone watching the displays in the first place, we wouldn't be in this pickle." Markham was fairly hissing by this point.

I grinned inanely and thrust my picked-over tray of goodies between the two of them. "Tonight we are serving mini Cuban sandwiches with mojo-marinated pork roast with maple mustard and pickles from our local Pickle Baron. And for the non–meat eaters, we are serving mini black bean burgers spiced with cumin and jalapeños."

Both Bill and Markham grimaced and refused my proffered nibbles. Fortunately, I was saved from babbling further inanities when the Key West mayor stepped up to the podium.

"On behalf of the staff of the Hemingway Home and on behalf of our conference organizers and all the people of Key West, I am privileged to welcome you to Hemingway's Key West home."

He went on to describe Hemingway's love for both the towns of Key West and Havana. Behind me, I heard a man whisper to his wife that Key West officials seemed to ignore the fact that Hemingway had spent little time on this island compared with the time he spent in his Havana home. More competition over Hemingway, but this time the two islands were jostling for position. It occurred to me that the folks who ran this home might feel a bit like one of Hemingway's earlier wives—left, by a man with large appetites, for something more alluring.

"While you continue to enjoy hors d'oeuvres," the mayor went on, "we welcome you to take a tour of the home. Your host will be one of our premier guides, Rusty Hodgdon." He pointed to Rusty, who waved and smiled, and the visitors began to cluster around him. "After the tour, you'll be delighted by our caterer's foray into Cuban sweets. I hear the guava pastries are to die for." He seemed to realize this was an unfortunate description, as he stepped down from the podium and melted quickly into the crowd.

"Tonight we will start our tour in the living room with the man who built the house in 1851, Asa Tift, a wrecker/salvager and marine architect," Rusty said in a booming voice. "He died in 1889, alone and without a will. The estate got tied up in litigation and remained primarily boarded up and empty for forty-two years until Ernest Hemingway and his second wife, Pauline Pfeiffer, bought it in 1931 for eight thousand dollars."

His words trailed off as he led the group from the porch into the house. I signaled to Bill and pulled him aside to see how his day had gone.

"Just about as well as you can imagine given that ugly exchange you overheard," he said, rubbing his hand over his face. "Poor Bob is so upset about the missing medal and the stabbing, he's rendered practically mute. We were hoping for all kinds of great publicity for the Little White House this weekend. Instead we've become the focus of lurid stories about theft and murder." He tipped his chin at the police officers checking visitors' purses and bags as they exited through the front gate.

"Are you worried something else is going to happen?" I asked Bill.

"That's a concern," he said. "Half the people involved with this conference want to cancel the rest of the weekend. But anybody involved in potential lucrative business deals, of course, thinks that's a terrible idea."

"Who's on that list?" I asked, my mind reeling with thoughts about how the murder might have hurt some attendees and helped others.

"Dana Sebek, who's working on access to Cuban coral reefs, wants the discussions to continue." Bill nodded at the attractive woman I'd seen in his group on Friday, and we watched her chatter with a little group of Havana visitors.

"How about Bob?" I asked.

"Of course he wants everyone to be safe. But canceling would be a big blow to our organization. We were hoping to not only score lots of new memberships but also secure corporate sponsorships.

"And I wouldn't say this to him, but now I'm a little worried about taking this group to the botanical garden. Our mayor's already declined to accompany us. And Markham doesn't want to go either. And who knows how many of the Cubans will come?" His eyes brightened. "Any chance you could come along tomorrow morning? I could use some extra help defusing the tension. Someone who could keep up a line of chitchat . . ."

"I'm not sure that's a compliment." I grinned, thinking about the obligations already packing tomorrow's schedule. But he looked desperate, so I didn't see how I could refuse. "Sure," I said. "Anything for you. What time?"

"Seven thirty at the entrance to the garden?"

I hurried off to load my tray with the sweet delicacies my mom had whipped up today. So far, her Cuban-style food was rivaling what I'd tasted this morning at El Siboney. I hoped my mojito cake could live up to her standards. I nearly flattened Lieutenant Torrence as I rushed back to the party with a full tray of guava pastries, rice pudding, and mini *dulce de leche* cheesecakes.

"You're in a hurry," he said. "Something important on your mind?"

"Pastries filled with guava and cream cheese," I said with what was certainly a silly grin. He had a sweet tooth, but his really soft spot was for my red velvet cake. And that would definitely not be on the menu tonight.

"Can you bring Miss Gloria to the police station sometime tomorrow morning?" he asked. "It's more or less routine. We'll be going over what you told us yesterday about what you noticed before and after the murder."

"More or less routine?" I narrowed my eyes and tried to read the real meaning behind his words. "I take it that means you're not close to an arrest."

He said nothing, but then zipped his fingers across his lips. "The investigation isn't going the way we'd hoped. The

Cuban visitors have buttoned up tight. Whether they were told not to talk or whether this is their normal reaction to police questions, no one seems to have seen much of anything."

"Hence, the second interviews," I said. "Maybe early afternoon, would that work? Morning is already more full than I can manage. I just agreed to go with this group to the botanical gardens, plus somehow they managed to get Gabriel's funeral mass scheduled on a Sunday morning. I'll make sure Miss Gloria is free as well. By the way, how are Zeus and Apollo?"

Torrence owned two elderly miniature Pinschers and doted on them the way I did Evinrude. He beamed. "They're doing well for old guys. I'll tell them that you asked. In fact, you might see them tomorrow and you can ask yourself. They're coming to the station for our 'take your dog to work' day."

* * *

We were puttering home to the houseboat by eleven, me wondering all the way how I'd get everything on tomorrow's to-do list accomplished. Somehow I'd make it work—the funeral, the cake, the articles, the chugs, the police, assisting with the dinner at the Little White House. Somehow it would all fall into place. Though tallying up the list made me feel anxious.

Once we parked at Houseboat Row, greeted the cats, and distributed bits of tuna, I felt exhausted but my nerves were jangling. "I don't know how I can sleep," I told Miss G.

"Me either," she said.

And she was the champion of sleeping.

"Plus," she continued, "I'm afraid that the police will want to hammer on me tomorrow, pressure me to tell them something about the murder. But it's all a jamble in my mind. I'd hate to make things up because I'm nervous." She looked so cute, with her quivery lips and white hair sticking up every which way. And so worried.

"They only push old ladies on TV cop shows," I said, trying to sound reassuring.

She rolled her eyes. "This from a woman who gets hysterical every time she has to set foot in that station."

"I've gotten better since I've gotten to know some of the guys."

But she had a point. I could still remember my disastrous first visit to the KWPD when they'd fingered me as one of the suspects for murder by key lime pie. Official police visits were stressful, for sure, no matter the circumstances. Truth was, I felt jumpy about separating fact from fiction, too. "What if we did a guided meditation?" I asked.

"What the heck is that?"

"Eric uses it sometimes with his anxious patients," I said. "He gets them to relax and then leads them through their memories of a traumatic event." This was not my worst idea ever—imagining what we'd seen and heard before the popping noises. Miss Gloria, especially, might come up with some clues about Gabriel's killer. She had been close to the storeroom where the murder happened.

"His most neurotic patients?" Miss Gloria asked with a giggle. "We would fit right in."

"I didn't ask him. You know how tight-lipped he is about his people. Probably."

"How does it work?" she asked.

"First we lie down somewhere where we can relax." We went back out onto the deck to our matching chaise lounges. There was no need to consult on this: this tiny spot of heaven drained the tension out of a tight body faster than any masseuse could have. I lit the candle that sat on the table between us, and it flickered softly in the darkness, reminding me of a gothic romance novel.

"What next?"

"Next we close our eyes and tighten and relax our muscle groups." I talked her through what I thought I remembered Eric telling me. "Notice your feet and toes, the cells, the skin, the muscles, the bones. Now tighten them as hard as you can, tighter and tighter."

"If this gives me a charley horse, I'm going to be peeved," said Miss Gloria.

"Shhh. Now let the tension go." By the time I'd moved up and down our bodies, I could feel my breathing getting slower and more even. Miss Gloria's sounded that way too. I was afraid she was falling asleep, although that wasn't all bad either. Sometimes, because she had more zip than a lot of women half her age, I forgot that she was on the far side of eighty years old.

"Now," I said, "picture yourself at the Little White House. There is Cuban music playing in the background, and you are carrying a tray with plates of flan on it. And then there is a popping noise—Ratatatat!" I shouted, startling both of us with my imitation of what had sounded like gunfire.

"Lordy lordy," said Miss Gloria, "you scared the bejeepers out of me. If this is supposed to relax a nervous customer, I don't see how Eric keeps any of them."

"Maybe that's not how he does it," I said, feeling discouraged. But suddenly I was flooded with the urgent tension of that moment. I remembered dropping to the ground and the way my tray of custards bounced off the ground and splashed onto the people around me. I saw my mother's auburn hair, Markham's gorgeous pink shirt, and a pretty flowered skirt. Maybe Dana Sebek's?

"I didn't hit the dirt when they hollered at us," said Miss Gloria. "I kind of started to slump and then Sam helped me to a chair."

"Do you remember hearing or seeing anything unusual before we heard popping noises? Did anyone come out of the kitchen who maybe didn't belong there?"

She closed her eyes and frowned, concentrating. "Do you know the men's room door is right next to the kitchen?" she asked. "I'm having trouble figuring out who came out which door."

I reached across the space between us for her hand. "Maybe you heard something," I said in a soft voice. Hoping like heck that she wouldn't come up with the sounds of a man getting stabbed.

She shrugged and opened her eyes. "Nothing's coming to me. But I know the mayor and Lieutenant Torrence were there almost immediately."

"The Cuban mayor?" I asked.

"Yes," she said. "And that woman we always see on the television commercials. The one with those pointy shoes? She's in real estate, I think. Or maybe she's the one who has the scuba diving company."

"Dana Sebek," I said. "She owns the dive shop over on Green Street, and maybe she works with Reef Relief, too? Her husband does something with dogs."

"I wonder why she was invited to the conference?" Miss Gloria asked.

"Don't you know that Cuba has the most pristine coral reefs in the world? I bet there are American companies chomping at the bit to get a claim on those reefs. And dollars to doughnuts, she's one of them."

"Anybody else?" I asked.

"Bill, of course, and Bob, and Turner Markham and Mayor Diaz and Irena, but she had a good reason to be going near the kitchen."

"One thing we can say for sure, the killer had to have been at the party," I said. "No one from the outside could have gotten in."

"Who knows? Security isn't perfect, you know."

I sat up, feeling my eyes go wide. "Wouldn't a person who stabbed another person be covered in blood?"

"Not necessarily," she said. "I've been watching that cop TV show, *Bosch*? Turns out a trained assassin can stab someone without leaving a drop of blood on his clothes. Something to do with cutting the bleeders on your chest first."

Chapter Thirteen

The tablecloth of certainty, with all its sparkly settings,
has been yanked, and not artfully. It's why people drink.
—Joan Frank, *All the News I Need*

I had set my alarm for 5:30, knowing I'd feel like limp celery that early but also knowing there was no other way to get those cakes made. When my alarm blared out, even Evinrude looked at me with disapproval.

"Et tu, Brute," I muttered and rolled out of my bunk. "All those mornings you've woken me up early and you can't keep me company this once?" He stretched his long legs out, extending his toes and his toenails—which needed trimming—then closed his eyes and went back to sleep.

The night still hung like a blackout curtain outside the houseboat. But I could smell the lure of freshly brewed coffee wafting in from the kitchen. Thank goodness I'd remembered to set the auto-brew. I poured a cup and sat at the banquette, slugging it down like an addict. As my body and mind perked up, I pulled out the recipe and then the ingredients for the mojito cakes we would serve tonight after dinner in the Little White House dining room. I would bake the four layers this morning and save whipping the cream, making the lime-mint glaze, and finishing the decoration for later this afternoon. All the fussy details of this cake were plenty of work, but the compliments I'd gotten when I served it made it worth the trouble.

In my KitchenAid mixer, I beat four sticks of butter with four cups of sugar, then began to beat in the eggs one at a time. When all that was a lovely, golden mass, I stirred in vanilla, rum, lime zest, and lime juice, and then set to work on mixing the dry ingredients. Once those were folded in and the milk added, I scraped the batter into four prepared cake pans. Our oven was too small for all that; there was barely enough space for two pans at a time. I could prepare the lime-mint syrup while the first cakes baked.

The plan was to put the cakes together now and paint them with the glaze later. I would slather them with whipped cream in between the layers and over the top, then decorate them with thin slices of lime and mint leaves right before my mother and Sam picked me up for the dinner. Even I wasn't crazy enough to ferry these beauties across town on a scooter.

Once the layers were cooling on the counter, perfuming the air with scents of butter and rum, I took a quick shower and trotted out to the parking lot to my scooter. The Key West Tropical Forest & Botanical Garden was located on the next island up from Key West, called Stock Island. I managed the trip in under ten minutes, as most of the traffic was coming south. I assumed the majority were workers who had jobs in town but couldn't afford to live here.

Bill was waiting at the entrance to the gardens with a small cadre of the folks attending the conference and a uniformed policeman. The Havana mayor and several other Cuban officials looked supremely grumpy. I imagined this tour of the boats fashioned by Cuban people desperate to leave their mother country and flee to the United States would make their blood boil. To tell the truth, I was surprised that any of them had agreed to come. The last of the conference group gathered, including those who'd complained yesterday about the tour. Even Turner Markham was there, though he hung back, working his smartphone with his thumbs.

I had seen these crafts before but not given them the attention they deserved. This was an outdoor exhibit, with the so-called boats arranged outside the perimeter of the garden. Left uncovered and open to the elements, they represented ingenuity and desperation.

Some had been built using the skeletons or frames of actual boats; others had been fashioned from tarps and hunks of Styrofoam and powered by lawnmower engines. I paused alongside one that had a beautiful mahogany deck. *Miranda* had been stenciled on the hull. I couldn't imagine setting off on one of these small, shaky crafts to cross the infamous straits that lay between Cuba and Key West. Ninety miles might not sound far, but I'd heard Diana Nyad talk about her attempts to cross the water between our town and Havana— powerful currents, stiff winds, deadly jellyfish, sharks. I wouldn't have been brave enough to get into one of these boats on a dare.

As we trudged along the perimeter of the garden looking at each of the boats in turn, I tried not to think of the people who had attempted this passage and failed. Imagine: months of planning and gathering materials, hours or days of rough seas, and then interdiction by the U.S. Coast Guard. Or a sudden storm washing the passengers into the ocean.

"This display should be moved indoors," I said to Bill. "The boats are getting ravaged by the elements."

Mayor Diaz muttered something in Spanish to his wife, the woman in a flowing white dress with gorgeous black hair who I remembered smiling at me before the first night's party. I caught him saying the word *bulldozer* and could guess the rest of his meaning. Bill had asked me to oil the waters—here was a chance to try.

I edged a little closer, smiled and bowed a bit, and then blushed, reminding myself that these people were Cuban, not Japanese. "*Hola*," I said. "*Buenos . . .*" I idiotically blanked on the Spanish word for morning. "Good morning," I stammered. "It's so nice to have you here on Key West. I hope you are enjoying your visit, in spite of the difficulties on the first night. And I hope you are enjoying our food. I'm sure it can't compete with authentic Cuban recipes from your island, but my mother is the chef this weekend. And she is trying her hardest to create some dishes that would make you proud."

Draw a breath, Hayley, I scolded myself.

The mayor looked at me as if I were speaking in tongues, and maybe to his ear I was. But his wife took a step toward me and shook my hand. "I'm Isabella Diaz. Your island is very beautiful," she said. "And your food delicious. I was just telling Eduardo on the way over that your *ropa vieja* reminded me of my *abuela*'s recipe. My grandmother," she translated. "I am only so desperately sorry we did not get the chance to sample the flan."

She smiled, her cheeks crinkling into appealing dimples. "I have a particular sweet tooth and I'm afraid that it shows." She patted her gently rounded belly.

I matched her grin with mine. "No, you're perfectly beautiful. I'm hoping you enjoyed the sweets last night, since you didn't get the flan. My mother insisted on making the pastry from scratch."

"Oh, certainly," she said. "The ones stuffed with guava paste and cream cheese were amazing. Reminded me so much of home."

"Tonight, I am the pastry chef," I admitted, wishing almost as soon as I said it that I'd kept quiet. "I'm making a mojito cake."

"Mojitos are my favorite!" she exclaimed, throwing her arms into the air in excitement. "I've never had the cake, only the drink." Her husband took a few fast steps ahead of us and began to chat with one of his colleagues.

"Your husband doesn't seem so happy this morning," I said, pasting a more serious expression on my face and gesturing at the chugs. "I imagine this history is difficult to witness."

"He didn't want to come," she said, lowering her voice so I could hardly hear. "But I told him he must keep his eyes open and listen. America has a lot to teach us if we only choose to learn."

"And I'm equally certain we can learn things from you as well," I said politely. And I meant it. America should be open to learning from any other country, no matter how small, or impoverished, or nondemocratic. "Isn't that the point of the weekend?"

"Has there been any word on the poor man who was killed the other night?" she asked.

"Nothing official," I said. "You were there at the party, I assume. I understand they're having difficulty identifying the assailant—the night was so special but also so chaotic."

She tipped her head and placed a hand on her cheek. "Someone wanted to sabotage—"

Her words were cut off by a protester outside the garden gates, who began to shout through a megaphone.

"This so-called cultural exchange is not bridging the gap between Cuba and Key West. This event supports the false notion that the current authoritarian regime is opening its doors to new ideas and new artists. We reject that fantasy! We are all putting blinders on regarding the vicious acts of the government in place now, and overlooking justice."

I noticed that Nancy Klingener, a reporter for the local National Public Radio station, had joined the group. She turned toward the protester with her camera and portable microphone.

Both Bill and Bob looked as though they were ready to crumble. The weekend was bringing out the worst of the tension between these two sides. But did this have anything to do with Gabriel's murder? Or the stolen medal?

We'd come to the end of the chug display, and Bill hastened to wrap up the tour with a quick reminder about tonight's dinner at the Little White House. I left the grounds determined not to let my chance to find out what had happened to poor Gabriel drift by me. Later on, when I got a moment, if that ever happened, I would call Nancy. As a reporter observing from outside the conflicts, she probably had a lot of insight into the stakes resting on this weekend.

Chapter Fourteen

The sad thing about all the Cuban food I eat outside Cuba is precisely that: it's outside Cuba.
    —Enrique Fernandez, *Cortadito*

I barely had time to hurtle back to the houseboat, take a shower, and change my clothes for the service. I tried talking Miss Gloria into staying home and resting, but she'd have none of it. As I dressed for the funeral, changing out of the shorts I'd worn to the botanical garden, I began to think about Gabriel. Truth: I had no idea who he'd been as a person, a human being. How had he felt about the country he'd come from? Had he been an activist? Or had he fallen in love with his new country and forgotten the pain of the old?

As for Maria, I knew only a bit more. She was the mistress of flan, of course. And devoted to her family. The funeral service might answer some of my questions, though you could hardly take remarks made at such a time at face value. No one ever said "He was a lousy father, tight with both praise and money," or "He cheated at golf," or "He drank away too much of his paycheck."

When Miss Gloria was ready, we hopped back on the scooter and zipped over to the church.

"I don't want people staying home for my funeral—that's why I go," she said as we dismounted. "It's an important ritual of life, like it or not. Although I don't think I really want a funeral; I'd prefer a party. Although if there's going to be a party, I'd hate to miss it." She paused for a minute, puzzling over this contradiction.

"So let's have a major party celebrating you when this crazy Cuban event is over," I said, hugging her shoulders. "And let's not talk about death and funerals. Because you're not allowed to die anytime soon. I'd be lost without you and you know it."

She nodded solemnly and shook her white curls out of the helmet I'd bought for her after the first few times we'd tag-teamed on my scooter. "I'm not going anywhere until you're safely married. And not soon after that either, because no telling what a hash you could make of that kind of commitment without me around to advise you." She snickered.

"I'm not that bad," I said, starting toward the parking lot. "We'll be late."

Gabriel's funeral was being held at Saint Mary Star of the Sea, the large Catholic Church on Truman Avenue. Outside the Catholic community, the church is perhaps best known for the grotto that contains statues of Our Lady of Lourdes and Bernadette. Fashioned out of natural island rock, the grotto was designed by one of the nuns in the early 1900s to protect

Key West from major hurricanes. When storms threaten, residents gather here to light candles and say prayers. I had been known to do this myself. Last year it had worked. Just barely.

We met up with Analise on the front steps and joined the line of people trickling into the church. After picking up prayer cards printed with Gabriel's photo and the Lord's Prayer in Spanish on the back, we took seats midway up the center aisle. The vaulted arches and high ceiling lent an airy sense to the sanctuary, which was exaggerated when the double doors lining both sides of the sanctuary were open, as they were today.

Two priests in white robes presided over the funeral mass, leading us through traditional Old Testament and New Testament readings, followed by the presentation of the gifts by Irena and two teenagers I did not recognize. After prayers, communion, and hymns, Irena came forward again to offer words of remembrance.

"I will be saying most of this in Spanish," she said, "as that is my family's native language." She offered a small smile, glanced at the paper on the podium, and began to speak.

Analise translated in a whisper: "To my cousin, everything was family. Family was everything. He was devoted to his sister, and his mother, Carmen, my own mother's beloved sister."

Irena's voice caught, and she dabbed at her eyes with the tissue clutched in her left hand. She took a deep breath and looked at Maria and her mother, huddled in the first pew. "In fact, he never started his own family, as he felt his primary meaning in life was to be found right in front of him."

A wailing rose from the family pew; I couldn't tell whether

it was Maria or her mother or some other bereaved female. Miss Gloria was sniffling too and dug around in her fanny pack to find another Kleenex.

"He was strong like a bull, always available to carry someone else's load. He was also an excellent cook. I'd put his *picadillo* up against that of any chef. He did not attempt to make flan, though he adored his mother's recipe and had been known to finish a tray of custard off on his own. He was also a talented carpenter. He loved his adopted country, while respecting the traditions and history of the country in which he was born."

Her voice broke again, and it took several moments for her to gather herself and finish. "He would have done anything for the happiness of his mother. He would be heartbroken to see her sadness on this day of mourning."

"That was a tough one," said Miss Gloria when we were back out in the sunlight. "A son should never go before his mama."

We followed Analise to the garden beside the grotto where the family would be accepting condolences. I was not surprised to see several Key West police detectives, probably friends of Nathan's, in plainclothes. If Gabriel's murder had been solved, I figured we would have heard about it. Nothing stays secret long in our little town.

We waited in the warm sun to pay our respects to Maria and her family. My mother and Sam had been seated some rows ahead of us in the church, but I knew they had to hurry off to work on tonight's meal. So I was the family representative. No matter how painful it might be to express condolences and be flooded with the agony of the bereft mourners, it would have been worse, far worse, to be in their shoes. We shuffled ahead, and I tried to think of words that might bring comfort.

"You know, there's really not a darn thing anybody can say at a moment like this," said Miss Gloria. "I've been through it, and it just hurts like heck. But when people show up at the service, it's like you can spread the pain for a moment—you get a little lift of the burden from your shoulders to theirs."

I looked at her in amazement. "You are like the Yoda of senior citizens, you know that, right? Sometimes you channel me the same way that Lorenzo does. It's a little spooky."

She tucked her hand under my elbow and squeezed, with a smile I could only describe as mystical. She trailed Analise through the receiving line of mourners. When my turn came, I took both of Maria's hands in mine, unable to keep the tears from running down my face upon seeing hers. "I'm so, so sorry."

She nodded quickly. And then glanced at her mother, a wisp of a woman swathed in a shapeless black dress and lace shawl. "This is my mother, Carmen," Maria said.

Then she leaned over to whisper, "Have you learned anything?"

I felt my face flush, and I gulped and stammered. "You know I'm not a police officer, right?"

She gripped my hands harder, and her tears came faster too. "Please help us. The police have been over to our house twice, asking where Gabriel might have hidden the medal. They don't seem to care that he's dead, only that he be blamed for stealing."

A memory from the first day of the conference flashed

through my mind: Maria saying that Gabriel would be accused for the disappearance of the prize.

"Why in the world do they think he was responsible for the theft?" I asked her. She bit her lip and shook her head. "If you want me to help, I have to know the truth. Is there any chance that he took it?"

But Maria just bawled. And her relatives and friends began gathering around, glaring at me with daggers of death. Her cousin, Irena, took my elbow and led me a few yards away.

"You have to understand that in these times, no one in authority cares about the truth if one of the parties is brown and even possibly illegal. We can't talk here. Come by the downtown Cuban Coffee Queen tomorrow and I'll answer whatever I can. I'm working from eight to three. I'll try to find out more from Maria, okay?"

"Please, please," Maria moaned as I started to walk away. "Closure is the only thing that might help my mother right now. It's not right that a mother's son should go first. It's not bearable."

I could only nod in agreement. I also wondered again how in the world the missing gold medal fit into his death. Or were they completely separate matters? The police didn't seem to think so. I met up with Miss Gloria in the grotto, where we said our good-byes to Analise and began trudging back to the scooter, feeling drained and light-headed. A text buzzed in. Nathan.

HEARD YOU WERE AT MR. GONZALEZ'S FUNERAL MASS. STAYING OUT OF TROUBLE?

I felt instantly guilty, and then outraged. REALLY? I texted back.

"Already he knows that?" asked Miss Gloria, peering over my shoulder. "What, does he have a mole watching you?"

I ignored the question. I didn't like the text, but I wasn't ready to explore my reaction in public. "We promised Torrence we'd stop by the police department, but I'm feeling weak. And ravenous."

"*Café con leche* and a Cuban mix?" she asked, eyes sparkling. She'd been helping me work through a list of restaurants that claimed to serve *the best* of these specialties. We'd already enjoyed the sandwiches at Cole's Peace, the Courthouse Deli, 5 Brothers, and Ana's. Sandy's Café on White Street was next on our list.

You could eat Cuban sandwiches (aka Cuban mix, aka Cubanos) every day for a year in Key West and still not scratch the surface of all the varieties available. Okay, that's a bit of an exaggeration, but they are common menu items. Today, Sandy's Café would work beautifully because it was on the way home and the coffee was powerful and delicious and the Cuban sandwiches authentic. I had tried making these sandwiches at home on the houseboat, but they had never quite tasted the same. What could be so tricky? Roast pork, ham, Swiss cheese, pickles, and yellow mustard, all layered on soft white Cuban bread. The secret must come in the grilling. Maybe the seasoning of a grill used for years' worth of sandwiches. My mouth began to water thinking about it.

Sandy's Café was more or less an open-air bar on White Street. Customers ordered at the counter and then sat at a barstool under the red-and-white-striped awning. I ordered two *café con leches* and a Cuban mix to share, then went to join Miss Gloria on a stool at the end of the bar.

"I'm wiped out and it's not even noon," she said.

"So you'll take a nap," I said. I wanted one too, but with the day I had scheduled, prospects were dim. "I have the very definite impression that Maria knows something about her brother's murder that she isn't saying."

Miss Gloria nodded. "You couldn't very well press her for details at the funeral. Don't you think they would tell the police if they had important information, though?"

"They don't seem to believe the police would give them a fair shake. But what are they afraid of? They can't deport him; he's already dead. And obviously the man didn't stab himself. Is there someone else in the family they're protecting from something?"

"Speaking of almost family, what's up with your Nathan?" my roommate asked. "I'd hate to find out later that he was one of those secretly controlling men who locked you away in a room, and once it's too late to save you, all the relatives and close friends report to the cops and the TV reporters that they had no idea this was happening."

I huffed and fidgeted with my napkin, wishing the food was already here so I could distract her from the conversation. "Obviously he doesn't have me locked in a room, because I'm right here with you. He doesn't want me to get hurt, that's all." Or so I hoped, putting the best possible face on it. My name was called and I scrambled off the stool to pick up our order.

We sipped scalding, milky, sweet coffee as I unwrapped the sandwich from its wax-paper cover. The tangy smell of the pickles wafted up in combination with the sweet mustard. Yellow mustard has gotten a bad foodie rap over the last ten years, with diners fleeing in droves to specialty condiments. But I'd learned to stay away from any establishment using fancy French mustard, at least on this sandwich.

I spotted Turner Markham at the end of the line of lunch customers at the counter. Should I flat out ask him what he knew about the murder? Generally Key West commissioners expect to be approached in this town. They don't hide away like congress people ducking town halls for their constituents. And he would've seen me this morning at the chug tour, and also at the opening event, though that had been a madhouse, so he couldn't be blamed for not noticing my presence. And sometimes the help blends into the wallpaper. Possibly he would remember me as the person who'd thrown a tray of flan on his shirt. Should I offer to pay his dry-cleaning bill? Not that it had been my fault, but it might be a good segue.

I balled up our trash, slid off the stool, and moved closer to him. "Turner? I'm Hayley Snow. I live on Houseboat Row. I wanted to apologize again for ruining your shirt with our dessert the other night."

It took him a minute to figure out what I was talking about. "Not your fault," he said, adding his trademark, winning smile. "We were all taken by surprise."

Dropping my trash in the receptacle near him, I said, "It was such a tragic ending to a fabulous event. Have you heard whether the murderer has been arrested? We're all kind of nervous about someone so vicious being out on the loose."

"Listen," he said, touching a hand to my back and smiling with reassurance. "We have an excellent police department in this town, and they are doing their job."

"But you do have a narrow list of suspects, right? Gabriel's people are concerned that this murder won't be taken seriously because of who he was. Or wasn't. I've told them this isn't so, but they are so distraught."

"You must know I can't talk about any details of an investigation with civilians," he said, his smile beginning to fade. "Gossip has never helped police work."

I tried another tack. "Have the authorities recovered the gold medal?"

He shook his head with a curt no, a super-annoyed expression creeping onto his face. I wasn't surprised—notwithstanding his comment about gossip, the way the coconut telegraph operates in this town, I would have known if the news had changed. And this weekend was probably wearing him out—he wanted these problems solved as much as the rest of us did.

On the other hand, why was he so testy?

Chapter Fifteen

Food was her finest expression of love, not unlike sex, yet longer lasting and more abundant.
—Jacqueline Sheehan, *The Tiger in the House*

The only positive thing about our impending visit to the police station was that it was close to Houseboat Row, so not out of our way. I was feeling both wired and exhausted. Honestly, Miss Gloria looked even worse. I had one scary moment on the ride over from Sandy's when her grip on my waist lightened and I was afraid she was dropping off the back of the scooter.

We approached the front door, and I picked up the phone that hung on the outside wall under the portico to speak with the dispatcher. "Hayley Snow and Miss Gloria here to see Lieutenant Torrence. I think it's him we're supposed to see. It's follow-up about the murder at the Little White House."

"I'll buzz you in. Come down the hallway to the left."

We heard a cacophony of barking when we stepped inside the building. Torrence met us about halfway down the hall and walked back with us to his office. His little dogs Zeus and Apollo danced along by his ankles. "It's 'take your dog to work' day," he explained again, slightly sheepish. "I didn't think I could handle both at once, and it turns out I was right."

"Don't worry, we love animals," I said. "Evinrude and Sparky will hate the smell of us when we get back home. But we all need to learn to be flexible, right?"

He stopped at the door rather than inviting us in to take a seat. "If you don't mind, I'd like to talk to you individually. Not that you'd hold something back with the other listening. I know you two don't keep secrets."

"Hayley doesn't keep any secrets," said Miss Gloria with a snicker.

Torrence laughed, too, and I shot her a glare.

"We get it," she said. "You don't want what we remember contaminated by what our good friend remembers."

Miss Gloria took her obligations as a citizen seriously. She had gone to jury duty as summoned last fall when many folks would have scrambled for an excuse to be dismissed. And if the officials had bothered to double-check the date of birth on her driver's license, she wouldn't have been called in the first place. In the end, she was selected as forewoman and sat through two ugly, draining weeks of testimony. She helped resolve a case involving manslaughter and a former city attorney when most of my friends and the media outlets had predicted deadlock.

Torrence's eyes met mine. "I think she should run for mayor," he said.

"Or president," I added. "Or world ruler."

"I'll move this chair just outside the door." Torrence dragged the more comfortable chair out of his office and set it up so my roommate could see everyone coming into the station and dispersing down either hall.

"I'll go second," she said. "I'll sit out here and take a little catnap."

"Would you like some company?"

Miss Gloria nodded her agreement, and after she perched in the big chair, he settled his elderly dogs in her lap. She and the dogs snuggled into a pashmina that she carried in her bag in case of overly aggressive air-conditioning. Torrence closed the door behind me, which I took as a measure of the seriousness of the conversation.

"I guess there hasn't been much progress on the murder," I said.

"Unfortunately not. And you can imagine the pressure with all the important people in attendance at this weekend's events. The Cuban security staff are really angry, and the feds want us to move the threat level to orange." He grimaced. "They really want us to call off the remainder of the conference. I don't know if Nathan mentioned that he's head of security this weekend, manning the mother ship in this building."

I gulped. No wonder he was even crankier than usual. And no wonder I hadn't seen a lot of him over on the Truman Annex grounds.

"The chief is pretty upset, too, and I can't say that I blame him. They're all in a meeting right now. In case you saw steam coming out of one of the second-floor windows, that would be what's happening."

He glanced down at the notes on his desk while I studied the photos hanging on his wall. There were former presidents, movie stars, and in a place of honor, several members of the police department with John Walsh, host of the TV show *America's Most Wanted*. Torrence had fingered criminal number 999 and often lamented that if it'd been number 1,000, John Walsh himself would have come to Key West with his TV cameras and his entourage and he would've been famous.

"Had you heard anything in advance that might have led you to believe there would be trouble at the Little White House?" he asked.

"Only from You Know Who," I said with a shrug. "Mr. Chief of Security. And that was before anything got started. He said there might be a problem and he asked us to step down from the catering. More than once. I have no idea what you guys heard in advance, or how you got the information," I said, surprised by a feeling of shakiness. I glanced up at the poster Torrence had framed and placed over his desk. IF YOU ALWAYS DO WHAT YOU ALWAYS DID, YOU'LL ALWAYS GET WHAT ALWAYS GOT.

"Of course, me being as stubborn as old baking powder in a failed cake, I told him absolutely not. We couldn't possibly bail out at that late date. We had all that food, and tons of people committed to work the weekend. But now I'm thinking . . . If only I had done what he suggested and talked my mother into canceling, Gabriel would be alive right now." My voice wobbled as I faced the possibility that I was obliquely responsible for this man's death.

"We don't know that and can't make that assumption,"

he fired back. "If someone was intent on taking him out, he would have been killed another way. Stabbing a man in the chest is not an incidental murder. That's a vicious act committed by a strong person." He patted the papers on the desk in front of him.

"If we can, let's review the time leading up to the incident." He looked down at his notes and then back to me. "You reported hearing the popping noises and then Maria's scream. Do you remember hearing any sounds of an argument or someone in distress before that moment?"

"I've been over and over this in my mind, searching my memory for what might be hidden there." I pressed my hands to my cheeks, which felt both warm and clammy at the same time. "We were so busy waiting on tables. And so excited about all the special guests."

"And you'd been dancing," he added with an impish grin.

"Yes." I sighed. "I was worried that my mother was annoyed with me for getting distracted. Right before hell broke loose, I had picked up the first tray of dessert. It was heavy, heavier than I would've expected, so not that easy to balance. My focus was on delivering the darn thing to the tables without spilling the flan and the caramel on our guests." Bigger sigh. "Which ended up happening anyway—I ruined our commissioner's silk shirt." I shook my head. "Nothing else comes to mind."

"Did you notice anyone in the Little White House, especially near the kitchen, who was wearing sequins?"

I tried to think that over carefully, picturing the various women who had attended the party. Assuming it *was* a woman, which was not always a fair guess in Key West. And then I remembered Miss Gloria's gift. "I suspect that question is a dead end. Both my roommate and I were wearing these really cute black sneakers covered in sequins." I knew this meeting was for him to interrogate me, not the other way around. But this question brought on a surge of curiosity that couldn't be denied.

"I suppose that means you found sequins near the body?" I asked.

His expression was pained. "Yes."

"What color, and what size?" I asked. "Because you know not all sequins look alike."

"We're aware of that." He grinned. "Believe it or not, a few of our officers have worn costumes during their tenure in this town."

"I guess that means you can't tell me anything more."

"You guess correctly. But we'll probably want to take a look at those shoes to be absolutely certain they are a match." He made a few notes, then set his pen on the desk and rubbed a finger across his mustache. "What I'm about to tell you is not going to be an official request." He paused, brown eyes intense. "Do you understand what I'm saying?"

"Not yet. I have not a shred of a clue what you're going to say."

"We'd like you to keep listening at your dinner tonight. You're working the party, right?"

I nodded.

"The Cuban delegation has shut down and won't say anything to us. And our Cuban-American residents on this island are not talking either. You, however, might be in a position to hear something that we might not." His voice had gotten fierce and tense. "We plan to have an officer working the event. I've already cleared that with your mother. But he'll stay in the kitchen. We can't have him waiting on tables in case one of the guests recognizes him as a cop.

"And there will be plenty of cops around the facility, and probably Cuban security too. I'm not saying you're investigating anything, I want to make that clear. You are listening only."

"I get it."

"Good. Then call or text me tomorrow and we'll talk. Collect impressions and we'll take it from there. Any questions?" He stood up and came around his desk to open the door.

I hesitated. Torrence wasn't the one I usually talked to about relationship issues. That would be Connie or Eric or Lorenzo or even Miss Gloria. But he knew Nathan better than any of my friends did. And I'd seen how kind he was last fall when we'd been trapped in the closet during a hurricane and he'd ended up performing my mother's marriage to Sam. And I was bothered enough that I decided I needed to vent, or burst.

"On an unrelated subject, I have a tiny worry." This was going to sound so ridiculous said out loud, even in a whisper. But it rankled me, and I knew it would only grow bigger if I let it fester. "You knew Nathan's first wife, right?" I knew he'd known her, because we'd talked about her in the past.

He nodded, though reluctantly.

"Things went bad between them after the home invasion, right?"

He nodded again.

"And I totally get why that freaked him out. And her too. I can't even imagine how scary that must have been, for both of them."

Another nod. He wasn't going to help me figure out what I was trying to say.

"Okay, bottom line. Do you think that still carries over?"

Torrence raised his eyebrows above his glasses. "What do you mean?"

"I'm wondering whether Nathan has someone watching me and reporting back to him about what I'm up to."

Behind his glasses, his eyes now looked worried. "What makes you feel that way?"

I glanced out into the hall. Miss Gloria had gotten up from her chair and was reading "most wanted" posters on a bulletin board, Zeus tucked under one arm and Apollo under the other. "I wasn't even off the grounds of the church when he texted me to see what I was doing at the funeral." My voice rose with irritation. "It's not just annoying, it's a little scary. I don't want to be involved in something where the guy is controlling."

Torrence looked instantly horrified.

"No, wait," I said, holding up a hand to stop him from cutting me off. "I never have really understood what happened with his first wife before the incident. Was everything hunky-dory in their marriage? Maybe he tried to manage her, too? Even Miss Gloria mentioned it this morning. That's probably why I reacted so strongly the other night when he asked us to withdraw from Mom's big catering gig. Again. I can't tell you how many times we'd already discussed that."

Torrence was shaking his head and I braced for a brush-off. Cops sticking with cops and all that.

He closed his door again. "As I mentioned, Nathan is the big picture security guy this weekend—he hasn't been down in the weeds, doing staffing for individual events. I'm the one who suggested we have someone looking out for you at the funeral, since he wasn't attending. We were very concerned that the murderer would be there and might follow you or try to harm you. I made the mistake of mentioning this to Nathan, and he went nuts over the idea that you might have been hurt. But listen, he's no stalker. It wasn't him who asked for a report from our guy at the service; it was me."

"Really? Wow, that's a relief," I said. "What about this plan for me listening in at the dinner?"

"He doesn't like it. But we'll have so many people in place, both uniformed and undercover, that chances of things going sour will be none."

I blew out some air and felt my shoulders try to move away from my ears. "Okay. If you're absolutely sure."

He laughed. "Who's sure of anyone in the end? We all have dark pockets in our psyche. But he's more likely to want to marry you than control you. Everyone knows you're not controllable. That's part of what he loves about you."

"He does? He certainly hasn't told me any such thing." I mulled this over. "Has he said anything specific to you about the future?"

"I have to draw the line there," Torrence said. "I don't want to incriminate myself or my friend." He grinned. "I'm sorry you were worried. I should have said something earlier."

Since we'd gotten this far, and since he'd married so many couples and must have seen it all—good, bad, and terrible—I decided to ask my other, bigger question. "I have to say, the idea of getting married scares me to death. Even if Nathan asked me, and I have no idea if he will or when—and PS, why is it that the man gets to decide all this anyway?" I glanced over at him. "I'm not asking you to tell me about anything you might or might not have heard."

"Sometimes it's hard to keep up with the way your mind works," he said, grinning.

I let go a great big whoosh of air. "Tell me about it. But what I'm trying to ask is, how do you know you will stay the same person that you were when you got married? Because if you change, the marriage becomes obsolete, right? Maybe that's why there're so many divorces. I think that's why my parents split up. Dad changed in one way that my mother didn't. Of course, they were also very young and getting married was not part of the plan." I stopped blathering and looked directly at him. "You conduct so many marriage ceremonies, I figure you must have some answers."

Torrence squinted. "You're giving me too much credit. I'm not a fortune-teller. I talk to couples ahead of the ceremony about how they communicate and when to get help and potential signs of trouble. Usually I get one shot with them— and how much can actually be accomplished in an hour? But from what I've seen, what you've described is not how marriages go. In a relationship that works, the marriage contract is a constant stream of renegotiation. Maybe it even feels like a series of marriages, under the cover of the one marriage. Do you understand what I'm saying?" He took one of my hands in both of his and squeezed.

"I think so. I think you're telling me that I don't need to panic. Although you're not telling me how to choose the right person in the first place."

He chuckled. "I'm wise, but I'm not the Dalai Lama. However, I do have a suggestion." He paused and rubbed his chin. "Can I be really honest?"

"Of course," I said. "I want nothing less." Though I had to admit that my heartbeat sped up a bit waiting for what he had to say.

"If your mind leaped right from his text to wondering if Nathan's watching you too closely, make sure you take a look inside yourself. Old baggage sometimes repeats itself, you know?"

"I know."

"And one more thing. If Nathan's text bothered you that much, you should tell him. That's the one piece of advice I give to my couples—talk to each other. Even about the hard things. Even if he scares you a little. And then reinforce him when he's able to do the same."

"Thanks. Like training a dog, then?"

He choked out a laugh, I gave him a hug, and we went into the hall to collect Miss Gloria. "I'm going to run upstairs for just a second and say hello to Ziggy Stardust while you two chat," I said.

"What about Nathan?" Miss Gloria asked.

I laughed. "I'll wave at him too, if he's not still in his top-secret meeting."

I took the elevator at the back of the building to the second floor and then turned left in the direction of Nathan's office. My heart had started to pound, and I couldn't pin it on running up the stairs, because I hadn't. Nor was it remembering how anxious I had been the first time I'd been called to the police department—about a poisonous key lime pie in which my knife had been found. Which, looking back, had been one of the most anxiety-inducing moments of my life.

More likely, I was nervous about seeing Nathan and telling him the truth about my feelings. We weren't together enough for that to feel routine. And half of the time lately, he had seemed to be scolding me for getting overinvolved. I tapped on his door, which was almost shut. I heard Ziggy's soft woofing and Nathan's rumbly "Come in." I pushed open the door. Ziggy's little brown ears perked up and his tail began to wag. He sprang from his dog bed to the chair in front of Nathan's desk and then into my arms. He began to lick my face with his rough pink tongue.

"When he sees you, all his training goes out the window. Happens to me, too," Nathan said. His smile went all the way to the green eyes that killed me every time. "What brings you to these parts?"

"We came in for our second in-depth chat about the murder," I said, "and I just wanted to say hi and see my buddy. I've missed you so," I told the squirming dog. When he'd calmed down enough that I could set him down on the chair, I went around the desk to give Nathan a kiss. "Fresh dog slobber." I grinned.

"My favorite," he said and smiled back. He held me at arm's length. "You're worried about something."

So I let it all burst out—how his text had troubled me, and how I had reacted badly to his last visit to the houseboat warning me off participating in the weekend. And how even Miss Gloria had been startled enough to ask if he was overly controlling. "I bet you didn't mean it that way, but I thought you should know."

He studied me without an ounce of humor, but said: "I can see how you'd feel that way. From my side, I'm worried about you running into a ruthless killer and getting in over your head."

"You guys think he was at the funeral."

He nodded. "Small town, and certainly if the killer was local, it's a good possibility."

"I can see why that would worry you," I said, remembering that I was supposed to reinforce his feelings too. "Torrence says you're having a rough day, so I won't stay. Just wanted to tell you both that I miss you."

His face looked blank for a moment and then he grinned. "I miss you too, even if you do drive me crazy." He hugged me so hard I thought he might crack a bone. And followed that up with a tender kiss.

Chapter Sixteen

While the quintessentially European flavors of onion and olive oil are satisfying, the sweet notes of the plantain are voluptuous. They are a siren call. Yield to the New World, they say. Yield to the tropics. Regress to your sugar-hungry infancy and childhood. Relax. Yield. Allow seduction.
—Enrique Fernandez, *Cortadito*

I'd missed two calls from my mother while we were at the police station, so I dialed her back as soon as we got to our boat. "Everything okay?"

"We'll see tonight," she said grimly.

Not an encouraging sign.

"How is the roast coming along?"

"We decided to do the cooking on site," she said. "It seems like too much of a risk to cook it here, drag it over there, and then warm it up. You know people freak out if they see pink, but on the other hand, it's so easy to overcook a pork roast. How about your cakes?"

"Almost ready for their close-ups," I said. "I baked the layers earlier and I'm about to whip the cream. Did you need something, or were you calling to chat?"

"Can you drive over in Miss Gloria's boat?" she asked. "It will save Sam the trouble of coming back up the island to pick you up." By *boat*, I knew she meant my roommate's vast, old Buick, with a front seat more comfortable than most people's living room sofas.

I agreed we would meet them at the Little White House at five and spent the next forty-five minutes finishing the dessert. So far, the cakes looked stunning—the layers of yellow infused with rum-mint syrup, mounded with whipped cream, and decorated with slices of lime. A few sprigs of mint would be the crowning touch. I walked out to our tiny back deck and chose the best-looking leaves from Miss Gloria's little herb garden. These I rinsed and artfully arranged around the limes. Then I fed the cats, changed back into my black-and-white server uniform, and woke Miss Gloria up from her nap. "Time to get ready, Sleeping Beauty," I said.

My mother had loaned me two BPA-free cake carriers, and I carefully fit in the cakes and covered them up. I scraped the last of the whipped cream into another container and wrapped up a few extra limes and mint leaves in case of dings or nicks. We loaded ourselves and our gear into Miss Gloria's Buick. Fortunately for my nerves, she hadn't taken this vehicle out by herself too often lately—only on occasional trips to lead one of her cemetery tours, or when it was her turn to be designated driver for her ladies' lunch group. Like a mom who doesn't want her teenager driving too soon, I'd learned to be liberal about offering rides.

Tonight's dinner was planned for a smaller crowd without surprise entertainment or outside guests, which we all desperately hoped would mean less stress than the opening gala. I dreaded revisiting the space where Gabriel had died, but hopefully a happy and successful event would banish the ghosts. Bill had told me weeks ago that the intent of this final evening was to cement any gains that the two sides had made. From what I'd been able to glean at the botanical gardens this morning, the gains were minimal. The evening might be short.

We parked on Emma Street and carried the cakes across the lawn to the back entrance of the Little White House. As we walked, I noticed at least four Key West Police Department vehicles and the officers I assumed must have come from them, along with a few residents of the nearby condos and gardeners working on the property next to the Little White House. Some, if not all, must be the undercover security that Torrence had mentioned.

Once inside, the comforting smells of delicious things cooking helped distract me from the door to the closet at the end of the storage hallway where Gabriel had been found stabbed to death. "Just don't look," I warned Miss Gloria, though I doubted there was really anything to see other than the remnants of yellow crime scene tape. And what was the point of warning her? Neither of us was the sort to avoid trouble. I concentrated on the scent of roasting pork to get my mind off the murder.

My mother had marinated the meat overnight in the traditional Cuban mojo-style sauce. The authentic base for this marinade was sour orange juice, which she had replaced with easier-to-find orange juice and lime to get a similar effect. Judging by the powerful and delicious scent of roasting garlic, cumin, and oregano, I suspected the dish was probably reaching its crunchy crescendo about now. The plan was to make the white rice on site and heat up the black beans. The only other ingredient we had to prepare in the kitchen was fried plantains, which did not travel well.

We bustled into the kitchen, each carrying a mojito cake. Sam took Miss Gloria's container and set it on the table. It was hard not to remember working right here with Maria and Irena on Friday before tragedy struck. We had felt so hopeful and excited about the weekend. Sam's eyes met mine, and I imagined he was thinking the same thing. He looked tired. I doubted he'd had this kind of life in mind for himself before he met the whirlwind that is my mother. As far as I knew, he'd had no experience with cooking beyond heating up his own takeout meals during his single years.

"Everything good here?" I asked.

"You can smell your mother's fabulous roast for yourself," he said as he took the cake I'd been carrying and laid it on the table next to the first. "Let me make some room in the refrigerator and we'll get these put away. The beans are simmering and the rice maker is set to run at six o'clock, and your mom is in the dining room setting the table. We've decided to bake bananas instead of frying plantains." He pointed to two Pyrex dishes filled with halved bananas, lying in some kind of sauce. "Butter, brown sugar, lime juice, and rum," he explained, anticipating my question. "It's not authentic, but the fruit they sent us from the wholesaler was unacceptable. And I convinced your mother we simply don't have time to go running around to the supermarkets all over the island."

"Smart man." I crossed the kitchen and removed the cover from the enormous pot of black beans. I could tease out the smells of onions and green peppers, ingredients central to my mother's Cuban-inspired recipe. Dropping my voice to a whisper, I asked, "Is she holding up okay?"

He forced a grin. "You know her, she doesn't stay down for long. Even if this weekend is declared a national disaster, we've learned a lot." He ran his fingers through his hair and lowered his own voice. "Things such as not bidding on enormous jobs that involve tending and carrying forward the relationship between historically hostile nations. Maybe cater a few five-year-old birthday celebrations?"

Miss Gloria and I laughed and he joined in, too. My mother was the type to be all in or all out. No way was she going to settle for providing punch and cookies to children's birthday parties. I pushed through the swinging door that led to the pantry and, from there, into the dining room. I was still in awe that we would be serving dinner at the exact table that had been used by Presidents Truman, Kennedy, Carter, and Clinton, as well as Secretary of State Colin Powell.

"How does it look?" my mother asked, glancing up from fussing over her table arrangements. She had chosen bright-red placemats and white linen napkins that echoed the colors of the white chairs with their red-patterned seat cushions. The centerpieces bristled with flowers and the flags of the United States, Cuba, and the Conch Republic of Key West. "Anthurium for hospitality and abundance, alstroemeria for prosperity, fortune, and friendship, and blue iris for hope."

"It looks amazing, and it smells that good, too. You've thought of everything." I picked up one of the white china plates to admire the line drawings of the building that danced around the rim.

"Can you imagine that Harry Truman and his family actually ate off those very plates? I had to beg for permission to use them, so don't drop one," she warned. "Wasn't that funeral just so sad? I can't honestly say I'm sorry that we had to leave early."

"It was brutal," I agreed, settling the plate back on the table. "And Maria and her mother are in despair. She said police have been to her house twice asking whether her brother stole the gold medal and stashed it somewhere. She's begging me to find out what I can about what happened because the police seem mystified. So if you hear anything funny tonight . . ." And that reminded me that I needed to keep an eye on Turner Markham—and make mental notes about who he was watching. Because I was pretty sure he had a murder suspect in mind, one that he wasn't willing to share with me.

"The problem is," I added, "everyone I talk to is acting suspicious. About something."

"I imagine we'll be way too busy to snoop—even you. We're all set in here," said my mother, perching her hands on her hips. "Now for the hors d'oeuvres."

As we returned to the kitchen, Sam was explaining the night's menu to a tall man wearing black pants, a white shirt, and an apron hanging from his neck and tied at the waist, like the rest of us. "We'll be serving the appetizers out on the front lawn," Sam explained as he pulled a tray of baked *picadillo* empanadas out of the oven.

"What's in the filling?" asked the man.

"Beef, onions, garlic, tomatoes, raisins, olives, spices, like that," Sam said. He turned to us and introduced Officer Tim Boyd.

"That will be plain Tim tonight," the man reminded us. "And I'm instructed to stay in the kitchen and do any scut work you need so I can be close by if needed."

"Scut work? Ha!" Miss Gloria pointed to the mountain of dirty pots, pans, and dishes that had already accumulated in the sink. She winked at him. "Game for starting there?"

"Whatever's needed," he said, his brown eyes twinkling back at her.

Miss Gloria finished arranging a tray of Cuban sandwich–inspired skewers—composed of squares of Swiss cheese, ham, and little chunks of dill pickle—on a flowered plate.

"What you can't see is a tiny dab of mustard between the cheese and the ham," Sam explained to Tim. "All made easy through the magic of a sous-chef such as myself."

"I thought you promised to make these simple," I said, turning to my mother.

"I made the filling for the empanadas last week and stuck it in the freezer," she said with a sheepish smile. "All we had to do was roll out the cornmeal crust and stuff the little devils this morning. Since you were making dessert, how else was I going to fill our time?"

"Next time, try a nap," I said. "Or a few hours at the beach? Or even read a good mystery?"

We heard the chatter of arriving guests outside on the lawn. "Show's starting," said Sam. "Man your stations!"

Miss Gloria and I each took a tray and headed out to the yard, where the dinner guests had begun to gather under the big tent. A trio of musicians was playing soft Cuban music. A hot flash of memory swept over me, the excitement and drama and finally fear from the Friday night event returning to me in a rush. I made a beeline for Eric and Bill, thinking Eric's calm demeanor would have a good impact on my nerves. Before I could reach them, Bob ducked in, grabbed Bill by the arm, and drew him away.

"What's going on?" I asked as I offered Eric the platter of steaming empanadas.

He shrugged. "They've been texting all day, so I don't know what could be new. In a nutshell, they were hoping the murder would be solved and all questions put to rest, but nothing appears to be happening. And the Cuban delegation is very withdrawn—in fact, everyone canceled except the mayor and his wife. I don't know what finally got to them, whether it was the chugs or the protesters or the murder or some combination. But if they weren't already scheduled to leave in the morning, I'm pretty sure they would be checking out early." He bit into the little meat pie and exclaimed with delight. "Oh wow, these are outstanding! I particularly love the saltiness of the green olives next to the sweetness of the raisins."

"Thanks, but no credit due to me this time. My mother and Sam made them. What's he most worried about?" I asked, tipping my chin at Bill, who was deep in conversation with a very animated Bob.

"The murder first and foremost, of course. But then, in the fallout from the first night, any goodwill between the Key Westers and the Havana people seems to have evaporated. And all of that stains the Little White House's reputation. The police are cranky too, but I suppose you have an inside track into that." He wiped his lips with a Little White House cocktail napkin and reached for a second empanada.

I cracked a grin. "I do and they are. What do you think was at stake for this conference, besides reputation?"

"On Friday night, Bob thought he had a couple of big donors to the foundation on the line, but they appear to have fallen through. You've been reading the paper?"

I nodded.

"They need a big win tonight—some kind of agreement with the Havana folks about something—something they can point to in order to say, 'See what a great asset the Little White House can be.'"

Behind Eric, I could see my mother twirling her finger— *Circulate!* "Enjoy the night; the boss is calling," I said, and headed toward the Havana mayor and his friendly wife, Isabella, with whom I'd chatted earlier this morning. She was wearing a sparkly, formfitting sunflower yellow–and–black dress that highlighted her dark hair and eyes.

"*Buenos noches,*" I said as I approached. "You look gorgeous! Tonight we've prepared empanadas stuffed with *picadillo*." I held my tray out along with a fistful of napkins.

"Oh, they look amazing," Isabella said, and turned to her husband. "Aren't these your favorites?"

He smiled politely but without warmth, and answered in accented English, "No, thank you. My mother's pastries were so flaky and crisp that I promised myself I would never attempt to compare. This could only turn out poorly for the competition."

What does a caterer answer to that? I couldn't think of a thing. "I hope you were able to take in a little more of our island today."

"I walked up and down Duval Street. My husband had to work," Isabella said.

"I hope you will excuse me," he said, pecking his wife on the cheek but not looking at me. We both watched him stride toward the men's restroom.

"Don't worry, I understand," I said, anticipating her embarrassment at his rudeness. "I've come to realize that some people visiting Key West adore it as much as we do, and others don't get it at all. I'm afraid your husband may be one of the latter."

She took a sip of her wine. "This trip has been very complicated for him. You must realize that not everyone in Cuba is in favor of this conference. And he is feeling a lot of pressure because he chose to come anyway. And then the stolen medal and that poor man dying. It's a bit much. All the other members of our group canceled from this dinner, but I insisted we attend. Maybe that was an error, but I apologize for his rudeness."

"Please—"

She cut me off and glanced at her husband's retreating form. "I spent a year in Miami as a high school exchange student, so I know how fraught this whole subject can be from either side. He finds it hard to see it more than one way. He can only imagine what another country wants from Cuba, rather than what we could exchange for mutual benefit."

"I wondered how your English came to be so excellent," I said. "What might your husband think our country wants?"

"That's a tough one," she said, fingering one delicate pearl earring. "The Cuban people would like some of what Americans take for granted—access to the Internet, ability to run and own businesses, higher wages, freedom to visit their relations in the U.S. And to import whatever they want from America, whether it's soap operas or televisions. Our government, I believe, is afraid that your country wants to control ours, in exchange for loosening trade restrictions."

"We've had a difficult relationship, so I can see why the trust would be missing," I said. Just then I caught my mother's eye. She whirled a finger in the air again, probably irked that every stop I made turned into a major conversation. "Excuse me, I need to get back to work. Enjoy your evening. I'll see you inside."

As I passed hors d'oeuvres to the other people gathered under the small tent in the side yard, I tried to listen to their conversations without getting drawn in. Bob, who was appearing progressively more disheveled as the weekend drew to its finish, was earnestly imploring Mayor Diaz to listen to or do something. Bill was talking to Rusty from the Hemingway

Home, and both of them looked unhappy. And, from the volume of Rusty's voice, I suspected that he had already downed a few cocktails. If I hadn't run out of empanadas, I would have hovered closer. Around the fringes of the group, several uniformed police officers lurked, adding another edge to the gathering.

I took my tray back into the kitchen, which was empty. I could hear Sam in the dining room, explaining the seating arrangements to Officer Tim. Since there was a slight lull in the action, I went down the hall to the storage area that housed the closet where Gabriel's body had been found. What could have happened between killer and victim that would result in such an ugly and violent outcome? It was unlikely that anything would have been overlooked by the heavy security presence the other night, but I needed to see for myself.

I eased the door open and flipped on the light switch. Then I closed the door behind me and began to sort through the stuff on the shelves. At the bottom were cans of paint, most half empty; I assumed these were used to touch up rooms at the house. Further up I found paint rollers, tubes of caulk, plastic trash bags, rolls of paper towels, lightbulbs, bathroom cleaner, and an orange hazard cone. I searched quickly behind all of the items, thinking of how expensive it must to be to maintain a historic building like this one. The door flew open behind me and I stifled a scream.

Rusty Hodgdon stood outside the door looking perplexed. "I'm sorry, I thought this was the men's room."

I gawked at him and stammered, "I was looking for the rum bottles my stepfather said he stashed here the other day.

I have a feeling the officers searching the premises might have impounded them."

He laughed and peered around. "We have a room very similar to this at the Hemingway Home—all the flotsam and jetsam of the work behind the scenes. Off to find the loo."

He staggered a little, and I wondered if he was pretending or was actually that tipsy. Could he really have thought this was the men's room, or was he looking for something, too? He'd shown a lot of interest in that precious, missing gold medal. Which might make him very dangerous. I felt a chill course from the top of my spine to my coccyx.

Chapter Seventeen

"A writer's personality is revealed by her connection to food," said Olivia. "Some people are feeders and some are withholders."

—Lucy Burdette, *Death in Four Courses*

I heard Sam announce to the guests outside on the lawn that the dinner was about to be served in the dining room. He ushered them in the front door and into the space where Jimmy Carter once hosted dinner with his family, where Harry Truman must have eaten many times with his wife and daughter and, more frequently, his cabinet along with members of the press. I filled the crystal water glasses on the table from a green pitcher on the sideboard. At that point, I realized there were five empty chairs.

"Should I take up the place settings so it isn't so obvious we're missing people?" I asked Bill in a whisper.

"There's no point in trying to hide it," he said. "Everyone's well aware." He didn't have to add another word because his face said it all—the big crescendo of the weekend was flatlining.

As my mother chatted and showed people to their seats and asked them about their preference for red or white wine, I went back in the kitchen to help Sam and Officer Tim plate the food. First we settled several slices of the roast on the dishes, then topped this with a spoonful of onions, soft enough to almost melt into the meat. Miss Gloria added a scoop of white rice followed by the black beans and then the perfectly sweet roasted bananas.

Sam picked up two of the plates to carry out to the dining room as my mother came springing back through the door.

"Easy," he said. "We almost had a casualty here."

My mother brushed past him and turned to me. "Isabella Diaz wants you to sit at the table during dinner. Since Rusty's wife didn't show up, along with the four Cuban people, there are too many men and five empty seats. She says it's terribly awkward and her husband is in a terrible mood, and Bill thinks it's a good idea too." She had a pleading look on her face. "We can handle everything from here. Please, whatever it takes to make this a success, we need to do it."

"It would make more sense for Miss Gloria to go," I said. "She probably needs the rest and she's a lot more lively than I am."

"I don't need any rest," my roommate said. "You keep saying that and it might get on my last nerve."

"Besides—" Sam shrugged. "If she asked for you, you should be the one to go."

"I'll be keeping a close eye on everything if you're worried about getting into trouble," the policeman said.

"But I'm not dressed for a party." I gestured at the spotted apron and plucked at my hair, which had frizzed to an auburn nimbus in the usual Key West humidity. "The other women are all dressed up. And on top of that, it would be too weird. I'm one of the servers; they are the honored guests."

I looked at the faces around me, all three of them hopeful. And thought about how much more I might hear actually sitting at the table than ferrying dishes in and out of the kitchen. "Okay." I pulled the apron over my head, folded it, and set it on the table.

"Here, take a seat for a minute," said my mother. "We'll jazz you up a little bit."

I slumped into the chair that she was patting. She took off her own string of pearls and fastened them around my neck. Miss Gloria hurried over with a hairbrush and my mother's makeup bag, and they buffed me up with blush and a swipe of lip gloss. Then my mother brushed my hair and tied it back away from my face with the green ribbon she'd had in her own hair.

"As good as gold," said Miss Gloria, grinning.

I took a big breath in and pushed through the swinging door to the dining room. All the diners turned to look at me.

"Hayley, we're so delighted you could join us!" exclaimed Mrs. Diaz. "I need someone to chat recipes with, and these fellows are simply not foodies. And Miss Sebek is busy talking fishing with the men. Leaving me in this wasteland devoid of female niceties."

She flashed another bright smile, and I slid into the empty seat next to Turner and across from her. Then I shook out the folded napkin that was at my place and bared my teeth into an answering smile.

"Thank you for inviting me," I said.

"At least this way, we know the food isn't poisoned," said Turner. He winked.

"Funny guy," I muttered under my breath.

Sam and my mother emerged from the kitchen with the last few plates, and Sam circled around the table, filling the wine glasses that had been quickly emptied. "Bon appétit," said my mother. "Oh my goodness, I should have learned how to say that in Spanish! But we hope you enjoy your dinner."

"*Gracias*," said the mayor's wife. "You could say *buen apetito* or *buen provecho*."

They hurried back through the door leading to the kitchen, and I yearned to follow them. For a few moments I heard mostly the clinking of silverware against plates and the gurgling of wine.

"The roast pork is phenomenal," said Eric from his perch at the end of the table. "Are you willing to share the recipe?"

"I'm betting it's marinated in our traditional sour orange juice with plenty of garlic," said the mayor's wife.

I nodded. "We've had such fun this weekend trying traditional Cuban recipes."

"When I visited Havana last year," said Turner, "the food choices seemed to be quite limited. I suspect that the government rations have had a distinctly and deliberately negative effect. Don't you think so, Mayor Diaz?"

What in the world was wrong with this man? Certainly, he was drinking, but so was everyone else at the table. Did that explain his behavior, or was he deliberately trying to be rude and offensive? If so, to what purpose? Fortunately, Bob was seated at the other end of the table, as he would have had heart failure if he'd heard.

"So what was your favorite part of Key West?" Eric asked, noticing the Havana mayor's red face. "In some ways it must feel familiar, and in other ways, quite foreign."

"Here's hoping it was Hemingway's house," said Rusty, raising his wine glass in a toast and then draining the last bit. All the guests turned to the mayor, waiting for his answer.

Dana took a sip of her wine and then said, "While he's thinking this over, may I be candid here?" She didn't wait long enough to allow anyone to say no. "I absolutely adore the cats at the Hemingway Home and find the man and his romantic escapades endlessly fascinating. But I don't enjoy reading his books."

She'd said this loudly enough to suck the wind from the room. As far as I knew, people in Key West and Havana did not criticize the master's writing. If they didn't care for it, they kept that opinion to themselves.

"Take *The Old Man and the Sea*, which I read last week because of this conference and because, after all, he did win the Nobel prize for it. Isn't it the writers' mantra that you're supposed to show rather than tell? But he goes all blah, blah, blah, telling us the old man is simple, but too simple to know he's humble, and so on. Doesn't that break all the conventions of good writing?"

I hadn't read this book—though I wasn't about to admit it. It hadn't come up in college, where I'd been most interested in culinary subjects. And lately, I'd been too busy with *Key Zest* and helping my mother get ready for the weekend to

155

do any extra reading. The closest I'd come to *The Old Man and the Sea* was visiting the Custom House Museum, where Hemingway's words were inscribed on the walls leading up to the second floor, showcased along with wonderful pen-and-ink sketches by Guy Harvey based on that very book.

"Maybe you have to be a man to love Hemingway," said Rusty. "All the macho posturing about war and bullfighting—testosterone helps with that." He rapped his fists on his chest like a big gorilla.

Mrs. Diaz laughed. "I loved *The Old Man and the Sea*. I don't know what that says about my hormone levels." She beamed at her husband. "Anyway, you asked about our favorite part of Key West. I did a bit of walking this afternoon. I adored the little neighborhoods with the wood homes decorated with gingerbread trim. Some of the woodwork is astonishingly intricate. And then all your little bursts of tropical foliage—those remind me of home. When I was finally able to drag my husband away from his work"—she patted his arm—"he admired your quaint harbor."

"What kinds of fish do the Cuban people love most?" Dana asked. "Here on this island, I would say yellowtail and grouper are prized for eating. I wonder how different it is in Havana?"

There was a dead silence for a few moments, and I wondered what land mine she had stepped on this time.

"The Cubans aren't allowed to go fishing," said Turner.

There was more pained silence in the group. I could imagine that the Castro government had preferred to limit access to boats so that people wouldn't use them to run for America. I could also imagine that the cost of power boats and fancy sport-fishing gear would be prohibitive for regular citizens. But why, why, why bring this all up at a dinner party planned around the concept of opening doors and cementing neighborly relations? I tried to focus on remembering every detail of the back-and-forth rather than on how uncomfortable I was feeling.

"I'm sure they eat fish," Eric said calmly. "Cuba is an island."

Finally Mrs. Diaz spoke up again. "If I might correct Mr. Markham's statement a bit, it's that the Cuban people don't ordinarily have the financial resources for sport fishing. But you will definitely see our countrymen fishing from the breakwaters and jetties right in the city."

Bill added, "I imagine that's one of the aspects of life that will change as the country slowly embraces commerce. I can understand why the authorities didn't much like people own-ing boats when emigration was such a powerful force. Now that the agreement between the countries has changed and the wet-foot, dry-foot law is no longer a factor, I should think access to boats will open up. Am I wrong?"

The image of those heartrending chugs at the botanical garden sprang to my mind again.

"Enough!" said Mayor Diaz. He threw his napkin on the table and pushed his chair away. "Enough about all the prob-lems and deprivations of the Cuban people, and how you do this and that better. I'm finished here." He threw a steely look at his wife, her horrified face and her sparkly sequins suddenly stark in the overhead light.

She glanced around the table, her expression apologetic. "I'm afraid we will be leaving." She came around the table, put her hand on my shoulder, and smiled. "I'm so sad that we will miss your mojito cake. I'm certain it will be devastatingly delicious, and I will regret its absence for the rest of my life. And finally I shall write my memoir: *The Middle-Aged Woman and the Cake*, by Isabella Diaz. It will be my fish that got away. Oh dear, that was a terribly awkward joke. I'm so sorry about all of this. *Buenos noches*."

They swept out of the room, past the Secret Service booth where the police officers had been stationed during the meal. I could hear the mayor's angry Spanish all the way outside.

Bob pushed away from the table and leapt up, then barreled down to my end. "What is the matter with you people?" Sweat popped out on his forehead and he wiped it away with his sleeve. "Are you deliberately trying to sabotage all the groundwork we've laid for months and months? And do you not realize how important the connection is between us and their country?"

"No disrespect intended," said Rusty, "But I don't believe Mayor Diaz had any intention of working with us. In fact, I wouldn't be surprised if he's the one who pocketed the gold medal on Friday."

Bob sputtered as he turned to Rusty, his spittle spraying onto me. "Are you mad?" He turned back to Eric. "You're the expert; have these people gone mad?"

Now Eric got to his feet and held his hands out in a calming gesture. "Let's everyone take a few slow and deep breaths," he suggested in his most soothing therapist voice. I knew it well from the times he'd used it on me when I was barely clinging to the cliff of sanity. "Maybe we can salvage something from this evening if we all work together."

"Why in the world do you think the mayor would have pocketed a medal that already belonged to his country in the first place?" Turner asked Rusty. "In what universe does that make any sense? I was a little hard on him, I admit. But I finally got tired of his Eeyore grumbling. I didn't hear one word about any projects that might have benefited our town."

Dana said, "I believe you shot yourself in the foot, my friend. Making some deals about common fishing grounds where the grouper and yellowtail still roam, that would have been amazing. And how about permission to study their coral reef? That could have benefited all of us. Have you not read the news about reefs dying everywhere? One third of Australia's Great Barrier Reef is bleached white, for heaven's sake."

Turner gave her a dismissive wave. "He was never going to lobby for anything that gave the U.S. any special access to something belonging to Cuba. I doubt very much that he even has the power to make changes. That's not how it works in his country. This whole event was a waste of time and money."

I thought he had a point, though bluntly and rather cruelly stated.

"Do you think Harry Truman settled everything in a weekend?" asked Bob, his words rising into an outraged squeak.

He stormed out of the dining room toward the stairs leading to the bedroom area where his office was located. Eric and Bill exchanged more horrified glances, excused themselves, and bolted after him.

I returned to the kitchen, where the others were carefully tipping slices of my amazing cake onto individual plates garnished with more mint. "Hold the dessert. There is no way to sweeten up that crowd. What few there are left."

"What's happened?" Officer Tim asked, stepping away from the cake to peer into the dining room.

"It's over," I said, sinking heavily into one of the kitchen chairs.

My mother began to cry. Sam hugged her and tried to comfort her, while I reported in a hoarse whisper on the conversations that had culminated in the mayor exiting with his wife.

"Sounds like those men were behaving like horse's asses," Miss Gloria said. "Though why would the mayor steal something that already belonged to his country?"

"That's exactly what Turner wondered." I dragged a finger through the whipped cream on the nearest piece of cake.

"Maybe because the medal was in the custody of the Catholic Church rather than the government, where he might have felt it belonged," Sam mused. "So this whole weekend could have been excellent cover to steal it back."

"And what if he was afraid he'd be found out and was looking for an excuse to cut out as soon as possible?" I asked. "Maybe that would explain why he's been such a sourpuss." I turned to our undercover cop. "Better text Torrence and let him know that the mayor shouldn't be allowed to leave the country until his belongings are searched. Yikes! That's going to go over like a sack of three-day-old dead bait fish."

Chapter Eighteen

Restaurant reviewing is a parade of the extraordinary, a half-dozen special-occasion meals each week. You hear a hundred explanations of how to order, smile your thanks at a thousand amuse bouches, read a million back-of-the-menu culinary manifestos. I texted to my boyfriend on my way from the office to review a dinner: I'm so tired of fois gras. *He replied:* Read back to yourself what you just typed. *You can have too much of a good thing.*

—Helen Rosner, "On Chicken Tenders,"
Guernica, June 2015

I woke up the next morning to a cacophony of barking, hissing, and the shrieks of a child. Based on the scent of coffee and fishy cat food along with the cheerful note on the counter, I deduced that Miss Gloria was already fully caffeinated, had fed the kitties, and had gone off on her senior citizen walk with Mrs. Dubisson. Feeling instantly guilty about having canceled my appointments with Leigh at the gym this week,

I poured myself a cup of coffee and went outside to investigate the morning ruckus and prepare to summarize my impressions of the night before for Torrence.

On the deck of their houseboat, Mrs. Renhart's two elderly cats were circling around her old Schnauzer, growling and hissing. The dog crouched low, barking furiously. A few feet away on the wooden catwalk, my friend Connie's baby was pointing and laughing from her perch on her mother's back.

"Good morning," Connie called. "I hope we didn't wake you. We're on our way to the playground, but we couldn't pass up the show."

"I had to get up anyway—I have two articles to turn in by the end of the day."

"How was the conference?" She peered more closely at my face. "You look a little tired."

"Honestly? I'm exhausted." I hopped up onto the wooden catwalk, gave my friend a hug, and kissed the baby's pudgy hand. She smiled and gurgled and kicked her legs in reply. "Catering is not for the faint of heart. Especially when we lost three of my mother's workers the first evening. And the wrap-up dinner party last night was an unmitigated disaster."

"I'm so sorry," she said. "Poor Janet. This was a big deal for her. Did the police figure out who was responsible for that murder?"

"As far as I know, they haven't even narrowed the field." I had the urge to tell her everything, which I usually did. But for once I imagined that the KWPD would appreciate some discretion. Though I could hint, right? "Unfortunately, the Cuban visitors are flying home today. Though I suppose that if one of them was a serious suspect, they'd be detained. Imagine the international chaos that could cause!"

The baby grunted and fussed and struggled to get out of the carrier that Connie had strapped to her back. "Let's have a drink tomorrow and you can tell me everything," Connie said. "I'll get Ray to babysit. He's been out so much, between painting commissions and working on his new studio, that I'm due for some adult time."

"Come here," I said, "we've got some nice rosé. And my mother was lamenting last night that she'd overestimated the hors d'oeuvres we needed for the party. She cooked for forty instead of twelve. You won't believe her empanadas. And she and Miss Gloria will want to see you, too."

Once my friend left and the neighbor's animals had retreated to their cabin, leaving only tufts of fur behind to mark the scene of the crime, I tapped out a list of notes on my phone to send to Torrence. They were just bits and pieces—his job would be to put them together into something that made sense. Or throw them out if they appeared nonsensical. Or if they didn't match up with what Officer Boyd reported. Though I couldn't really imagine what he'd have to add—he'd seemed more interested in culinary insights than police work.

IT WAS A LOUSY NIGHT, WORSE THAN EXPECTED. FIRST OF ALL, FOUR OF THE INVITED DIGNITARIES NEVER SHOWED UP. THE REMAINING TWO CUBAN GUESTS STORMED OUT BEFORE DESSERT. WHERE TO BEGIN? RUSTY HODGDON, WHO WORKS AT THE HEMINGWAY HOME, SCARED ME TO DEATH WHEN I WENT LOOKING FOR RUM IN THAT CLOSET. HE CLAIMED HE WAS LOOKING FOR THE MEN'S ROOM. AND HE DID SEEM

LIKE HE'D BEEN DRINKING, SO IT'S POSSIBLE HE WAS TELLING THE TRUTH. BUT THE CLOSET ISN'T ANYWHERE NEAR THE MEN'S ROOM, SO I DID FEEL SUSPICIOUS.

I figured Torrence would know which closet I meant. And I wasn't going to volunteer that I was also snooping among the supplies. That in fact I had gotten there first.

THE HAVANA MAYOR WAS COLD AS ICE, THOUGH HIS WIFE THINKS THIS HAS TO DO WITH POLITICAL PRESSURE FROM HOME AND MAYBE THE VISIT TO THE CHUGS. IT SEEMED TO ME THAT HE WOULD HAVE PREFERRED TO BE AMONG THE MISSING, TOO. (SHE IS A DARLING WOMAN WHO SPEAKS PERFECT ENGLISH AND SEEMS CAPABLE OF UNDERSTANDING ALL SIDES OF A PROBLEM. WOULD EITHER ONE OF THEM BE CAPABLE OF MURDERING A MAN IN COLD BLOOD? IT'S HARD TO PICTURE.)

I thought hard about how to phrase the next part.

BOB WOLZ APPEARED VERY WORRIED ABOUT THE FACT THAT NO DEFINITE AGREEMENTS WERE MADE BETWEEN THE TWO CITIES. MAYBE THIS IS RELATED TO FINANCIAL PRESSURE AT THE LITTLE WHITE HOUSE? ANYWAY, HE WAS APOPLECTIC BY THE TIME THE DINNER FIZZLED OUT. EXCUSE ME, BLEW UP.

I deliberately left out mention of Bill Averyt. I couldn't see throwing my friend under the bus when I was certain he couldn't be the killer.

DANA SEBEK IS EXTREMELY GUNG HO ABOUT MAKING A CONNECTION OVER FISHING AND WATER SPORTS AND LEARNING FROM THEIR HEALTHY CORAL REEFS. BUT IS THERE SOMETHING MORE PERSONAL IN IT FOR HER?

And more to the point, was she as clueless as she'd appeared last night? I thought not.

TURNER MARKHAM WAS FULL OF HIMSELF, AS USUAL. IN FACT, I'D SAY HE MADE A JACKASS OF HIMSELF BY CRITICIZING THE WAYS THE CUBAN GOVERNMENT WAS SCREWING ITS PEOPLE. I CAN'T IMAGINE WHY HE WOULD HAVE BEHAVED THIS WAY, EXCEPT IT'S BEEN A LONG, EXHAUSTING WEEK AND THE ALCOHOL WAS FLOWING FREELY.

Torrence wasn't a big fan of Markham either, so this probably wouldn't come as much of a surprise.

OMG, I JUST NOW THOUGHT OF THIS. YOU KNOW THOSE SEQUINS YOU WERE ASKING ABOUT? MRS. DIAZ'S DRESS WAS SPRINKLED WITH THEM. AND NOW THAT I'M THINKING, DANA'S SKIRT WAS MADE OF TULLE, STUDDED WITH BLACK SEQUINS. THEY BOTH LOOKED SO CUTE—THEY HAVE THE FIGURES TO CARRY THOSE DRESSES OFF.

TMI, no doubt. But that stream of consciousness led to the next question: what female would have been strong enough to wield that knife? Both Mrs. Diaz and Dana looked fit and well toned. And I'd heard that acting in self-defense brought surges of adrenaline. Heck, I hadn't just heard it, I'd lived it. More than once. But I couldn't picture Isabella Diaz stabbing someone. And I didn't know Dana well enough to make that assessment.

AND PS, YOUR OFFICER TIM WAS A BIG HIT WITH THE KITCHEN STAFF. HE'D LITERALLY DO ANYTHING MY MOTHER SUGGESTED, INCLUDING SCRUBBING POTS. AND, HE WAS VERY INTERESTED IN THE RECIPES. LET'S HOPE THE POLICE

DEPARTMENT DOESN'T LOSE HIM TO MY MOTHER'S CATERING COMPANY LOL.

After those notes were cleared out of my mind, I relaxed a few more minutes with a second cup of coffee, pining for a real *café con leche* and avoiding my real work. The day was calm, and warming up. The water glinted with flashes of light in the sun, sea gulls cawed and swooped, and I barely noticed the hum of traffic from Palm Avenue. The conversation I'd had with Torrence about marriage and the possibility of my own baggage getting in the way of seeing things clearly kept churning through my brain. Why had my parents gotten divorced? I knew the story that had always been told— my dad finally left when he became convinced they had nothing in common. What exactly did that mean? Was there more?

I punched my father's speed dial number. He usually seemed happy to hear from me, though he was abysmally poor at calling himself. His second wife, Allison, often phoned to fill me in on what he would have said. But this topic I needed to broach directly with him. Thank goodness she had not been part of their breakup story. He'd married Allison quite a few years after divorcing Mom, acquiring a stepson, Rory, in the process.

Once he picked up, I asked if he had a few minutes to chat. Which he did. "I know you don't really like to rake the past over the coals, but I was thinking about your marriage to Mom. I wondered why it really ended?"

The silence that came from his end of the line fell cold and heavy like an ice-bucket challenge. I could have filled it up with my own speculations and musings, but this time I felt brave enough to let my question sit.

"Why in the world are you thinking about that now?" he asked.

"It's an important part of my history," I said. "You know what the shrinks say: those who ignore the past are destined to repeat it. Or something."

"The truth is," he said after clearing his throat half a dozen times, "we'd grown apart. We didn't have much in common anymore. We were so damn young when we got married— we didn't know each other very well. Heck, we didn't know ourselves."

"Yes, but you had *me* in common."

He sighed. "Yes, we did, and as I've told you before, missing out on parts of your life is one of my great regrets. And it always will be. And I'll always be grateful to your mother for the amazing person you turned out to be. Why are you asking? Did she put you up to this?"

"Of course she didn't," I answered quickly. "She is delightfully, exquisitely married to Sam. And you're happy too, I presume."

"Of course." He rustled and harrumphed. "Back then, we had no idea what made marriage work. Neither one of us knew how to talk."

I murmured an encouraging *mmmm*, suppressing the urge to mention that he wasn't all that great at it now either.

"Looking back, which I don't like to do because it's over and done, I suppose we could have learned. But I had in my mind a career-minded wife who could share the financial responsibilities of a family and our life together. Not a happy homemaker. And that's what I thought I was getting. And neither one of us was mature enough to have a baby. Fortunately for you, Janet adapted into a wonderful mother. And I suppose some part of her did want a career, as she has one now. How is that going, by the way?"

"Very well," I said, mulling over whether to discuss the problems of the weekend with him. I decided not. He sounded normal and supportive right now, but often he couldn't keep his critical side from coming out. Especially where my mother was concerned. He'd home right in on the fact that maybe, just maybe, she'd gotten in way over her head.

"It sounds like you're saying that it was hard to accept who she really was at the time; instead, you focused on your expectations for your fantasy wife, and those weren't met."

"Yes," he said, "and if you hadn't happened along, perhaps we wouldn't have gotten married at all." He hurried to add, "Not that I'm saying in any way that I wish you didn't exist."

Another call came in, which my phone identified as Bill Averyt. "Dad, it was great talking with you. I have to take this call. Give my love to Rory and Allison."

I hung up and accepted the call from Bill. After a perfunctory good morning, he began to pummel me with questions. "Have you heard from the police? Is there any news about the murder? How about Mrs. Diaz, did you hear from her this morning?"

He was obviously stunned by what had happened at the dinner. "Slow down," I said. "I can't answer questions that fast. First, I haven't heard anything from the police. I sent some notes over to them this morning about what I noticed. But I honestly didn't expect anything back. It's not exactly a two-way street."

I snickered. Then, before he could ask, I summarized what I had observed. "I was sorry to even mention Bob, since he's your friend and your boss and he was so distressed."

"And that was nothing compared to what he's like this morning," Bill said. "A big meeting of all the foundation's board members has been called for tomorrow. He's afraid they're going to ask for his resignation. Or worse. I can't believe this is happening. He's dedicated to that place; he knows the history and the stories as though he's lived each of them. Losing him would be like a death in the family. And if he's canned, the rest of us will be next."

"I'm so sorry," I said. "Hopefully the police will have sorted this out before the meeting."

"We're not optimistic," said Bill. "In this case, optimism would be based on a major case of denial. I hoped you'd have something new."

I heard a voice in the background.

"Eric wants to know what you're doing with those beleaguered mojito cakes."

"Sadly, those sat out so long, we had to throw them out last night," I said. "No one wanted to risk the warm whipped cream. Call it another death in the family," I added, trying too hard to leave him with a laugh.

Chapter Nineteen

If you wish to make an apple pie from scratch, you must first invent the universe.

—Carl Sagan

After hanging up with Bill, it was past time to buckle down to work. I'd probably get more done at the office, and besides, showing my face would be a good thing for my employment future. But first, I would stop by the Cuban Coffee Queen off Southard Street, buy a large *café con leche*, maybe with an extra shot of espresso, and attempt to understand what Irena had been trying to tell me yesterday.

I parked in my spot behind Preferred Properties, home of *Key Zest*, figuring it would be faster to walk than to weave around downtown looking for parking. And besides, a few extra calories burned would be only good news.

This branch of the Coffee Queen was located down a small alley lined with local businesses. Irena waved as she saw me coming. I passed through picnic tables of breakfasting tourists and approached the counter.

"Good morning," she said. "Geoff will be making your coffee today. He's in training. It's actually his first morning on the job, but he's showing great promise."

Inwardly, I groaned. No one could be much good brewing specialty coffee on his first day. Geoff, a wiry guy with his hair shaped into a blue Mohawk, looked absolutely panicked and frozen. He was likely to be overwhelmed if I asked for extras, like the second hit of espresso.

"Start by packing the grounds into the cup. Remember what I showed you earlier?" Irena asked gently. He spooned ground coffee into the cup, leveled it off, and twisted it onto the espresso machine.

"Don't forget to put a little pitcher under the spigot and then start it," she said in a sweet voice, though at the same time rolling her eyes at me. "Milk is in the fridge. Pour some into the large metal pitcher and dunk the steamer rod into it. Hayley takes one sugar, which we know—and you will learn—because she's a regular." She winked at me and watched as he did the work and the machine began to work its noisy magic. "While you're waiting for that to brew, you would take her money. This time her coffee is on the house."

When my drink was finally ready, she told the man she was training that she was taking a break. "I'll be sitting right there in case you need me." She pointed to the picnic table closest to the exit, but not more than ten yards from the counter.

Once we were settled at the table, she asked, "Have there been any arrests?"

I shook my head.

"How did it go last night?"

I took a sip of my coffee, hoping for an instant rush. "The food was fabulous but the company, atrocious. Most of the Cuban delegation declined to attend, and the mayor and his wife left early. It's almost as though the weekend was cursed—and this dinner was the perfect bookend to that horrible Friday night party." I hadn't meant to sound so negative, but what was the point of sugarcoating the truth? Her own cousin had been stabbed to death opening night—she couldn't have positive feelings about the event.

The smile that Irena had kept on her face until now faded. "My aunt feels hopeless about the authorities figuring out who killed Gabriel. She doesn't even believe that they're trying. I'm beginning to think she's not paranoid; she's correct."

"I know quite a few cops in this town," I said, reaching across the picnic table to squeeze her hand. "There's no way they're going to let the murder investigation slide. It's dangerous. It's bad for residents and tourists alike and it would make them look like fools. Your aunt may not see what they're doing, but I know they're working behind the scenes." I didn't think I should say that I'd just sent in a set of notes about my observations from the night before. It would not be reassuring to hear that I was helping them investigate—observing only, as Torrence would have corrected me.

Irena merely shook her head and withdrew her hand from my grasp. "You can tell her all day long that Cuban-American people are just as important as plain Americans in this town and she'll never believe it. I honestly think she'd return to Cuba if she could. I've got to get back to work," she said, gesturing at the customers who were stacking up by the counter, fidgeting and grumbling. "This new guy can't tell spent grounds from fresh beans. Let me know if you hear anything else, okay? Anyway, thanks for trying."

She was trying to appear cheerful, but the disappointment she felt about my lack of news was plain on her face. I couldn't blame her. TV cops seemed to arrest murderers within the first twenty-four hours. We were eons behind that schedule. I felt guilty and sick about failing her and her family.

She returned to my table one more time. "Can I just add that Maria seems terrified? She won't tell me of what, but I can take a wild guess."

"I'll keep working on it," I said.

The customer who'd had this table before me had left a copy of the *Key West Citizen* on the table, so I paged through it while I was finishing my coffee and attempting to shift my focus to planning the day. Two articles about the Cuban conference dominated the front page. The first mentioned the conflict of ideas between the protesters—those who supported rapprochement between our countries versus those who felt any softening of sanctions and regulations only fed the communist government. NPR reporter Nancy Klingener had supplied photos of the group protesting yesterday's visit to view the refugee boats at the botanical garden. The second article, illustrated by a photo of police tape around the Friday's crime scene, contained optimistic updates from the police chief.

"We are pursuing all leads and expect to have suspects in custody shortly," he'd said. "Citizens who may have information about the murder are encouraged to contact the police."

Two sentences that didn't necessarily go together, I thought as I turned the page.

The outlook for the weather was more sunshine and warmer temps. "This day in history" showed a photo of President Truman in shorts, a guayabera shirt, and a pith helmet, chatting with reporters on the front lawn of the Little White House, who likewise were wearing shorts. Just above the photo, the usual cranky suspects had filled the "Citizens Voice" comment line with complaints about rude taxi drivers, loud leaf blowers, and tourists too inebriated to check for traffic. The final remark caught my eye.

Money, money, money, isn't that what the Beatles sang? To solve the horrific and embarrassing murder at the Little White House, our chief needs look no further than to who the conference benefits. It certainly doesn't appear to have helped the citizens of Key West.

This might be true. And most likely, the people who were hoping to make money had been gathered around the table last night. And Bob's stewardship problems had to have a place on the list. Though it would seem counterproductive to murder someone at the event where he hoped his fortunes might be restored. Why Gabriel? It didn't compute.

Still, wouldn't it make sense to look into Little White House finances?

Who could help? The name that came to mind was Palamina. She would know where to go and how to do this, but she'd have mixed feelings, of course, not wanting me to butt in where I didn't belong. And I didn't want to raise Wally's ire again by speaking to her separately. But, on the other hand, what if this was a big story, and I broke it or added material above what had already been gathered? What if I came up with leads crucial to the murder investigation? Not only would I be helping Irena and Maria and Carmen, but I could be saving Bill's job, and providing publicity that our little e-zine didn't often get. I decided I'd continue to puzzle over the murder as Gabriel's family had asked. If I discovered something new, I could turn it instantly over to the police. No one could fault me for thinking, right?

I left the coffee shop feeling mostly sad. I hoped the caffeine would hit hard and soon so I could get my work done in time for the deadline. And I hoped that reading cookbook introductions and looking at pictures would whet my stalled writing whistle.

I power walked over to Books & Books, a bookstore founded by Judy Blume and her husband, to check out their selection of Cuban cookbooks. After that, I planned to hit Key West Island Books on Fleming Street and look at their quirky cookbook selection. It was such a relief to have two successful bookstores in town, steaming ahead.

Books & Books was located in a corner of The Studios of Key West, a Miami deco building on Eaton Street that had been rehabilitated and filled to bursting with art, music, artists—and now books. In the cookbook section, my attention was drawn to a small white volume called *Cortadito: My Wanderings Through Cuba's Mutilated Yet Resilient Cuisine*. Skimming through the first chapters showed me that the author felt considerable grief about the state of Cuban food today due to the economic problems in the country, though he had great memories of Cuban food in Miami. The author's powerful yearnings for the old Cuba reminded me of Maria and Carmen. His doubts about the quality of Cuban food reminded me of Turner Markham's comments last night.

I bought that and also a book called *Cuba! Recipes and Stories From the Cuban Kitchen*. This was a beautiful hardcover with pictures of food that kicked my salivary glands into high gear.

On the way out, I remembered that Nancy Klingener's radio studio was right here in The Studios of Key West building. I decided to take a detour and chat with her about what she might have noticed at the tour of the chugs yesterday morning. Would that count as investigating, which Torrence had warned me not to do? More like chatting with a friend. And besides, if I learned something crucial to solving the murder, I could pass it right on to the police, along with any residual guilt.

I exited using the back door of the bookstore, walked through the main gallery of TSKW, paused to admire local Key West artist John Martini's eccentric metal sculptures, and went up the stairs to the second floor. I knocked and popped my head through the open door. Nancy was working at a laptop on her desk, set to the side of her recording equipment. Gorgeous photographs of the island were displayed on the walls above her.

"Do you have a second?" I asked. When she nodded, I stepped inside and gawked at more photos hung on the other walls—birds, Key West nature, and local island color. "These are amazing," I said. "A local photographer?"

"My husband," she said with a proud smile. "What can I help you with?"

"Nice job on the front page reporting on the visit to see the chugs yesterday," I said. "I thought you were mostly radio?"

"I am," she said. "Though we do post our stories often to Facebook. And when the print media comes knocking, I don't turn them away." Her eyebrows drew together over the top of her glasses. "You were there too. What's your angle? How are you involved?" she asked, not sounding suspicious or hostile, more matter-of-fact.

I hemmed and hawed. "It's complicated." I sighed. "It's not sheer nosiness, though the police probably think so. The whole conference thing has turned out to be such a disaster, and honestly the investigation appears to have stalled. Gabriel's family asked me to keep my eyes and ears open, as they don't believe the authorities care much about the outcome. Maybe you heard about how badly last night's dinner went?"

She shook her head; she hadn't. So I filled her in on the infighting.

"So I wondered whether you noticed anything at the garden that I didn't."

Her eyebrows peaked again. "Like what?"

"Things like tension between the attendees. Or maybe you overheard comments? Anything that might shed some light on the murder. Or the theft of the medal."

"Do you have a personal stake in all of this?" she asked.

I squirmed a little; I could see what made her a good reporter.

"My mother had the catering gig for the weekend. And my friend Bill Averyt is one of the organizers. So if the conference bombed, so goes my mother's catering business and Bill's livelihood. But most painful to me would be disappointing Gabriel's family." I perched on one of the chairs in front of her desk without being invited. At least she hadn't thrown me out.

"Everybody's at each other's throats, but I can't really find a personal connection between Gabriel and any of these people," I continued. "I'm kind of stuck on the disappearance of the medal and whether and how that might intersect with him getting killed. They weren't absolutely linear timewise, but in the same ballpark."

"That makes sense," she said.

"Did someone need money so badly that they were willing to grab that gold? Did Gabriel witness the theft, and that happenstance get him killed? And if so, how did the rest of us miss it?"

I paused to give her a chance to comment on my stream of ideas. And realized in the short moment of silence that if he died because he saw something he shouldn't have seen, it could have been any of us stabbed to death in that kitchen. It might have been absolutely random. A case of there but for the grace of god . . . I felt absolutely leaden with fear. But wouldn't any of us have reported the theft immediately? Maybe he didn't have the time . . .

Her reply cut off my scary line of thinking. "This has to be off the record," she said, "because I haven't had the chance to poke around and find enough evidence to substantiate the rumor." She stopped and waited for me to agree. After I nodded, she said, "I have heard rumors from several sources that the Little White House Foundation might be in some financial hot water. Expensive repairs to the building were needed this summer, rentals of the facility were down, and they spent too much on a couple of premier events."

"So who would be on the hook for that?"

She shrugged her shoulders, took off her glasses, and pinched the bridge of her nose. "I hate to even say this, because he's a friend of mine. But Bob Wolz leads the charge over there. And don't get me wrong, he's done wonderful work as the executive director of the foundation. He has been very involved in restoration, as well as developing educational exhibits."

"Aside from Hemingway Home, it's my favorite place to visit on the island," I said. "I learn something new about our history every time I take that little tour."

Nancy tapped her fingers on her desk. "I admired his plans for this Havana/Key West conference. We are so close to Cuba that we definitely should have some connections. And we share common assets. And if we don't share common problems now, we will in the future. Tourism, the environment, they were hitting all the right notes."

Again she paused, waiting to see if I was following. "But?"

"But look at the way the opening night was presented. Did it need to be that lavish? I know they wanted to make a splash, but can you imagine what it cost to bring in Jimmy Buffett and President Obama? The line item for security alone must have been off the charts. I bet they were staggering numbers."

"Yes. I had the distinct feeling there was a lot at stake

here, and they felt they needed a big fuss to attract the right donors, now and in the future."

She turned her laptop so we could both see the screen. "But here's the thing. I do a fair amount of surfing through financial records filed by the nonprofits in our community. Because you never know where you might stumble across a story. An interested citizen can find a lot of fascinating information right there in plain sight."

She clicked through a couple of screens until she reached the website of the Community Foundation of the Florida Keys, and from there to the Little White House Foundation, and from there she brought up a page filled with pie charts and a spreadsheet of numbers. Small numbers. Lots of them. "You should study this if you're interested in the subject, as you seem to be. I can send you the link."

"Wow. Looking at those might cause my brain to freeze," I said with a chuckle. "My father has always been disgusted by my lack of mathematical skills. But I come by this honestly—directly from my mother."

She began to get the glazed look on her face that suggested that, once again, I was yammering mindlessly. "Enough about me. Yes, please send it." I recited my email address. "But it sounds like you were saying you noticed something off about the Little White House Foundation?"

"According to these numbers, in the red in a big way," she said flatly. "In other words, more than a lot was likely riding on this fancy weekend. They were desperately in need of a big influx of cash."

"Which does explain why Bob was so upset last night. But

what's the worst that could happen? We get a new executive director? Isn't the White House itself listed on the historical registry, safe and sound?"

"Not so fast," said Nancy. "The structure is protected, but maybe not the property surrounding it. Assuming that's the case, what if a far-thinking developer gets the idea that he could lease or even buy the property and build more condos? You weren't in town when Pritam Singh bought up all the land where the Truman Annex lies now. No one else had the vision to see what it could become. And now it might be the most desirable real estate on this island. And it made him a fortune."

I chewed my lip. "More condos in that location would go for a lot of money."

She nodded slowly. "Boatloads of money. And a slick presentation could ensure people involved both with zoning and with the state that the Little White House would remain in position, untouched. I'm sure a case could be made that it might even be improved by the influx of cash. An historical site in the tropics takes oodles of cash to maintain."

"It makes me sick to think about it, though," I said. "No wonder Bill and Bob are so upset."

I left the office confused about what this new insight could have to do with the murder. And more determined than ever to find out what had really happened this weekend. Perhaps a good start would be visiting every guest I didn't really know from last night's dinner. Since I was so close to Caroline Street, I decided to start at Dana Sebek's dive shop.

Chapter Twenty

"Oh dear, no, I can't possibly eat that," she said, her voice gone dangerously sweet. Sweet as icebox pie. Sweet as sugar tea.

—Joshilyn Jackson, *The Almost Sisters*

Dana looked completely different than she had in the official meetings and parties throughout the conference. No sequins, no tulle, no flowery girl dresses. She wore tan hiking shorts, a crisp white T-shirt, and serious water sandals. As I came into the shop, she was helping a customer sort through shelves of masks and bins of snorkel fins.

"I'll be with you in a few," she told me with a friendly smile.

I wandered around the edges of the small shop, looking at flippers and masks and tanks and wetsuits. And then, since the chances of me going scuba diving were zero, I studied the photos on her wall. Most of them were underwater pictures of colorful coral reefs, tropical fish, and even the dreaded invasive lionfish. Another wall was covered with photos of Jimmy

Buffett and his band, and his fans in bright tie-dyed shirts and funny hats featuring stuffed animals. She scared the heck out of me when she approached me from behind.

"You know, those spiny lobsters are absolutely delicious, by the way. We love the lionfish too, though it's a harder sell because they're so ugly."

I pointed to the photo right in front of me, a happy-looking man who posed with a pack of dogs of various shapes and sizes. He wore a gray felt hat shaped like a shark and his T-shirt read IT's FIVE O'CLOCK SOMEWHERE. "Who's this character?" I asked.

"That's my husband, Joe," she said.

I looked at her with astonishment. "And these are all your dogs?

She laughed. "No way, he drives for Mobile Mutts. He picks up dogs that have been rescued all over Florida and delivers them to no-kill shelters or foster homes. He's my hero. Though if I'd allow it, he'd move them all in."

"I didn't mean to keep you from a paying customer," I said, gesturing at the man who appeared to have left without buying anything. "I came to ask you some questions about the conference."

She nodded. "Not a problem. That fellow couldn't find anything right with any of my equipment. I finally figured out that he's been reading about all the weekend warriors who come down here to snorkel or dive and end up dying of heart attacks. It doesn't happen that often, but of course it always makes the newspaper. Turns out, he never learned to swim."

I shivered, imagining how terrifying it would be to go

underwater with only a tank of air on my back and no confidence that I could make it back to the boat. "That would take the fun out of spending the day in the water."

"Absolutely. So I referred him to our resident swimming lesson expert, Steven Callahan, and told him I'll be here to sell him equipment and set up a trip when he's ready. Steve didn't learn to swim until late middle age—and he was afraid of the water. You should never overestimate the effects of fear on any situation. Our bodies are designed to react quickly to fear, flooding us with adrenaline, and that causes sweating, rapid heartbeat, weakness . . . And as a result, people tend to panic, as he knows well. So he understands what people are facing. He has a one hundred percent success rate with my hapless customers so far." She had a good belly laugh—not laughing at her customer, but laughing with him.

All very interesting, but somehow I needed to get her to explain her presence at the conference. "I was curious about why you're so interested in Cuba?" I figured if I asked a general question, she wouldn't feel as though I was accusing her of anything.

She squinted, studying my face. "I thought I recognized you, even before you sat down with us last night. You were one of the caterers—the food was delicious."

"Thanks," I said. "My mother deserves most of the credit. She's the chef, I'm just a minion. I'm actually a writer for *Key Zest* magazine, doing a background story on effects of Cuban culture on our island. That's why I came to talk with you."

"Sure," she said. "I'd be happy to help with that. It's so important that we make a connection with the Cuban people. You may know that they have the world's only untouched coral reef. And this is because their government hasn't allowed fishing and tourism and manufacturing to ruin it. My concern, and not only mine, is that if the wrong people weasel their way into that situation, that reef could be devastated." She was shaking her finger and her voice had gotten loud. The freckles on her face popped into greater relief as her face flushed bright pink.

"Not only would it be a special place to visit, but we could learn so much about the way it's been preserved. And that information could be critical to helping us understand what we can do to bring ours back. If that's possible. It's like the other treasures that might be opening up in Cuba—they can be protected or they can be decimated. The jury is out."

"So you're basically an environmentalist?"

She laughed again. "I'm not totally altruistic. I realized when this conference was first being proposed that if my shop could team up with some Cuban boats, we could offer amazing trips. Other water sports vendors in Key West were very interested in this kind of opportunity too."

"So you were representing Key West boating and fishing types—I imagine there are a lot of them. Who did you have to lobby to get selected?"

She grimaced and crossed her muscular arms over her chest, studying me. "I suspect your mother went through a similar process—a proposal of interest with supporting references, including the green light from the Chamber of Commerce.

I made it very plain that while I did have a dog in this fight, I could also speak for the other vendors." She paused and leaned in closer. "I had another motive, though."

Good gravy, what now?

"My husband and I are huge fans of Jimmy Buffett's music. Parrot Heads through and through. You probably didn't know because we keep these things quiet so that outsiders don't rush him, but the local club had a meet and greet with Jimmy Friday night after the conference. Honest to gosh, it was a life list experience. And the only way I could be sure to get tickets was to be working at this conference. So I pushed hard to get accepted."

She led me back to the checkout counter of the shop and pointed to a signed photograph that hung on the wall behind the cash register. Dana and her husband wore colorful hats with parrots on them, along with a James Bond–style tuxedo for him and a sequined sheath for her. Jimmy Buffett, the famous singer who'd gotten a huge career boost from his songs about Key West—and also put the city on the tourism map—had his arms around their shoulders.

Unless my bad-guy radar was completely off base, I thought she sounded sincere. "How did you feel the conference went overall?" I asked.

"You were there last night," she said. "Very little good could come out of that. And the murder put a damper on everything."

"Such a tragic situation," I said. "Did you know Gabriel?"

She was quick to shake her head. "Have you heard anything about an arrest?"

"Nothing, other than what was in the paper this morning. And they like to keep up an optimistic front when there's been a tragedy. Understandably. I'm sure the police have already asked you, but you have a different perspective on the events than most people, as one of the attendees. Weren't you there for the Little White House tour on the first day when people realized the medal was missing?"

She nodded, but her brown eyes narrowed. "Did you say that this interview was for a piece on Cuban influence on Key West? You seem very curious about the murder."

What could I say? I explained my connection to Gabriel's family, without mentioning what Irena had said this morning—that Maria seemed scared witless.

"I told his cousin I wouldn't give up, so that brings me to you. Did you notice anything off? Someone who wasn't acting the way you might have expected?"

She slid onto the stool that sat behind the checkout counter. "Naturally, there was tension right from the beginning. I'm sure you saw the protesters outside the Southard Street gates?"

I nodded my head yes, hoping she'd have more than general impressions. More descriptions of the police and Secret Service presence weren't going to help me figure out what happened.

"Were you seated close to the back of the Little White House during dinner Friday night?" I hadn't remembered seeing her near the kitchen or the restrooms, but the night was so chaotic and I'd been so caught up in dancing and waiting on tables and gawking at the celebrities that I must have missed many details.

She folded her arms over her chest again, for the first time looking uncomfortable. "To tell the truth, I was a little upset being seated practically on top of the restrooms. Though we did get served first and had excellent access to the bar, which I may have utilized a little too freely." She grinned. "Throbbing headache all day Saturday. I was actually in the ladies' room when all the hubbub erupted. I was shocked when I came rushing out and saw everyone on the ground."

If this was all true, she might very well have seen the murderer come out of the kitchen. If it wasn't true . . . I tried to picture what she had been wearing Friday night, but all I could remember was last night's sparkly tulle. And I couldn't think of a reasonable way to ask about her other outfit. Was the Jimmy Buffett photo taken that same night? With her wearing sequins?

"Could you possibly have seen Gabriel arguing with someone before he was killed?"

She looked embarrassed again. "Honestly, I was very busy hobnobbing with the Cuban delegation, because getting in on the ground floor when those reefs are opened up is so crucial. And it wasn't only me; everyone at those tables wanted something from Cuba."

A chime sounded and two Asian young people came into the shop.

"You'll need to excuse me," she said, gesturing in their direction. "I really wish I had seen something helpful. I might have if I'd been paying attention to what was around me. But I wasn't. I was very focused." She began moving toward her customers. "Please let me know if I can set you up with snorkeling equipment or a tour."

"Maybe," I said. "I'm a Capricorn. We feel a lot more comfortable on land."

She laughed along with me, but this time her amusement sounded forced.

Chapter
Twenty-One

Se formó tremendo arroz con mango. (*A sticky situation is brewing.*)

—Cuban saying

I left the shop and stood out on the sidewalk blinking in the bright sunlight. A half block from here, gaggles of tourists were packed onto Duval Street, carrying drinks in plastic cups as they navigated from one bar to the next. How many of them knew there was so much more to our town then this tacky street? How many would bother to visit the other local places I loved, the historical sites that made it special? This was one reason that I always directed first-time visitors to the conch tour trains. Although residents complained about the incessant noise of the trains passing through their neighborhoods with their drivers on loudspeakers, at least visitors got a balanced overview of the island.

Since I'd ended up so close to the Truman Annex, I couldn't help wondering whether my ex-boyfriend, Chad, had seen anything unusual Friday night. He lived in the former

Naval Administration building that overlooked the Little White House grounds. Sometimes he worked at home; was this one of those days? After going back and forth in my mind, I called his office phone, knowing he rarely answered. He left that kind of work to his secretary, Deena Smith, with whom I'd been friendly until Chad and I blew up.

"It's Hayley Snow," I said when she answered. "Good morning!"

"Long time no hear from you," she said, sounding astonished. "I hope you're not in the market for a divorce lawyer."

"Not a bit," I said, hurrying to add, "Though I have a terrific guy in my life, and maybe someday we'll get married. I'm in no rush—don't want to make another dumb mistake." Though on general principle, I hated the idea of her reporting something pathetic about me to Chad, I honestly no longer cared about the relationship. It had been a brief but spectacular failure, but it had gotten me here to this island, and for that I would always be grateful.

After I asked about her own romance and heard a bit about its progress (slow but steamy), I asked if Chad might have been on the Truman Annex grounds this past weekend and whether he'd reported any insider news about the murder.

"Insider? Nothing that he shared with me," she said. "He's working at home today. Knowing him, if you call ahead and he recognizes your number, he'll ignore the phone. If you're in the area, maybe drop by?"

"What if I brought him a coffee?" I asked.

"Coffee won't get you too far. But remember how much

he loves those glazed doughnuts from that shop next to the Tropic? He won't buy one for himself, but he can't resist if someone offers him one."

"You're a sweetheart," I said, beginning to walk in the direction of Glazed Donuts. "We should get together soon and have a drink."

Which we probably wouldn't, not while she still worked for him. One thing he understood was her value as a secretary. And front woman. She had the people skills that he lacked—he was the shark in the back office, she the soothing goldfish swishing through the water out front. For those reasons, he paid her very well. My stomach flip-flopped wildly as I got closer to Eaton Street, thinking about Chad's possible reactions to seeing me. I lectured myself about ingesting pure sugar and carbs when I wasn't hungry, but my anxiety and the memory of those light pillowy doughnuts won out.

Glazed Donuts was operated by an adorable young couple, who usually sold out of their amazing treats by midafternoon. Today the chalkboard outside the door described the specials as a key lime pie doughnut; a thick chocolate option with chocolate icing and covered with big, round chocolate sprinkles; and a maple-glazed doughnut with candied bacon, which I'd had in the past and swooned over. But since Chad preferred plain glazed, I ordered two of those and a latte to go and continued on my mission.

I hurried past the post office and through the gates into the Truman Annex. All of the side gates leading to this complex were locked at six PM except during the Fantasy Fest Parade, when none of the residents wanted rowdy, partially nude revelers to get trapped inside. These same gates had all been locked during the day and evening of the first fancy party of the weekend.

When I reached the grounds of the Little White House, I paused to take in the view of the lawn. This was truly a lovely green space on our crowded little island, and it would be a terrible shame to lose it. It was hard to picture more condos getting shoehorned in around the White House, but I did not have a developer's eye.

I circled the lawn and approached the front door of my ex's condominium. I pulled in a deep breath and pushed my shoulders away from my ears. It wouldn't do to look nervous in front of Chad. He had a nose for weakness, finely honed from years of representing angry parties in nasty divorces. What could I say to convince him to talk about his impressions of Friday night, assuming he'd been here watching? He was predisposed to think of me as pointlessly nosy. I picked up the phone and pressed the numbers for his apartment. No answer. I hung up and tried one more time. Nothing.

As I was about to give up, a tall, older woman approached, pulling a red wagon that contained an elderly Jack Russell dog with a cast on his back leg. I recognized her as Molly Shallow, the neighbor who lived directly under Chad's apartment on the first floor. Maybe she'd been here Friday night—and maybe she'd be less wary about talking to me than Chad would have been.

I broke into a huge smile and explained quickly who I was and why I was there, skipping over the low point in our nasty breakup that she had probably witnessed when Chad put all my belongings out on the sidewalk. And glossing past the fact that I had no official reason to be poking around, instead giving her the explanation about my article on Cuban influences in our town.

She cocked her head to the right and then the left, like a wary bird. "Were you the girl whose stuff my neighbor stuck out on the curb?" She pointed to the cut in the cement that was reserved for short-term loading and unloading and handicapped residents.

What could I say? It wasn't going to work to lie, so I nodded.

"Honestly," she said, her eyes narrowing as if to size me up, "I didn't think you'd last around here. I thought you would have left the island not long after what he did."

"Turns out I'm more stubborn than that. I love this place, and I found a job at *Key Zest* that I adore, and I'm not going anywhere."

"Good for you. I'm not going anywhere either. Tell me again what you want to know?"

"I'm trying to get a sense of some of the people who attended this weekend's conference. And also wondering whether you were here for the big event on Friday?" I kept chattering about how tragic the events had been and how terrible the effects might be on our island if this wasn't resolved quickly. "Do you have a few minutes to chat? I come bearing doughnuts." I held up the white bag.

She nodded after a bit, and gestured at the little dog. "Come in. This is Paddy. He tore his ACL two weeks ago." We entered the vestibule of her apartment, which was old-fashioned yet comfortable, reminding me of my grandmother's home.

"We can sit outside," she said, leading us through the living area and out onto a large deck overlooking the harbor. The dog hobbled over to a bed shaped like a bone and settled in as we took seats in metal garden chairs. An enormous Disney cruise ship was docked at the nearby Margaritaville Westin, and the notes of "When You Wish Upon a Star" began to ring out.

Chad had grown to hate the cruise ships that filled the piers on this end of the island, but I'd enjoyed watching the tourists disembark—all part of the tropical island charm. I opened my bag and handed her one of the doughnuts on a napkin.

"Thank you," she said. "When the universe brings you a doughnut, or a cookie for that matter, I think she expects you to enjoy it."

I grinned and set upon my own sugary orb.

When we were finished eating, I repeated my first question. "Were you here Friday night for the opening party?"

"I wasn't an invited guest, but a few of us residents sat out on lawn chairs and watched for a couple hours." She brushed a few flakes of sugar off her lap. "We felt like kids watching a baseball game from the roof next to the stadium. Only of course they wouldn't let us anywhere near the roof or even the balconies. I would have given anything to shake Mr. Obama's hand, though not all of my neighbors were fans. And the music from Jimmy Buffett—that was a treat! I'm no Parrot

Head, but being so close to a legend was special. We could smell the Cuban food and wished we could be eating it. Torture!"

"My mother was the caterer," I told her. "She and her sous-chefs did an amazing job, and it was all going so well. Until the end, of course. Those popping noises were so puzzling and disturbing. Did you happen to see what happened?"

"Of course, the police have been here several times already asking that very question." Her little white dog struggled to his feet and hopped over to my chair to snuffle my fingers, then lick them clean of sugar. "I have a feeling it was unauthorized fireworks. We had some atrocious renters in this building last week who didn't seem to understand civility. First, they threw a wedding right on our pool grounds." She threw her hands up in disbelief. "They didn't ask anyone for permission; they just did it. The filters have been clogged with hideous plastic flowers ever since. And there was trash everywhere. And all throughout the week, their teenagers were caught trying one prank after another, including setting off fireworks and sending drones out. The president of our condo board finally had to ask the family to check out early."

Her renter scenario would mean that the popping sounds were unrelated to the murder. And that the timing of Maria finding her brother's body was simply a rotten coincidence. Possible, I supposed. But surely the police would have explored this avenue? Nothing else seemed to be turning up.

"Have you thought to ask Rusty Hodgdon? I believe he was attending the party."

"I've talked to him a bit. How do you know Rusty?" I asked. The web of connections on this island should never be surprising.

"I've been a member of the Key West Writers Guild for years and years. And he's our president at the moment. How do you know him?" she asked.

"I met him at the Hemingway Home," I said, "where he's a wonderful tour guide. He can really spin a tale. What's his writing like?"

She peered at my face. "You don't plan to print this in your paper?"

"Of course not," I said, scrambling for a plausible reason to be asking. "I've seen his books displayed at the Key West Island bookstore, and I wondered if they were good."

She thought this over. "He's a bit like the girl with a curl in the middle of her forehead."

I must have looked puzzled, because she continued right on.

"When he shares his own work with our group, mostly thrillers, it's very strong. Even gripping. But when he tries to imitate Hemingway"—she made a face—"I mean, who's good at imitating Hemingway? Even Hemingway's own work sounds stiff and stilted to my ear sometimes. And what the copycat writers lack is a lifetime of feelings about what it meant to be Hemingway. His intense admiration for macho pursuits. His love of women and his inability to remain faithful. It's hard to channel all that while copying a master's spare style."

I couldn't think of any more reasonable questions and she seemed to be tiring, so I thanked her for talking with me and started back toward the office. I wasn't sure I'd learned much new. Certainly a man wouldn't have murdered another man because his copycat writing wasn't up to snuff. And besides, I'd found the lines Rusty had quoted hysterical. But suppose a man was obsessed with the whole concept of Ernest Hemingway?

Stealing the gold medal, that could have been in Rusty's wheelhouse. And then suppose Gabriel caught him at it?

Chapter
Twenty-Two

My pastry chef says the more battle scars, the better the food.
—Amy E. Reichert, *The Coincidence of Coconut Cake*

Drooping a little from the letdown after my sugar dough-nut high, I took the stairs to *Key Zest* two at a time. Wally, Palamina, and Danielle appeared to be having a staff meeting in the vestibule.

"Oh my gosh," I said, feeling my stomach clunk to my knees. "Did I forget a meeting?"

"Impromptu," said Palamina. "We know you're working hard out in the field."

"But since you're here, I can ask instead of emailing: possible to have all three of your articles in by end of the day tomorrow?" Wally asked. "Everything else is already laid out."

He jerked a thumb at Danielle's computer, open on the desk. He was wearing his palm tree–dotted *Key Zest* shirt, which had been our team uniform until Palamina arrived at the magazine with her more highly developed sense of style.

Whatever was going on—and maybe it was just me being paranoid or guilty about all the time I'd missed here lately—I sure didn't feel like part of the team right now.

"Absolutely," I said, trying to sound confident and competent though I felt neither. "Three, though?" I finally added, because as stupid as it sounded to be asking, it would be altogether worse to have promised something that I didn't deliver. "I've got the one on Cuban influence blocked out"— so not true, I had the introduction only—"and I can quickly finish up the Cuban food visits tomorrow."

"Of course, yes on those," said Wally in an impatient voice. "But we also discussed the roundup on Cuban mix sandwiches. Aren't you about ready to wrap that up, too?"

Palamina smiled graciously, softening his blunt words a little. "It would make sense to run that piece in this issue, since our focus is on Cuba."

I tapped the side of my head with the palm of my hand. "Oh yeah, got that one almost in the bag, too. Miss Gloria and I hit Sandy's yesterday, so I'm certain I have enough material."

"We're eager to see how you'll spin it so it's not just a list of sandwiches and their ingredients," said Wally.

Did that mean he found my last roundup article lacking? This, of course, was the challenge of every food writer—how to write about the food but also make the piece about something bigger. Had I gotten too small? Or was I getting insecure and overly suspicious and reading too much into every word?

I retreated down the short hall to my tiny office, feeling unsettled and scattered. Why were they being so hard on me?

Or were they? There was no way I could get my work done sitting in this cubby only feet from my bosses, speculating about what was wrong. When I heard the door to their shared space close, I grabbed my stuff and returned to Danielle's desk at the top of the stairs.

"Is it just me, or are they acting weird?" I whispered. "I feel like Wally's mad at me, but he won't come out and say it. But it makes me feel like he and Palamina are on the A team and I'm on the bench. Or some other kind of dumb sports metaphor."

Danielle snickered, but then her face got serious. "I think Wally does feel like you left the team. But it's not work, it's personal. And I suspect he's not evolved enough to recognize what he's doing." She ran her fingers through her blonde curls. "You've fallen in love, and he's a little sad about it. And he's a guy, so it's hard for him to talk about."

Yikes. And here I thought we'd sorted all our previous relationship stuff out. Plus, I thought I'd been pretty circumspect about my romance with Nathan. "What am I supposed to do about that, Miss Ann Landers? Do I come right out and confront him?"

Danielle gathered her hair into a ponytail and then let it drop down her back. "If you're by yourself with him sometime, maybe mention that you miss his friendship? It would only embarrass him if you pointed out that he seems jealous."

I nodded. She was right, as usual.

"And meanwhile, work your tail off, girl!"

"Got it. I'll be home writing if you need me." I trotted down the stairs to retrieve my scooter. On the slow traffic-ridden trip up island, I mulled over what Danielle had said about Wally. He and I had never experienced the passion that I felt now with Nathan. And it seemed possible that Wally could sense that and was regretful or envious. Was I falling in love? I thought maybe she was right. In fact, if I was being honest with myself, I'd already fallen. That thought felt like touching a hot stove burner with my finger. I pushed my mind back to this past weekend's tragedy.

While waiting at the light on the corner of Eaton and White streets, I realized that in the matter of Gabriel's murder, I'd been looking for the money trail. Maybe I needed to be searching for the passion there too. Because I couldn't think of a reason that any of the people I'd met or chatted with would want to stab Gabriel. Right smack in the middle of the biggest party of the season. Yes, Bob was passionate about the Little White House and obviously worried about funds. Yes, Dana was passionate about diving and fishing and Cuba's coral reef, and maybe expanding her own business to amazingly fertile new oceans. And yes, according to Molly, Rusty was passionate about Hemingway and his own writing and how the two compared.

What did any of that have to do with the man who was killed?

Not one of them had mentioned anything that directly associated them with Gabriel. Maybe I was asking the wrong question. Maybe the better question should be phrased: Who else knew Gabriel, and what was their history together? Who had the kind of intense connection that could have led to murder? Because it seemed true, at least in our little patch of paradise, that murder was rarely incidental. Unless the incident involved drug dealers or other inherently violent and ruthless criminals, the victims and the killers knew each other in some intimate or compelling way. Or in this case, unless Gabriel had witnessed someone stealing the priceless gold medal.

The problem was, I didn't know much about the man, other than that his family adored him and he was a good worker. Like most people, Gabriel had probably spent a lot of his time at work. Maybe his boss would be willing to talk.

While waiting through the second red light in the cycle, I looked up the address for Gabriel's former employer, Fogarty Builders. They were located on Stock Island, past the golf course off a little street on the right, where many small businesses found land they could afford to rent or buy. Stopping in person was likely to yield better results than calling on the phone. When my turn came at the light, I roared over the Palm Avenue bridge, past the bobbing houseboats, and out toward Stock Island. I took a right off Fifth Street to Fifth Avenue and parked in the lot behind a group of unassuming industrial buildings.

A tall, dark-haired man with sleeves of tattoos on his arms was talking on the phone at the desk inside the door. He held up a finger and smiled, then disappeared through the inside door, still talking.

The room was decorated with photographs of projects I assumed this company had worked on—lots of bright tropical colors, tropical wood, porch swings—along with quotes from happy customers. On the man's desk was a photo of a beautiful, slender, curly-haired woman in a lacy wedding dress, her arms also covered with tattoos. She was toasting something on a stick over a campfire.

Finished with his call, the man returned and noticed me studying the photograph.

"My wife," he said, grinning. "Her one requirement for our wedding was toasted s'mores rather than a cake."

"Now that is thinking out of the bridal box," I said, grinning back.

"Chris Fogarty." He stuck his hand out and I shook it. "What can I help you with?"

"I'm not likely to be a client, unless I come into a windfall. I live on Houseboat Row." I introduced myself and explained that Gabriel's family had asked me to explore the circumstances around his death. "I realized that I didn't know much about him. And then I thought, who would? His boss. So that brings me to you."

His forehead wrinkled in puzzlement. "You're an investigator working for the family?"

Here we went again. *Tell the truth, Hayley.* "Actually, I'm a food critic. I was working the event where the murder occurred, and I became friendly with a couple of Gabriel's relatives. So, odd as it might seem, I hoped you would be willing to talk to me a little bit about what he was like as a person."

"What happens with the information I give you?"

"Very reasonable question," I said. "Anything that sheds

light on the murder goes directly to the Key West police. I promise." I said this in my most earnest voice. I meant it, too.

"Okay. Let me think," Chris said. "He was quiet. Even though he worked with us for years and years, I wouldn't say that I knew him particularly well. He was that quiet. The kind of guy who doesn't make a splash, but he leaves a hole. You know? He was an incredibly talented carpenter and it's going to be hell to replace him."

"What kind of work did he do?" I asked.

"We are known for the level of finish on our projects," he explained. "And he was often involved with that final phase of the work. He made exquisite gingerbread trim and sometimes even pieces that went inside the homes."

"Anything I could recognize him by?"

He thought this over. "In his own work, he might use different species of wood in the same piece. Or, say, big slabs of wood for a bar top, with unfinished edges, the bark still on it. He was also a shipwright."

"Explain, please?" I asked.

"A carpenter who worked on ships. Which you can understand takes a particular kind of person. A ship is only as seaworthy as its carpenters—worthless if it's full of leaks."

"Sounds like a wonderful employee. Were you aware of any conflicts that he might have been involved with? Did you notice difficulties with other staff?"

Chris fell silent, running a hand across his chin. "Like I said, he was quiet. Never had any fights with people here. Though maybe I got the sense that he was not a happy man.

Pleased when he did good work and got complimented for it, but underneath, he was not happy. The happiest I ever saw him was when he was working on the Harry Truman poker table restoration."

"He must have been quite talented," I said. I was feeling hopeless about gleaning anything useful from this visit, but since I was here, I might as well pursue this to the finish.

"The original table was given to Truman by three guys who worked in the U.S. Naval Station cabinet shop. It's made of mahogany. You've visited, right?"

I nodded. "Of course, many times."

"Then you probably noticed the ashtrays, which were made out of discarded mortar casings. Remarkable piece of work, truly. Gabriel was involved in taking it apart, replacing it with a replica, and then working on the repairs. He was skilled enough to do all of that. We framed the photo of the finished table—you can see it over there." He pointed to a photograph mounted on the wall behind his desk.

I got up and walked over to look. The photo had been taken inside the Little White House after the table was returned to its rightful place. Gabriel and Chris were standing on either side of it, beaming. Bob Wolz hovered in the background.

One highlight for a man with a lot of tragedy in his life. But all of this was getting me nowhere fast. I returned to my seat. "Did he talk about his family? Did he ever have a girl-friend that you know of?"

"No women that I'm aware of. He was devoted to his family, of course, as are all the Cuban-American men I know. Since his father had been lost at sea when he was a boy, he saw himself as the man of the family. Or that's the sense I got. He was very proud of his mother's cooking and we were fortunate enough to enjoy several of her flans."

"Makes my mouth water just to think of that dish," I said as I stood up. "I appreciate your time." I handed him one of my business cards. "Let me know if you think of anything more?"

Chapter
Twenty-Three

*That's another advantage of conspicuously avoiding seri-
ous cuisine: If anybody points out an imperfection, you
can say, "Look, it's just dinner."*
—Pete Wells, "We'll Always Have Paris," *The New
York Times*, March 29, 2017

B y the time I finished talking with Chris and had wended
my way through the fierce traffic running from Stock
Island into Key West, it was almost four o'clock. And I had
not written one more word of my three assignments. As I
dashed up the finger to our houseboat, a text came in from
Miss Gloria.

I WILL BE FINISHING UP WITH THE CEMETERY TOUR AT 6 PM. ANY
CHANCE YOU COULD PICK ME UP? ARE WE EATING IN TONIGHT?

I honestly didn't have time either to run around town or
to make dinner, but there was no way I would respond in a
negative. How many years did I have left with my dear friend?

You never knew when anyone's life might end, but I wasn't going to lose precious moments with her. Or my mother. Or my other favorite people. Gabriel's death had reminded me how fragile life was. I texted back.

OF COURSE. AND HOW ABOUT A HOMEMADE CUBAN MIX?

The sandwich shouldn't take long to put together and it would help me punch up the last article, the review of places where we'd tried a mix. And then I could finish up with some philosophical musings about this signature Key West delight. I pulled a small container of leftover pork roast from the freezer that my mother had packed up for us after the party Friday night. Then I checked the fridge. We had the yellow mustard and a jar of the Pickle Baron's dill pickles. And I could run by Fausto's for the ham and cheese and Cuban bread on my way home from the cemetery.

I went out on the deck, where both Sparky and Evinrude were doing their sleepy iguana imitations on my lounge chair in the brightest patch of afternoon sun. "Move over, you big lugs," I said, and shuffled them to the side. Sparky stretched and purred. Evinrude didn't even open his eyes. I plugged in the fairy lights that we had wound through the big houseplants we kept on the porch, flipped my laptop open, and began to write.

Tampa, Florida, claims to be the home of the Cuban mix sandwich, but Key Westers know the truth: it was served to cigar factory workers in Havana and Santiago de Cuba in the 1800s and from there imported to this island. These days, you might find the sandwich offered at diners and restaurants across the state—and even the country—that are reaching for a Caribbean flair. And those appearances might cause you to believe there's not much to this sandwich. But buyer beware!

I spent the next three hundred words describing the perfectly melted cheese and toasted bread found at Cole's Peace, versus the outlier lettuce layered into the product at the Courthouse Deli and the strictly traditional nature of the 5 Brothers offering. I loved these sandwiches as much as anyone, but some days this job felt positively inane. Did Pete Wells ever feel this way? That he had not another word to say about food? I thought he must. He didn't make the mistake of taking his work too seriously. And besides, someone, somewhere would be grateful for my sandwich guidance.

The alarm on my phone beeped, signaling that it was five forty-five, time to swing over to the cemetery and pick up Miss G. I hopped onto my scooter and zipped down Truman Avenue and across on Frances Street to the back entrance.

Inside the wrought-iron gates, I saw the tiny form of my roommate a stone's throw up the main drag. She had a small group of tourists gathered around her, leaning in to catch her words. Once I'd caught her attention, she flashed ten fingers, signaling that she needed about ten minutes to wrap things up. Since I was so close, I made my way to the Catholic cemetery. I didn't remember there being a strictly Cuban section the way there were Catholic and Jewish enclaves. But I figured that since the funeral had been held at St. Mary's, Gabriel's grave might be located among the Catholic markers.

Some folks find the idea of a cemetery morbid or terrifying, but I found it mostly peaceful. The company was good (quiet but thoughtful), the history amazing, and the architecture and stories behind the stones fascinating. I'd even grown to appreciate the enormous, prehistoric iguanas that often sunned themselves on the warm cement or marble crypts. There was only one section that I avoided, the area that was home to the gravesite where I'd once found a new body stuffed into an old crypt. That had turned into one of the more horrifying moments of my life so far, and even getting near it gave me the creeps.

The monuments in the Catholic part of the cemetery were adorned with praying hands, crosses, angels, and many faces of Jesus. I wandered through the gravestones, silently sending my respects to the people ensconced under the stones and in the vaults. In the far corner near the street, I spotted evidence of a recent burial—disturbed earth and a pile of sweet, decaying flowers, along with several stuffed animals. Next to this grave was an older stone, with the name Ernesto Gabriel Gonzalez engraved on it, along with an etching of waves, a sailboat, and a cross with beams of light emanating from it. The epitaph was in Spanish, but I thought it translated roughly to "Brightly Beams Our Father's Mercy," the title of a hymn my grandmother used to sing about sailors lost at sea.

Obviously, I'd found Gabriel's father. Which meant most likely Gabriel himself had been buried here too.

"Ready to go?"

I clapped a hand to my chest. "You startled me!" Miss

Gloria had come up behind me and I'd been too wrapped up in my thoughts to hear her.

"Sorry," she said, taking my hand. "Let's roll. I'm hungry enough to eat a whale, blubber included."

We made a quick stop for supplies at Fausto's on White Street, then buzzed home to the houseboat marina. As we strolled up the finger to our boat, saying hello to all the neighbors as we walked, I thought again what a miracle it was to have landed in this space. Even the worst eyesore on our walkway, a boat that had been abandoned and filled with trash, had been removed. A well-cared-for two-story houseboat had taken its place, owned by a nice couple with a cat. They adored living on our row, and were terribly proud of the children's book that had been written and published about their new home half a decade earlier.

Once we got home, Miss Gloria fed the cats while I layered the sandwiches together. Pickles, yellow mustard, Swiss cheese, ham, and pork—the ingredients were simple but the end product more than its parts. While we waited for them to grill, I called my mother and put her on speakerphone.

"Checking in to see if everything got cleaned up okay and whether you've heard any feedback from the weekend?"

"You wouldn't even know there'd been an event at the Little White House, which is kind of miraculous considering all that went on." Her voice started out sounding chipper, but at this point, it broke. "As for feedback, I haven't had any. I can't say the phone has been ringing off the hook with bookings of repeat business either."

She had absolutely counted her chickens before they hatched on this topic—making lists of the invitees for each of the Cuban conference parties who might hold social events this winter, and committing those lists to memory so she and Sam would remember to chat them up.

"These things take time," I said. "I don't think anyone rushes home from a party to call the caterer." I made goo-goo eyes at my roommate, signaling for help.

"We are about to have a Cuban mix using your roast pork," said Miss Gloria. "We can hardly wait. I had a long shift at the cemetery this afternoon, and I bet I walked five miles."

"Good for you," said my mom in a distracted way, which was not like her. "Any news about the murder on your end?"

I gave her a thumbnail sketch of where I'd been and what I'd heard, which didn't amount to a hill of beans in the end. "No one's got an obvious motive to kill Gabriel, from what I've seen. There's something we don't know."

My mother heaved a big sigh. "And hopefully the police will do their job. How did your visit to the station go? We never got the chance to catch up with all the hubbub yesterday."

I summarized my interview with Torrence, telling her about the sequins and his questions about what I might have seen but not mentioning either our discussion about Nathan or the fact that he'd asked me to be the police department's eyes and ears at last night's dinner.

"My chat went pretty much the same way, except . . ." Miss Gloria paused, her eyes darting back and forth, left and then right, so she appeared a little shifty—as shifty as a sweet old lady in her eighties can look. "I didn't want to tell you this, because I was afraid you'd feel left out, Hayley, but . . ."

Another pause. "But what?"

"He asked me to take notes, mental or otherwise, about what I observed, and then pass them along to the undercover cop."

"Good gravy," I said, a little embarrassed that I'd felt so important. "He asked me to do the same thing! I sent my notes off to him this morning. I think this means they basically have no clue who murdered that poor man."

The timer on our grill went off, and we said good-bye to my mother and sat down outside to eat our sandwiches. The boat rocked as though the bight was being jostled gently by a giant-sized mother. And we could hear the hum of voices on the neighbors' televisions and the ever-present tinkle of Mrs. Renhart's wind chimes. We'd been so lucky not to have thoughtless people move into the neighborhood. We'd not had to suffer through late-night beer pong or drunken fights or even garbage thrown in the recycling bin. And that bit of gratitude brought up a wash of dread. I glanced at the boat next door, but there'd been no new activity as far as I could tell.

"Mom's awfully disappointed," I said to my roommate through bites of crusty bread, crisp pickles, and oozing cheese.

"But Sam is so good for her," said Miss Gloria. "He'll have her thinking philosophically in no time. It's good to have a husband who complements your fiery nature, like he does hers." She winked at me. "I had that, too, and I wish it for you as well."

Chapter Twenty-Four

They were like chunks of pineapple and honeydew in a fruit salad—tart and plump but there merely for the collective purpose of volume.
—Rakesh Satyal, *No One Can Pronounce My Name*

A text message chirped from my phone on the bedside table, waking me from a deep sleep. Very little light seeped through the slats of my Venetian blinds: it was still pitch-dark except for the flickering streetlights on the dock reflecting off the water. I groped for the phone and squinted at the screen. Irena.

CALL ME, she'd written, followed by six exclamation points. And no apologies for jolting me awake at five in the morning. So I dialed her number.

"Maria is missing and my aunt is hysterical. Can you come over right away?"

"What do you mean *missing*?" I rubbed my eyes, trying to

shake the groggy feeling of a head stuffed full of cotton batting.

"Aunt Carmen says Maria got a call late last night, and she heard her leave the house. She heard her scooter engine start up. And she never came home. She waited until now to call me and she's completely undone."

My stomach clenching into a knot, I grasped at the only straw I could think of. "Probably a boyfriend, no? Maybe she went out to meet him and fell asleep and—"

"This wouldn't happen." Irena's voice was definite.

Was she protecting Maria's reputation or was she right? She had told me only yesterday that Maria was afraid.

"Can you stop by? Please?"

I thought about what I had planned for the day and how far I was behind. Not to mention the fact that it was five in the morning and I was utterly exhausted from the week we'd had.

"She won't talk to the police, if that's what you're thinking should happen. I already suggested that. She knows it's too early to file a missing person report." Irena hesitated. "And besides, they haven't found Gabriel's killer. What if they think she did it? Or was in cahoots with someone who did it, and now she's running away to protect herself?"

"She killed her own brother? That seems unlikely." Ridiculous was more like it.

She cut me off. "Probably they just don't care. Not enough, anyway. And if they don't care about a dead man, why would they care about a woman gone out in the middle of the night? In Key West?"

She had a point there. Lots of people stay out until crazy

hours on this island, but it's usually visitors overdoing vacation revelry rather than residents. I threw the covers off and swung my legs out of my bunk. "I'll come. Give me fifteen minutes to get dressed and make a cup of coffee."

"I'll have one here waiting for you."

"You're an angel," I said.

Both cats had stretched their way out of their early hour stupor, so I fed them and left a note for Miss Gloria, whose gentle sleep noises wafted out from her bedroom. Then I sputtered over to the small concrete block home where Maria lived with her mother, and formerly her brother as well.

Their house was located in the part of Key West called New Town, found at the waist of the island, pinched in by the Garrison Bight on one side and salt marshes bordering A1A and the Atlantic Ocean on the other. Much of this land was constructed from landfill, and it lies lower than the neighborhoods in Old Town. It had been hit hard by the back surge of hurricane Wilma, though fortunately the storm surge was smaller during Irma. Most tourists don't get to this part of the island, unless they take the Christmas trolley to view the amazing show of lights residents put on every December.

In the glow of their porch light, the yard looked as though it hadn't been mowed since last week—probably Gabriel's job. There was a small plaster shrine that held a prayerful Mother Mary in the front yard near the stoop. Irena was waiting for me at the door.

"I'm so sorry to wake you this early, but she's absolutely distraught. I just didn't know who else to call." She took hold of my left forearm and led me into the dim and cool living room. An air-conditioner labored in the corner window, and Maria's mother, Carmen, was huddled on the couch. I'd only seen her once before, at the funeral, wearing a lace veil that covered most of her face. Now, even through her mask of grief and worry and age, I could see that she must have been a stunning woman.

I crossed the room quickly and crouched down in front of her. "I'm Hayley Snow," I said. "We met very briefly at the church. And I'm very sorry for your loss."

She shuddered, tears trickling down her softly wrinkled cheeks.

"Let me get you some coffee," said Irena, retreating to the kitchen.

"Your niece tells me that your daughter didn't come back last night. Was this unusual? Was she seeing someone? Maybe she met someone for a drink and tried to call you?"

She nodded yes, this was unusual. Then shook her head twice for no, she wasn't seeing anyone. And no, she wouldn't have met someone for a drink. I heard the noise of grinding from the direction of the kitchen and then smelled fresh coffee beans releasing their heavenly scent, followed by the sweet sound of steaming milk. Irena returned to the living room with a large mug of perfect coffee and I sipped it gratefully.

"Irena said there was a phone call last night. Tell me everything you remember about that, even something that might seem unimportant."

Irena translated my words into Spanish and her aunt

answered back, unleashing a torrent of words I hadn't a chance of understanding.

"She says Maria was a good girl," Irena said. "They were both devoted children. They refused to have families of their own because they insisted on taking care of me. Now what will I do? Everything is lost."

The woman began to wail, and Irena hurried over to sit on the couch next to her, where she gathered her up and began to rock her like a baby. Maybe it sounded to her, as it did to me, that she believed her daughter wasn't coming back anytime soon. If ever. Irena murmured to her, smoothing the hair away from her face.

"Did Maria say anything aloud when she was on this phone call?" I asked.

Carmen trembled and snuffled and finally whispered an answer.

"She thinks Maria said something about a pier."

Carmen nodded vigorously, her face tear-stained and limp with grief and a dim flicker of hope.

"*El muelle de pesca.*"

"A fishing pier," Irena repeated, and she looked at me expectantly, too.

"Did she say this in English or Spanish?"

"English," said Irena, after checking with her aunt.

We lived on an island. Piers were everywhere. Piers were us. And who was to say her daughter hadn't said another similar word, like *beer* or *dear*? Or *fear*? "Has she been acting like she was afraid of something or someone?" I asked. "I mean, before Gabriel?"

Irena shook her head. "Never, not until Gabriel was murdered. Since then, of course, we've all been frightened. Maybe she most of all. All week she seemed so nervous and I told her it would be all right. But it's not, and it will never be, will it?"

This brought a fresh onslaught of tears from Carmen. "And she was obsessed with the gold medal."

The gold medal again. What did this have to do with anything? Did she think her brother had stolen it? Or was she going to meet someone who had taken it about retrieving it and returning it to the Cuban delegation? Or could she have been handing it over? There didn't seem much chance that she'd taken it—she'd been very busy in the kitchen all night like the rest of us. But what if Gabriel had really taken it? Maybe she'd even seen him with it, either that day or later, here at home.

My head was spinning.

"I am lost," I said.

"I am, too," Irena admitted.

"May I look at their rooms? Both of their rooms?" Both women nodded their assent.

Irena led me down a short hallway and showed me her cousins' bedrooms. Maria's was plain but pretty, with a pair of white terry bed slippers sitting by the bed and gauzy white curtains at the window. Her white eyelet coverlet had been thrown back, and a well-worn teddy bear had toppled to the floor at the end of the bed. Other than that, there was nothing out of place. Nothing in disarray. I shrugged, not even sure what else to look for. It appeared as though she had left in a hurry but planned to come back to bed. I thought she was the kind of woman who wouldn't leave a bed unmade for long, or her nightgown thrown carelessly on a chair.

"Gabriel's room is just across the hall," said Irena, leading me out. Carmen shuffled along behind us, snuffling.

Gabriel's room was simple as well: a wood-framed twin bed covered with a faded blue denim quilt, a crucifix hanging over his bed on the wall. But after a few minutes of taking in the room, I could see that while the furniture was simple wood, it wasn't cheaply made. I suspected these pieces had been built from recycled Dade County pine, a hardwood highly prized for building conch homes in Key West. A wooden dresser had hand-carved knobs and beveled edges, the seams interlocking, not glued or nailed. Some of the raw edges actually still had the bark of the tree on them. Just as Gabriel's boss had described.

"He built all this," Irena said after watching me absorb it. Her aunt nodded proudly.

I opened the top dresser drawer and glanced through, which didn't take long—this was where he had stored notes about ongoing construction projects. There were also some drawings of his own work, including a diagram of the restoration of the Little White House poker table. The drawers underneath held neatly folded underwear, rolled socks, pressed pajamas, and several pairs of blue jeans. I felt through all the clothing; there was certainly no gold medal here.

On the nightstand, Gabriel had left a short stack of books, including some of Hemingway's novels, books about Cuba written in Spanish, and a Bible. In the bottom drawer of the nightstand I found a metal box with a key protruding from the lock. I glanced up at Carmen and Irena, and they nodded that I should open it if I wanted. Inside was a collection of articles about Cubans who had immigrated to the United States on chugs. Some of the clippings had yellowed with age, but many had more recent dates. The *Key West Citizen* often carried stories about the boat people who'd successfully landed in the United States. And since we were the closest land to Cuba, Key West had often been their target.

"He had something of a fixation on these refugees," Irena said. "Every time he heard of a chug landing, he would go to meet them, bringing drinks and snacks before the immigration people took them into custody. He made phone calls for them to relatives in the continental U.S. He used to argue with his mother about this." She put an arm around her aunt and squeezed her shoulders. "She would tell him it's time to bury the past. And he would say, it's already buried you. *Ya te ha enterrado.*"

The whole thing made me sick with sadness, as if their collective pain had infused the house, ready to flood anyone who visited. I looked away and continued to page through the articles in the box. At the bottom of that stack, I found a photocopied clipping about the award of the 1954 Nobel prize to Hemingway for *The Old Man and the Sea*.

"Was your cousin a writer?" I asked.

"I don't think so." Irena's forehead wrinkled as she repeated my question to Carmen, who also shook her head.

"Why was this clipping important to him?"

Neither of them had a clue.

"You say the police have been here twice, asking. Do you

think it's possible that Gabriel did take the medal?" I hated to push this, but I felt I had to know.

"I can tell you this, he'd never stolen anything in his life. Not even a piece of candy as a boy. And now we only know that he is dead and she is missing." Irena's eyes shone with tears.

"I understand that. I believe it. But what if he thought he had a good reason, the right reason? And what if someone saw him and confronted him later at the party? And that got him killed? Maybe Maria found it here in the house and was meeting someone who would return it to the rightful owner, where it belonged?"

Irena just shrugged, but her jaw was set like iron. "I thought the convent owned it. We have no idea who would have been the rightful owner. But he wouldn't steal something, we know that."

The women stared at me, their anger and desperation and grief all plain on their faces. I was beginning to feel desperate too.

"Did he have any other conflicts with anyone that you're aware of? Like at work?"

"They adored him at work. He was a finish carpenter for Fogarty Builders. He could handle jobs that were too intricate or delicate for anyone else on the island."

Again, this confirmed what I'd heard yesterday. I was retreading old ground and getting nowhere.

Carmen said something in Spanish.

"She says her husband was a talented carpenter too, so Gabriel came by it naturally," Irena translated.

I looked at her sad face and back to the sadder-still face of Carmen. "Okay. We can spend a little time looking for her, but I think you should call the police if she doesn't turn up quickly. This feels like a needle in a haystack, you know? Just two of us whistling in the dark. And if she was as afraid as you say she was, we shouldn't waste time. The police have the manpower to really mount a meaningful search."

Carmen clutched my hand and pressed it to her forehead, weeping and talking to her niece in fast Spanish again. All I understood was *thank you* and *coffee*.

"My aunt says to tell you please come back when this is over. She would like to make you her specialty *café con leche* and a flan." She patted her aunt's hand and smiled. "See, I come by my talents naturally, too. Back in Cuba, they called her the Cuban Coffee Queen. There was even a poem written about her."

"Not the one on the menu at the Cuban Coffee Queen shop?" I asked them in amazement.

"That's the one," Irena said, and they both grinned. "And don't ask how it happened to get there, because she won't tell. Not even me." Then she leaned over to stage-whisper, "I think the owner of the Coffee Queen had a crush on her back in Cuba."

Chapter
Twenty-Five

Food may just be fuel for some people, but for many marginalized communities, it represents community, connections, a way of expressing your culture in public without care or concern for how it might be received by those who do not share it.

—Mikki Kendall, "Hot Sauce
in Her Bag," Eater.com

We decided to split up the work: Irena would zip over to the boardwalks across town by the harbor known as the Key West Bight; I would check out the White Street pier on my way to the piers along Mallory Square and the Margaritaville Westin. These seemed like unlikely places to meet for something shadowy—too many windows overlooking the water, too many people potentially watching—but I'd take a quick spin around and then check the big concrete pier that ran parallel to the Navy's Outer Mole, their private quay across the small Key West harbor. We would text each other if either of us found something related to Maria—either her turquoise scooter with the ¡Viva Cuba! stickers on it or Maria herself.

The only other obvious fishing piers I could think of were those running on both sides of Palm Avenue, close to House-boat Row. If we hadn't located her in any of the other places, I could check that on my way home. Irena agreed that that would be as far as we would take it. Then either she had to call the police or simply settle in to wait for her cousin to return.

I started with the White Street pier, officially named the Edward B. Knight Pier, known for its poignant AIDS memo-rial and popular with locals as a good place to watch the sun-rise with a dog. Even though it was well before the official sunrise, light was beginning to dawn, revealing a few early birds on the benches along the pier. I puttered slowly all the way to the end but saw no sign of Maria.

I continued across White Street to Eaton on my way to Mallory Square. At this time of the morning, downtown was not yet clogged with tourists and workers. I rode right through the parking lot off the square and drove over to the water, looking for a blue scooter or a small woman with raven hair. I managed to startle a few homeless men who were tucked in behind some palmetto bushes, and they stepped out, blinking and cursing. Homeless people are discouraged heavily from spending the night on public or private property, but not every person without a home chooses to hike out to the shelter on Stock Island to bunk down in a Quonset Hut with several hundred other folks. For the cops, it's a delicate balancing act: tourists and residents versus the folks who need a place to rest overnight.

"Good morning," I called. "I wonder if you've seen a woman with dark hair on a turquoise blue scooter this morning?" They just glared back.

No dice. A ghostly wave of seagulls and skimmers swerved across the water and landed on the pier. The sight of this square at this time of day couldn't have been a starker contrast to the bustling crowds that gathered during the evening sunset celebration. I paused for a minute to listen—for what? I wasn't sure. If I hadn't been searching for a woman in trouble, this scenery would have felt peaceful, not spooky.

It wasn't legal to ride a scooter or a car or even a bicycle on Mallory Square or the piers along the Margaritaville resort, but I wanted to cover as much territory as quickly as I could. And be ready to bolt if I needed to. Within minutes, I reached the water closest to the Truman Little White House, near my ex's condominium complex. I peered over the edge of the dock to check on the boats bobbing along this stretch— mostly Danger snorkel tour boats, a few small yachts, and two rental fishing crafts. No sign of a woman in distress. Remembering that my access to the other side of the Navy Mole was blocked by a cut in the concrete and that the gates to the Truman Annex would be locked this early, I circled back alongside the Custom House Museum to Whitehead Street and over the access to the new city park via Southard Street.

I paused by the new park and the controversial amphitheater and squinted at the walkway across this small harbor. Maria should not have had access to the Outer Mole, the pier belonging to the Navy. Occasionally, cruise ships docked there, but the passengers were not allowed to disburse on their own. Rather, they were ferried back to Key West by trolleys or conch trains.

I tried not to think of the body that I'd seen in the water at the other end of town during that frightening time leading up to my friend Connie's wedding when my brother had disappeared. We'd found a runaway girl, floating, her hair drifting out like a mermaid or a Gorgon, but not breathing.

The sky had lightened enough that I could see the details of the Coast Guard's *Ingham*, a hulking gray battleship, retired now except for tours and occasional cocktail parties. I checked the bike and scooter racks near the eco-discovery center but found only a couple of old bikes lacking critical parts, such as one of the tires. Sometimes even a good lock took you only so far in this town.

But my heart sank as I spotted a scooter parked at the end of the road leading to the battleship that looked much like what Irena had described as Maria's. I considered hopping off my own scooter and starting along the pedestrian dock toward the Westin cut. The posted sign said motorized vehicles were forbidden here, too. On the other hand, if I found Maria in trouble—or if a killer was still lurking—I wanted to be able to move quickly.

From this side of the cut, I could see my ex's condominium complex again, the same buildings that backed up to the Truman Little White House. A few lights had flickered on, but most of the apartments were still dark. I wished I were back in my berth, a purring cat stretched along my side. I drove along the edge of the foliage, one hand on my phone ready to punch 911 if needed, and headed down to the end of the pier, where the pass-through ended. This was definitely a fishing destination. When I first arrived on the island, I'd been astonished to see a man dressed as Elvis casting his line into the water.

Why in the world would Maria have come out here in the pitch-dark? Something to do with her brother's killer—that was the only reason I could imagine. Which made the urgency for me not to do something stupid more salient in my reptile brain. My heart began to pound harder and my mouth felt suddenly dry. I made it all the way to the end without seeing any sign of her, nor of any possible assailant. I crossed the last few yards of concrete to the water.

Just on the other side of the jetty, where one of the water sports companies stored their standby Jet Skis, I spotted something bobbing in the water. Not something, someone. A glob of seaweed and assorted trash obscured the face, but the hair was coal black like Maria's.

Chapter
Twenty-Six

*Come along inside . . . We'll see if tea and buns can
make the world a better place.*
—Kenneth Grahame, *The Wind in the Willows*

Maybe five minutes had passed since I'd dialed 911 and
reported the presence of a body. I crouched behind a
palm tree trunk along the edge of the concrete, listening to
the splash of water on cement, listening for sirens over the chattering of my teeth, trying not to think about whether it really
was Maria and whether she'd already drawn her last breath.
And whether I was in danger now too if someone thought I
knew too much.

"A body?" the dispatcher had asked. "Are you sure it's a
body? Is this person alive or dead?"

I didn't know. I couldn't get close enough to her to check
this out. But I wasn't feeling optimistic. Two police cars came
screaming across the pier, followed by one of our fire department's ambulances. It occurred to me that I should text Nathan

now, rather than having him hear about this through the grapevine.

DROWNING WOMAN. MURDER VICTIM'S SISTER. PAST THE INGHAM NAVY BIGHT. I'M HERE.

"Where is she?" the cops yelled as they flung themselves out of their vehicles and I came out of my hiding place to meet them.

I pointed.

A young cop with a blond buzz cut hopped onto the fence separating the pier from the cut, where the woman floated. He propelled himself over, landing in a crouch, one foot on a Jet Ski and one in the water. He caught his balance and leaped to a paddleboat, closer to the woman. Another cop passed him what looked like a pool skimmer. He leaned over the water and nudged the woman closer.

"I could be wrong, but I think she's breathing," he called as he pulled her closer. "Possible head injury. Bring the stretcher and the C-collar." As he tipped her head out of the water, I saw a stream of seawater gush from her mouth. The other cop and the paramedics hoisted a stretcher over the fence and onto the paddleboat. They gently loaded her onto the stretcher, and the paramedic began to administer CPR.

As they carried the stretcher over the fence, onto the pier, and into the ambulance, Nathan's SUV pulled up alongside me. I felt an instant flood of relief mixed with the tiniest bit of trepidation. He sprang out of the vehicle and clasped my shoulders.

"Are you okay?"

I nodded. "Just shook up."

He didn't say anything more, only hugged me hard and fast. Then he lifted his right eyebrow and leaned in to kiss me on the forehead. "I'll be right back."

He jogged over to chat with the officer, who was soaking wet from the waist down, as they watched Maria's stretcher slide into the back of the ambulance. Once they'd closed the doors and sped away, Nathan returned to me.

"You called this in."

I nodded.

"And you found her by accident? You were out for a morning drive?"

I rolled my eyes. "Not exactly." I explained how Irena had called me, and what her aunt believed that Maria might have said, and how we'd made this plan to take a quick survey of piers based on what Carmen had reported. "A total long shot. I never thought I would actually stumble across her. The plan was to call the cops as soon as we surveyed the possibilities and didn't find her." I shrugged, then wrapped my arms around my shoulders, as I was beginning to shiver.

"And that's it, you have no idea who made the phone call or what this is in reference to?"

"No idea, although it's hard not to make a connection between this and her brother's murder. Right? Two people in the same family brutally attacked? It can't be coincidence." Based on the Weather Channel report I'd watched last night with Miss Gloria, it couldn't have been much colder than seventy degrees. But it felt like thirty.

When he noticed me shivering, Nathan gave me another quick hug, then held me at arm's length, his hands on my shoulders. "We'll need you to come down to the station and give us a statement. Do you have time for that later this morning?"

I nodded.

He pulled me close again, this time for long enough that I could feel the warmth of his body solid against mine. "I'm glad you're okay. For now, I suggest you go home, take a hot shower and get a cup of coffee, and maybe a breakfast sandwich, extra bacon, extra crispy."

That made me smile, though his gaze was level and his tone flat.

"Later on, we'll talk about how you could have been killed by the same person who attacked her." He walked back to the cut to talk to the other cops.

But how could he not be annoyed? I would've been annoyed with me for taking a risk. On the other hand, if Maria did survive, it might be thanks to the fact that I'd arrived exactly when I did.

When I reached my scooter, I texted Irena.

FOUND HER. I THINK SHE'LL BE OKAY. TAKE CARMEN AND MEET THE POLICE AND EMTS AT THE HOSPITAL. I'M GOING TO RUN HOME THEN WILL JOIN YOU.

Irena texted me back when I was warming my bones in the shower. Maria had been transferred to the ICU, and there was no point in showing up at the hospital now. If she was able to speak later or if they had some other news (darker, I assumed), I would be the first one she'd contact.

I seesawed back and forth about whether staying home was the right thing to do when a woman's life lay on the line. But I couldn't help with that, plus, I had articles to write. A job to keep. Hovering around the waiting room pouring my anxiety into the stew of feelings that was already bubbling would not help anyone.

I drove back to town, parked behind Preferred Properties, and trudged upstairs to *Key Zest*. Even early-bird Danielle was not in yet, so no coffee, no doughnuts. Then I remembered that she and Wally were presenting at the Chamber of Commerce open house and were not expected back until after lunch. I started the coffee maker and raided Danielle's emergency snack drawer for a half sleeve of Oreo cookies. Coffee and cookies in hand, I shut my door, glanced over my sheaf of notes, and tried to plan an attack on the day.

I worked for several hours formulating the draft of the article about the influence of Cuban culture on Key West. Without parroting the entire history of the two islands, I noodled over the contradictions between them. How Havana had started out as a glittering Camelot—a place for steamy nights and sultry music and tropical food, and how that had changed as the political regime changed and Cubans began to leave to escape oppressive government policies. How some saw Havana as a golden treasure winking with promise while others saw her as a fruit rotting from the inside out.

I wrote about roast pork and flan and the best coffee in the world bridging the gap between those views—and carrying the memories of home for people yearning to revisit their homeland.

All of this brought me circling back to Carmen and the tragedies of her family. It was hard not to shoot off on thought tangents. My mind kept returning to the political conflicts, including the passionate disagreement between a contingent of Cuban-Americans who felt that supporting their former country essentially resulted in feeding a wicked government, versus the people who believed and possibly lived the idea that punishing the government really punished her people. As far as I could tell, there was no single truth. The intractable knottiness of the problem—never mind what our own country's politicians decided to do—left me feeling sick and sad.

As I wrote, I grew hungrier and hungrier. The store-bought cookies were not enough to stem the tide. I should take a break, grab a bite. Who knew if I'd be needed later at the hospital, or when they'd want me at the police station? On the other hand, all of this was due tonight. I switched gears and looked over my notes for the Cuban food piece—skimpy at best. I had eaten at El Siboney and sampled a smattering of Cuban mix sandwiches. And those sandwiches and my recipe had now been written up in a separate article. Using that material twice would not earn me a coveted spot in *Best Food Writing*, nor the accolades of my bosses.

Feeling guilty about writing a column mentioning only one real restaurant, lost about questions around Maria's attack, and now officially starving, I had the bright idea of having a bite at Frita's Cuban Burger Café. I could solve all my problems—or most of them—with one quick stop.

* * *

Located in the block of Southard just below Duval Street, Frita's doesn't look like much from the street. A prospective diner can order standing outside on the sidewalk or step inside. Dining options are sitting at one of the picnic-style tables outside by the grill or eating inside a cavelike room decorated with a dizzying array of Cuban artifacts and artwork. To taste a variety of things on the menu, I ordered the famous Frita's Cuban burger, a mango, pineapple, and avocado salad with grilled shrimp, a chocolate milkshake, and a flan. Then I went inside to take a seat in the deserted dining area, soaking in the bright colors and mementos from Cuba—artwork, a painted coconut, a napkin holder shaped like a pair of pink flamingos.

But the thought of the shimmering flan pulled me back to my sadness about Maria's attack, especially since it had happened so soon after Gabriel's death. Surely they were connected. So far, I hadn't gotten much of a clue about people who might have wanted either or both of them gone. Carmen had suffered some great losses in her life; it didn't seem fair that this was the way things might end for her daughter. I scrolled through some of the notes I'd taken on my phone, searching for something I could have overlooked.

But before I got very far, a friendly woman with long dark hair delivered the food I'd ordered. The scent of grilled meat and spices wafted up from the first plate, a burger covered with shavings of irresistible crispy potato strings. I took a big bite out of the combination pork and beef burger seasoned with Spanish spices and slathered with Frita's secret sauce. I needed to save room for the other items, but it was hard to stop once I got started. But then I took my first sip of chocolate milkshake and knew I'd be forced to face the food critic's dilemma—how to avoid indigestion from overeating. Every dish I'd ordered was good enough to finish.

I paused to look through the notes I'd made while attending the tour of the chugs at the botanical garden. I had taken photos, too. Some of the rickety homemade boats were starting to sink into the land, rusting out, returning to their original elements. I hesitated on the photo of one that had seemed better built than the others, with a teak floor that actually resembled a boat more than a floating piece of trash. Although the writing had faded almost to illegibility in the fierce South Florida sun, I remembered seeing the name yesterday. I zoomed in with my camera app. *Miranda*.

The woman behind the counter, who also served as waitress, came over to check on my lunch.

"Everything is incredibly delicious," I told her. "I spent the past few days working the events at the Little White House, and I believe the stress alone burned through my week's calorie allotment."

"Poor Gabriel," she said, shaking her head sadly. "And I'm so sad about Maria. I hope she can pull out of this. Her mother must be devastated. She is a gentle soul with a lot of heartbreak in her history."

Obviously, news had traveled fast about the attack on Maria.

"About that," I said, "do you mind telling me about the heartbreak?"

I'd asked this same question over and over of Irena, always getting the sense that she was holding something back. Maybe a stranger to me would say something new.

"You probably know that Carmen and her son fled from Cuba during the sixties, leaving everything they owned behind?" I nodded. "She was pregnant with Maria. Her husband went into hiding, waiting for the break that would allow him to escape. And terribly afraid they would never let him go." She let out a hiss of breath and wiped her eyes.

"My mother tells the story of how the Cuban community got the news that he was crossing the Straits of Florida. But a terrible storm had been predicted, and no one understood why they launched their craft in that kind of weather. Two days later, the people here heard that a boat was headed for Fort Zachary Taylor, and everyone rushed down to the beach to welcome the sailors. Five men made it ashore; the other twenty had drowned on the second night, when the worst of the storm blew through. Carmen's husband was one of them. His boat is still on display at the botanical garden."

"Was it called the *Miranda*, by any chance?" I asked, thinking of how I'd learned that both Gabriel and his father were shipwrights.

She nodded. "His pet name for his wife was Carmen Miranda. All that to say that this talk about improving the U.S. relationship with the Cuban government has brought up a lot of hard memories. That country owes her."

A boisterous group of tourists came to the sidewalk window to order, and she excused herself to wait on them. I finished my lunch, took some photos of the room, and went outside. I simply couldn't believe that Carmen and Irena had told me everything about their family's tragedy. Irena must know something more. By now, I strongly suspected that the old loss would shed some light on the newer ones, if only I had all the puzzle pieces. I texted her to ask about Maria's condition. And then told her I hoped to have a chance to talk with her. Her reply came in quickly.

MARIA STABLE. LOTS OF RELATIVES AT THE HOSPITAL WITH MY AUNT, SO I CAME BACK TO WORK FOR A FEW HOURS.

So I returned to the Cuban Coffee Queen, waited for a slow spot in the rush of customers, and then approached the counter.

"I can't believe they didn't give you the day off."

"There was no one to cover this shift with Geoff, and he's simply not capable of managing on his own. I'll go back to the hospital when the owner gets here. They'll let me know if she takes a turn for the worse. The show must go on. You know that's true, especially on this island."

I didn't believe the hearty cheeriness she was attempting to display.

"Was Gabriel always angry about what happened to his father?"

Irena took her time to answer. "The anger was there in the

239

background, always. But it would bubble to the surface from time to time. I would definitely say that this Key West/Havana conference business churned everything up. For the whole family, but especially for him. And Carmen too," she added, with a little lift to her brows.

"I think there must be something more to this story, something you aren't telling me," I said. Flatly, as though this was a fact she couldn't refute.

Marius, the owner of the coffee shop, appeared behind the counter to tell Irena she could go. She thanked him, took off her Cuban Coffee Queen apron, folded it neatly, and stashed it on a low shelf near the souvenir ball caps. Then she came out of the shop to join me.

As we walked toward the street, she said, "I've told you everything that I know. Which is not to say that I know everything." She swiped her hand across her forehead. "My aunt might be ready to tell us the rest of it. Shall I meet you at the hospital?"

Chapter
Twenty-Seven

Before the doorbell rang, Ivy had been regarding Norbert
with a tenderness he had never known. He was serving
her breakfast, and could not be sure if the love in her eyes
was in fact for him, or for breakfast.
—Keziah Frost, *The Reluctant Fortune-Teller*

Fifteen minutes later, I arrived on Stock Island, zipped
around the perimeter of the golf course, and approached
the royal palm-lined drive leading to the white-and-blue
stucco hospital. A pit of dread gathered in my stomach, which
I imagined most customers and visitors felt, though for different reasons.

I signed in for a guest pass and took the elevator to the
third floor. As I approached the nurses' station, I saw Irena
leading her Aunt Carmen to a small waiting area and followed them in.

"She's holding a vigil by Maria's bedside," Irena told me
softly. "But now that they've upgraded her condition to
serious," she added, "I assured her that's it's okay to leave

the room so we can talk for a few minutes. Better for Maria not to hear something upsetting right now. Even if she's not conscious, she might understand."

I nodded vigorously and sat on a green vinyl chair across from the two women. "It's freezing in here," I said, shivering. "Why do they always keep the temperature so low?" I wasn't expecting an answer to my question, merely nattering to fill the silence.

"Aunt Carmen." Irena took both of her aunt's hands and held them firmly. "It's very important that you tell me everything now. We want to punish the man who killed your son and tried to kill Maria." She repeated those words in Spanish.

Tears seeped out of Carmen's dark eyes and then she began to weep, gulping big noisy breaths of air. Irena rubbed her back until the sobs abated. Carmen reached into her skirt's pocket for a white handkerchief and swabbed at her face. Then she began to speak in Spanish, her gaze cast down at the linoleum floor. Irena waited until the tumult of words had come to an end.

"Oh my god, I should have known something was terribly wrong," she said to me. "My mother knew something dreadful had happened, but she didn't want to pressure her sister. Even as she was dying of cancer, she refused to talk with me about this."

Now Irena, too, directed her gaze to the floor as she began to tell me the story.

"Carmen says Mr. Markham's father was on a business trip in Cuba in the early 1960s. It had become clear that for political reasons, the family could not stay in their country, and they approached Markham and begged for his assistance. Carmen was able to get safe passage with Gabriel, who was only two years old, and Maria, her unborn baby. The government wouldn't allow her husband to leave, but he insisted they go without him. Once they'd made it to Key West, Carmen went to Mr. Markham's father and begged him for help again."

Irena took a deep breath and looked at me, her eyes now brimming with tears, too.

"He made her do things, unspeakable things, things she's never told anyone, in exchange for allowing her husband to leave on the boat he'd been secretly building.

"In spite of his meticulous handiwork, the boat was unsafe for the passage in rough waters. It was simply too small and too light. The weather was terrible that night, and most of the men perished, including her beloved husband. Why did Markham insist that they travel only on that night? My aunt believes he wanted her husband to die so he would not learn what he had done."

She took her aunt's hand and pressed it to her cheek.

"But she felt she could do nothing about it. Who would believe such a story? Who would believe that she was anything but a whore? And who would believe that such an important man would behave so badly? Her husband was gone and she was deeply, deeply ashamed about what she'd done."

Irena glanced up at me again. "You can see why I didn't know the rest of the story either. Carmen never told a soul, not even my mother. But Gabriel guessed it, when this Cuban conference stirred up his mother's memories and her grief. He found her weeping over a photo that had been taken in Havana of our current commissioner's father and her husband in the historical column of the paper. She can only imagine that Gabriel must have offered to work with your mother's staff for the weekend in order to have access to Turner Markham so he could confront him."

"Obviously, his plan went terribly wrong," I said softly. I squatted down and placed my hand on Carmen's knee. "I'm so sorry for your loss." How many times could I repeat this? But each time I meant it, felt it a little more deeply. I glanced back up at Irena. "Please tell her it wasn't her fault; she was doing everything to help her family."

Irena repeated this to Carmen, who only shook her head and wept. "You'd better go," Irena said to me. "I'll stay here with her."

I exited outside to the bright January day, the contrast with the sickness and grief inside inevitable. So many questions remained. Why in the world would Markham stab Gabriel after he confronted him about his father's brutal behavior? Wouldn't he simply laugh that off?

I puttered back to the houseboat, poured a glass of iced tea, added sprigs of mint and a slice of lemon, and went outside to think and to work. Carmen's story loomed in my head, filling me with sadness and anger. As I sipped, a snippet of gossip about how Turner Markham's father had been a hack writer niggled in my mind. I did a quick Google search on Markham Sr. and scrolled through the multiple references to his political career and various activities in Key West. A perusal of those left him looking like a local hero.

Finally I came across a little piece that referenced him as a

Hemingway wannabe. And the item beneath that mentioned an interview with Markham Sr. in which he proclaimed that he was a better writer than Hemingway. Unlikely. Absurd.

I tapped the number for Joan Higgs—a friend I'd met while getting a flu shot at the health department—into my phone. I'd seen her across the aisle at Gabriel's funeral. She was a conch, born and raised in Key West, so she would probably have more accurate stories about Markham Sr. than what I could find online. When she answered, I explained what had happened to Maria and how I was helping the family figure out who was behind the violence.

"This may sound odd, but I wondered if you remembered Turner Markham, the father. I'm trying to understand what he was like as a commissioner. And a man."

"It's hard to put this politely," she said. "He was a turd."

I laughed, though it wasn't the least bit funny, not when I knew how he'd behaved with Carmen.

Joan continued, "He was a blowhard, very interested in publicity. Always telling people what a winner he was and how many helpful things he'd done for the island. In fact, what he did was drum up publicity opportunities—I've never seen anyone before or since who managed to get his photograph in the paper as often as he did. He had some bubba friends on that staff, for sure."

Bubbas were good old boys, in Key West–speak. "Do you remember anything about him writing fiction?"

She snorted. "He fancied himself as a Hemingway kind of figure, and from the gossip around town, his womanizing was legendary. And his drinking, likewise. So he resembled

Hemingway in that way. But his writing was just dreadful. My mother tells me of the night he made the entire city council and everyone in attendance at that meeting listen to a reading. What could they do? They all clapped when he finished, but I suspect more than one citizen was choking his laughter down. She remembers him as a miserable human being. And she was shocked at the way he was verbally abusive to his son."

I'd never heard Joan speak so bluntly about anyone.

"So I'm not surprised that his son turned out the way he did," she added.

"Meaning?"

"Meaning he turned into a bully, too."

After a few more minutes of chitchat and my promise that I'd let her know if I learned anything new about Maria, I hung up. Her impressions and memories led me to wonder whether Mr. Markham Sr. would have pined for the gold medal that had been awarded to Hemingway, even convincing himself that he deserved it?

I could imagine that Turner Markham Jr. heard about this miscarriage of justice all his life. And that Turner himself might have seen recovering the medal as a holy grail. From there, it didn't take a huge leap to imagine that Turner might have stolen it on the first morning of the conference and stashed it somewhere safe to pick up later.

But what came after that? What made sense of the senseless murder?

Suppose Gabriel had seen him hide it and gotten the idea that if he stole it back, he could go to Turner and taunt him as payback for how his mother had been tortured? Or maybe Gabriel, being more of a man of honor, would have suggested that he'd return the medal to Turner if proper apologies and reparations were made to his mother? And in that kind of moment, I could imagine Turner's heart filling with rage, and then, him lashing out.

Maybe this theory was preposterous, but had any better ideas or solutions been floated? Not that I knew of. The key to solving the murder might lie in finding the medal and using it as bait to reel Turner in and get him to talk. But we had to find it first. If the medal was not at Maria's house, there was a good chance it had never left the Little White House.

I texted Bill and asked if he could meet me at the White House. It was late enough in the day that tours shouldn't be a problem. I glanced around to see whether any of my neighbors were out on their decks. GOT A BIG IDEA ABOUT THE MURDER, I texted into the phone. BUT I'D RATHER TELL YOU IN PERSON. I was starting to feel a little paranoid, afraid that somehow Turner Markham would realize I was on to him. Maybe he'd even seen me find Maria on the pier. If my theory was correct, he'd proven himself ruthless and vicious already.

MEET ME AT TLWH, Bill texted back.

* * *

I waited for Bill at the back of the property on the bench where tourists gather to meet their guides. Relieved to see his familiar form materialize, I explained to him what Carmen had finally confessed: that Turner Markham's father had taken advantage of her and then essentially signed a death warrant for her husband.

I explained about the boat and the weather. "Once he was drowned in the Florida Straits, she was emotionally and psychologically ruined."

"And this relates to Gabriel's murder?"

I nodded my head in a vigorous yes. "Maybe Gabriel only recently discovered this connection between Markham and his father, or maybe this conference brought it to the front of his mind. Somehow, I think he must have confronted Turner with some evidence of wrongdoing. Like maybe he even saw Turner steal the medal. And Turner, with too much to lose if this story was revealed, killed him on the spot."

"It sounds bizarre and unbelievable," Bill said with a sigh. "But no one's come up with anything better so far, right?"

I nodded.

"What kind of evidence?" Bill asked. "Photos? A letter?"

"Suppose Gabriel took the gold medal from the place where Turner had hidden it and hid it somewhere else, planning to confront Markham later?"

"But I'm sure the authorities have gone over this property with a fine-tooth comb. I know they did. I was here watching them."

"So we'll search again," I said, trying to sound more confident than I felt.

"Okay, let's do it," he said, leading me up the stairs to the entrance. "We can't lose anything by looking."

The inside of the house was cool and dim, and I smelled hints of must and maybe even a whiff of cumin and garlic left over from last night's dinner. It felt peaceful, not hectic and crazy the way the past few days had been.

"The second floor was roped off that morning," Bill said. "And Gabriel was working like a fiend for your mother all day. People would have noticed him creeping upstairs. And he wouldn't have gone into the gift shop, because it was staffed. So I imagine if it's anywhere, it's got to be here on the first level."

"I already searched the storage closet," I admitted. "The other night, before the dinner started."

"And I pawed through the director's office and the kitchen," Bill added with a guilty smile. "At least we've got it narrowed down."

So we started in the former Secret Service booth and searched side by side, working around the living room, the dining room, the barroom, for over an hour. We picked up every single glass, ashtray, and bauble, felt through every one of Mr. Truman's desk drawers, examined every book. I felt sweaty and tired and discouraged, and Bill looked just as bad. I leaned against Harry Truman's bar, looking over the rooms we'd been through, wishing for a little nip of the president's bourbon.

I couldn't keep a Cheshire cat smile from creeping onto my face.

"What?" Bill asked.

"I was thinking about Harry Truman's poker table, and how they took it apart to make the replica that would stand in while the original was refurbished? Gabriel was a master finish carpenter who worked on that table. I imagine there might be nooks and crannies where something, some kind of evidence, could be hidden. He would have known where to stash the medal."

"Farfetched," said Bill. "But I'm willing to look."

We circled the table, tapping all the wood, listening for the hollow sound that might indicate a small space where something could have been left behind. Then I saw, really saw, the cigar ashtrays recycled from brass shell casings inset into each of the card players' places. My breath caught; this was surely it. But we lifted every metal cup out of the wood and found—nothing.

So I dropped to my hands and knees and crawled underneath the table. I felt around, working my fingers along the joists, feeling for an open crevice. And finally there was a slot, big enough to insert two fingers. And something moved when I stuck my fingers up there, and it made a small *thunk*, like metal on wood.

"I've got it!" I said, so excited that I slammed my head into the underside of the table as I scrambled out. "Ouch! But I think it's really there."

Bill got down on all fours and felt the same thing I had. "I'm going to try to work it out. Can you grab a knife from the drawer just left of the stove?"

"Thing is," I said as I returned from the kitchen and handed him the cutlery, "how do we get Markham to make a move that proves he was looking for the medal?"

Bill grunted and wheezed, now lying on his back underneath the table.

"What if I told him I'd found it and then see if he responds?"

I took out my phone, found Turner Markham's Facebook page, and tapped out a message.

I'VE FOUND THE MEDAL.

"Wait," I said, pausing before I hit send. "I think it would be smarter to call Nathan and Steve Torrence. The old me would have texted Turner Markham and told him to come over immediately. The new me believes this is a police job. That way, we can let them extract the medal and avoid contaminating it with our fingerprints."

Bill grinned as he wormed out from under the table. "The new you is a lot smarter than the old you."

But as I fumbled to exit from Markham's page to get to my contacts, I heard the whooshing sound of that message getting sent.

* * *

Three police cars and Nathan Bransford's SUV were parked on the drive alongside the Little White House less than fifteen minutes after I reached Steve Torrence and explained what Bill and I thought we'd found in the poker table. They gathered in the barroom, and Nathan got down on his hands and knees with a flashlight and an evidence bag. He backed out with a small package wrapped in blue tissue. He set the package on the table, and the other officers clustered around to look. Using a pen, he unfolded the paper to expose the medal.

"I'm ninety-nine percent sure it's the actual gold medal, the one we saw in the case the first day," said Bill.

251

"But how did it get here?" Torrence wondered.

"I have a theory," I said. "If anyone is interested."

"Go ahead," he said, and Nathan nodded in agreement.

"I'm thinking that Gabriel might have seen this event as a chance to avenge what happened to his parents."

"Meaning what?" Nathan asked.

I gulped. It felt wrong to tell a roomful of strangers about Carmen's history. I looked around the faces at the table. She'd held this as a shameful secret for so long. Nathan noticed my hesitation.

"This is all confidential," he said gently. "We can't act if we don't know the facts."

So I explained about Turner Markham's father's broken promise, and the abuse, and the death at sea. "He would have known they couldn't reasonably have survived the passage. He was the one who insisted they had clear passage only that night." I felt tears choke my voice, and I took a minute to calm down.

"Another thing I'm guessing is that the elder Markham felt he deserved that gold medal. And, by extension, our Turner Markham felt that way too. So when our commissioner saw a chance to palm it Friday morning, he took it. Maybe Gabriel caught Turner in the act of stealing the medal, and he threatened to expose him for his father's sins. Maybe he was holding the knife? Who knows? But more likely Gabriel watched Turner hide it, and later stole the medal back and hid it here." I tapped the table. "Gabriel used the distraction of the party to confront Turner. And that went badly."

"The question is, why would a Key West commissioner risk ruin by stealing the Cuban medal?" Torrence asked.

"His father was a blathering narcissist who somehow imagined he deserved the Nobel prize the same year Hemingway won. He was a sour, angry man who expressed his disappointment by making his family pay. I've heard he had a tendency to hold a grudge. Turner tried to avenge his father's failures by writing his own Hemingway-style book. But face it, he's a hack, too." I grinned.

Another man detective piped up, directing his question at the others, not me. "Now the question is how we get him to confess, if this is in fact what happened. Which to my ears sounds ridiculous."

Nathan snapped, "We bring him in to the station and we hammer at him until he gives us the truth. Just like any other suspect."

For a few moments, they argued back and forth. Would Markham ever tell the truth, and did they owe him any different treatment because of his position and his service to the town?

"The answer on that last part is absolutely not," Torrence said. "A criminal is a criminal, period. And a man in a position of authority, with the trust of his voters, should be held to the standard of any decent human being. Maybe, in fact, that standard should be higher."

"I have an idea on this, too," I offered, once it became clear that no one else seemed to have a good approach. "You won't like it when you first hear it, but"—I shrugged—"might be worth a try."

Nathan gestured for me to spill. I suggested that I might be the logical person to contact Turner Markham, tell him I had recovered the medal, and offer to meet him here.

"We can't and won't put a civilian in the position of sitting duck," Torrence said. "I like the idea, but a cop has to lure him in. There's no reason it has to be you."

Exactly at that moment, a message whooshed into my inbox.

I'M LISTENING.

And I had to explain to them all how I'd thought I could handle this myself, and realized immediately what a lousy idea that was, but then my clumsy thumbs hadn't gotten the message . . .

Chapter Twenty-Eight

What you have with a restaurant that you visit once or twice is a transaction. What you have with a restaurant that you visit over and over is a relationship.
— Frank Bruni, "Familiarity Breeds Content,"
The New York Times, September 18, 2013

Sweat seeped through my T-shirt and ran down my back as I heard the rumble of Turner Markham's jeep on the lane in front of the Little White House.

Nathan had been the last of the police to get into position. He'd crossed the room to put his hands on my shoulders and look deep into my eyes. "You don't have to do this," he said, his voice quiet and kind. "We can just bring him in for questioning like any other person of interest. The text doesn't matter; you do."

"You know how slick he is," I said. "Has anything ever stuck when he's been accused of something? All those resolutions he pushed through because they benefited his businesses? He shouldn't get away with murder. Especially almost twice."

He cupped my cheek in his palm and sighed. "You're too brave. Do you understand that when I get angry with you about doing something risky, it's not that I'm so angry, it's that I love you? And I'm afraid I'll lose you?"

My throat closed up and I leaned forward to kiss him. "I love you, too. Nothing risky, I promise. You'll be right here, only feet away, true? So go."

I heard the click-clacking of the tires on Turner's truck hitting the driveway, then the silence as he shut the engine down. In a rush of claustrophobia, I had the urge to run outside to meet him. But I knew that would screw up the plan, make it harder for the police hidden in the living room and kitchen to protect me. And deviating from what we'd agreed on would panic Nathan and Torrence. And panic has never enhanced good decision-making. So I sat like bait fish in a bucket and waited. I heard heavy footsteps on the short flight of stairs that led past the Secret Service booth.

"Hayley?"

Markham's voice sounded normal, and I tried to make mine match. "In here." That came out as a whisper. "In here, in the poker room," I called.

He came in cautiously, looking all around him as if I'd set a trap. I pictured the two uniformed cops squatting behind Harry Truman's bar, ready to heave themselves out with guns flashing at the first sign of trouble. I pictured my trusted friend Steve Torrence poised behind the swinging door that led to the kitchen. And I pictured the strong shoulders of Nathan Bransford crouched down in the Secret Service booth. Nathan who loved me and would never allow me to be hurt.

Markham stopped to look the space over. Then he glared at me. "I hope this isn't a wild-goose chase."

"It's—" My mouth felt too dry to finish one short sentence. I swallowed and tried again. "It's not."

"Here's what I want to know: why did you think of me when you found the medal?"

"I knew you and your father were both big Hemingway nuts. I'd heard you talk passionately about how this prize really belonged in the United States, not Cuba. And I agree completely with that. Why should they hoard this precious symbol of one of our country's great writers?" I forced a grin. "Besides, you were one of the few people who was in the house when the thing disappeared. You and Gabriel. And he's obviously dead."

He didn't look convinced.

"Let's call it woman's intuition."

"Even supposing that's all true, which seems unlikely, why did you contact anyone? Why not take the medal and sell it and then keep the money yourself?"

"Because I'd have no idea how to unload the darn thing. I was hoping you would."

As we'd planned the sting, we'd gone round and round and finally decided that he might bite if I told him I thought I knew where the medal was but would have no clue how to dispose of it.

"It must be worth a ton, right?" I continued. "And there's no way that kind of money should be buried down there in the southern netherlands of Cuba. One day that dreadful government will swoop in and pluck it out of that convent anyway, right?"

"You got that right," he said.

But cautiously, as though he was checking me out. Was it possible that I was setting him up? I had to imagine that was going through his mind.

"The point is," Nathan had said half an hour earlier, "sound as dizzy as you possibly can. Like you're a helpless female who can't possibly figure out how to solve this knotty problem without him."

I'd made a face. *Really?*

"I'm not saying you *are* dizzy, I'm saying you're a good actor," he'd added quickly.

"Nice save, Bransford," one of the other cops had said.

Another policeman had snickered. "He'll find out later if he's made the save or not."

At that point I was peeved, dog-tired from getting up so early, and on a knife edge from the stress of the whole week. I wanted to pitch a little snit and say, "Really? I'm the one who found the dang medal and now you'll make fun of me? Fine, how about you all handle this on your own without the dizzy broad involved. Take him down to the station and watch him deny everything."

But even more, I'd wanted to stop Turner Markham.

Torrence had stepped forward and circled his arm around my shoulders, a placating look on his face. "Everyone's a little tense right here. Let's all stand down a minute and work together on this."

So we'd made the plan and everyone had agreed it was the best chance for nabbing him. And now I was stuck living with it, even scared out of my gourd.

"So here's the thing, I believe the medal has to be in this room. Because there were too many people around right after it was stolen for someone to smuggle it out of the house without being seen, remember? You were here with the entire Cuban delegation and the folks from Key West as well."

"I remember," he grunted. "I assume the cops searched everywhere, though."

"Dollars to doughnuts, cops being cops and a little bit dumber than usual in this town, I bet they didn't think to look inside the poker table."

Not true at all, but that was payback for Nathan's dizzy comment. I explained the same thing I had told Bill only hours earlier, then repeated for the cops when they'd shown up. "I think it has to be hidden right here in plain sight. But suppose we make a deal? You tell me what really happened and I'll share the money once we sell it."

He rubbed his jaw, thinking that over. "If I'm selling it to my contacts, we split it seventy percent me, thirty percent you. Especially since I'm the one who took the biggest risk and knocked off that lying bastard before I could get it back from him. Believe me, he was going to sell it and keep the profits. That's the kind of family he comes from."

"I thought that's what happened," I said, feeling a surge of outrage. "I thought you were the one who stabbed Gabriel. I wasn't exactly sure why, though."

"What's your guess, Little Miss Smarty-Pants?" he asked.

"You were the biggest Hemingway scholar I've seen, for one," I said. "Though in a different way from the people who fawn all over the man and his work."

Turner's face flooded red and the muscles in his neck bulged with tension. "You and I both know he was a cheating hack. He won the prize for being Mr. Macho, Mr. Bullfight, Mr. Sexy Ladies' Man. Dana Sebek was right about her theory. That's what people really love about Hemingway. They want to *be him*, right up until the point where he blew his brains out," Turner said. "They don't care about his stupid, stilted writing. My father had more talent in his pinkie than that man had in his whole brain and his whole life. And, for that matter, so do I." He paused, pulling back from his lapse into a full-bore rant. "But that doesn't explain why you think I killed a guy."

"It was the small splotch of blood spatter on your silk shirt." He looked shocked, glanced down, and brushed at his green golf shirt. "At first I thought maybe the caramel sauce from the flan I dropped splattered over your clothes and that was the sum total of it. Honest, I only thought of it because I was going to offer to pay your dry-cleaning bill."

But his face had gotten even redder and beads of sweat popped out, and as I opened my mouth to continue to talk, he cut me off.

"That bastard ruined everything. It was almost like he was lying in wait, watching me, hoping I'd trip up."

I didn't say that Gabriel *had* been lying in wait for him, in fact had waited a lifetime for that moment. But he probably hadn't counted on the possibility that Turner Markham would act as completely ruthlessly as his father had, years before him. That taking another human life meant very little to either of them if they could get what they wanted in the end.

I gutted back a wave of sheer panic, realizing that Markham would stop at nothing. If I hollered for help now, the cops wouldn't have enough on him to put him away. There was nothing to do but slog ahead with what we'd planned. Nathan would call this off if he thought I was in any danger. Any danger at all.

"Anyway," I said in the dizziest voice I could muster, "I think the medal is hidden in this table." I rapped on the top of the mahogany. And then explained about the reconstruction and how Gabriel had been part of the crew that did the work. "So he might have known of a cubbyhole where he could hide it. And I'm assuming that's what he did—after you stashed it someplace less secure."

He didn't answer, but got down on his hands and knees and crawled under the table as Bill and I had. I heard him suck in a little breath of air when he found the medal tucked away in the tiny opening where Nathan had replaced it. He scrambled back out, grinning, the gold winking in his left hand. And a gun in the other. "I'm sorry about that thirty percent, but I don't believe you've earned it," he said.

But before he could raise the gun to level and shoot me, a phalanx of angry cops piled on top of him. And Nathan grabbed hold of me and whisked me out into the sunlight before I had time to really breathe or speak another word.

I stood there shaking in his embrace, half scared to death, still, and half inordinately proud of my part in the takedown.

"You know what," I asked, starting to giggle uncontrollably. "That was by far the dumbest thing I've ever done. Let's don't forget in the future that you helped set it up."

Chapter Twenty-Nine

As I ate the oysters with their strong taste of the sea and their faint metallic taste that the cold white wine washed away, leaving only the sea taste and the succulent texture, and as I drank their cold liquid from each shell and washed it down with the crisp taste of the wine, I lost the empty feeling and began to be happy and to make plans.
—Ernest Hemingway, *A Moveable Feast*

Even with Maria's condition upgraded, first from critical to serious and then late this afternoon to fair, and with Turner Markham ensconced in the Stock Island jail, I wasn't much in the mood for a touristy party scene. Plus, my mother and Sam were sharing drinks with Miss Gloria and Connie on our houseboat deck to celebrate the end of the Havana conference and Turner's capture, and I couldn't think of a place I'd rather unwind from a difficult week. And the sign on the boat next door had been marked this morning in bright crimson letters: Sold! We all wanted to cheer my housemate up about the unknown new neighbors. She was trying so hard to put on a sunny front, but we could all see her dismay, plain as daylight.

But Nathan had astonished me so thoroughly with his reservation for dinner at Hot Tin Roof that I couldn't refuse. Especially after he'd described his schedule for the next two weeks. Because he was in charge of ten days of SWAT training for the whole department, this little window of time was his only real availability. Hot Tin Roof's second-floor restaurant was located within the Sunset Pier complex only a stone's throw from Mallory Square, and conversations could sometimes be overwhelmed by the music from the stage in the outdoor bar below. Definitely not Nathan's style.

This time, fortunately, the performer was a well-known soul singer named Robert Albury. And Nathan seemed so pleased about having scored a table on the deck overlooking the water. We ordered appetizers and drinks—a mojito for me and a nonalcoholic beer for him—from a waiter with a Russian accent, and settled in to watch the busy scene below us. Our order came out quickly and we filed our dinner choices with the server. Out on the horizon, a variety of boats plied the harbor, taking advantage of the impending sunset.

"You see that yacht out there?" Nathan asked, pointing to the enormous blue-and-white boat moored farthest out. "I heard two different stories this week. One said there was a Russian oligarch who lost his wife and came here to drown his sorrows. The other claimed the boat is owned by Norton Revson, you know, the high-end cosmetics magnate? They say he loves drag bars and comes here to get his fix. Or is it *café con leche* that he loves?"

I tried to smile. He could tell I was down and he was doing his best to jolly me up.

"I know you're sad about Maria," he said, reaching for my hand across the table. "And after all her family suffered, it doesn't seem right that she ended up almost drowned. But she's going to be okay, right? That's what the doctors said?"

I nodded and swallowed a big gulp of my drink, not wanting my words to wobble when I spoke. "The good part is that that awful man will really get punished, right?"

"He may think he's got friends in high places, but the negatives are pretty damning," he agreed.

The dinner food was delivered—crab cakes for me and a rare steak for him. He ordered me a glass of rosé. We ate in silence for a bit.

"How do they rate on the famous Hayley Snow crab cake scale?" he asked.

He was *really* trying to cheer me up—even pretending that he cared about food.

"Right up there," I said, smiling. "Lots of crab, not much bready filler, and a crunchy crust. And their remoulade sauce is very good too, with a nice zip that sneaks up on you after finishing each bite."

"And tell me again how you ended up figuring out that the medal was in the poker table," he said.

"Really?" I asked, looking under our table and pretending to search. "Who are you and where did you hide Nathan Bransford?"

He smirked. "Yes, really. I'd like to hear how your complicated brain works."

"Everyone wants to know that, but it's a mysterious being, my brain."

"Come on," he said. "You're good with words. Describe it."

"It was like what I do when I'm working on a review. I don't know immediately how I feel about a restaurant and its food and its chef. I taste lots of dishes and take notes about my reactions and pictures to document everything. And then I step back for a bit and let my subconscious go to work. And a couple of hours or days later, the truth is revealed. Maybe the chef was trying too hard to imitate a Michelin-starred restaurant. Or maybe the chef cares more about volume and money than he does about food. Or maybe the owner is too cheap to buy good stuff, when every home cook knows the end result can't transcend lousy ingredients."

The whole time I talked, I watched his face to see if he was listening, which he seemed to be. And then whether he cared. Which, who could really tell? That would come out in time. And as long as he cared about me, I could let the food part go.

"Interesting," he said. "You work bits and pieces of information around until it all drops into place—like a detective would do. Or maybe even a psychologist."

"You're full of surprises," I said, sipping the last bit of wine from my glass.

"I like to keep you guessing. What say we move downstairs for a nightcap?"

"Really? You want a drink here?" I gestured at the crowd below, swilling, smoking, yakking under bright-yellow umbrellas on a finger of the pier that extended out into the water. "You can't even indulge tonight anyway."

"I like Albury's music," he said a little sheepishly, anticipating my astonishment.

This was altogether strange. He wasn't the kind of man who liked lingering in a crowd. Especially in a crowd of tipsy tourists. Too many bad possible outcomes circled through his mind, and he preferred to be on the outside watching for one of them. I was certain he'd already pictured the panic that could occur if something went wrong and the crowd tried to crush farther inland for safety. Bottlenecks and potential problems waited everywhere, as customers could only get to the bar via narrow boardwalks. But he paid the bill quickly, then grabbed my elbow and led me downstairs.

"Look," he said. "Our lucky night. That couple is leaving." He pointed at two brightly painted stools close to the stage that had just been vacated.

"Isn't that Officer Ryan?" I asked.

"Oh, maybe you're right." Nathan waved at the other cop, and we made our way over to sit. "I'll have to thank him for his excellent timing when I see him tomorrow."

He ordered us drinks from a chipper waiter as we watched the singer. This performer was quintessential Key West—an older black man, dressed in baggy shorts and a T-shirt, crooning his heart out with old bluesy classics. He had the most soulful, pained expressions on his face as he met the eyes of various women in the audience.

"He's working the crowd," I said.

Nathan laughed. "He's a master. I could learn a lot from this guy."

"This next song," said the singer in his deep and husky voice, "goes out to Hayley Snow." He looked over at me, winked at Nathan, and began to wail: "Try a little tenderness."

I felt tears prick my eyes. "You set this up?" I asked Nathan, moving now from a little surprised to utterly stunned.

"I got scared in the Little White House yesterday. Scared I might lose you," he added. "I wanted to do something special." He took my hand and squeezed. "You seemed so pressured this week, and sad about Maria and Gabriel."

I nodded; their story was so tragic. "You can't imagine how painful it was to hear Carmen talk about what had really happened those years ago. And Gabriel dying while trying to avenge his mom—that was the exclamation point on an awful story," I said, squeezing back.

"There's more, isn't there?"

I bit my lip, weighing whether to tell him. "It's not only Maria. And this will seem so ridiculous in comparison to what they lost. The houseboat next door sold," I said. "Miss Gloria is really worried about the new neighbors. I know it sounds silly to you, but it matters to me if she's happy. And she's happy on Houseboat Row. For now, anyway."

He nodded and looked back at the stage. He'd tried hard with the impromptu dinner and the special song, but he wasn't an emotional man, and I needed to accept that if I planned to stick with this relationship.

"It's not sentimental, no, no, no," belted Robert Albury, staring right at me.

When he'd finished the song, I looked back at Nathan to thank him. He handed me a pale-blue box, about the right size for a watch or a necklace—definitely not a ring—tied up with a white ribbon.

"I have something for you."

"What's this?"

"Open it," Nathan said.

I untied the ribbon and took off the lid. A key. I looked up, feeling confused. I already knew where he hid the spare key to his equally spare apartment. Not anywhere a normal person would choose, by the way. Not underneath a potted plant by the door or hanging from a nail on the fence, for example.

"What is this for? Don't tell me you bought me that yacht after all?"

"I bought the houseboat next door to yours," he said. "You've made it very plain that you won't move out, so I'm moving in."

"But you hate Houseboat Row," I said, still not understanding why he'd even consider such a move.

"You've probably noticed that my job isolates me. But you bring me back to the world. I see the worst that people do to each other. And you see the best."

He continued, "You've stayed at my apartment. I'm not good at making a place feel like home."

He was right about that—guy-style leather furniture, a minimally stocked kitchen, and nothing on the walls. One time earlier in our relationship, I'd stayed over and offered to make scrambled eggs in the morning. I'd found his kitchen lacking butter, salt, pepper, and a spatula. Even his little dog,

Ziggy Stardust, spent as much time out of the house as he could manage.

"If Houseboat Row is home to you, I know it will become home to me."

"So what," I joked, "you can borrow a cup of sugar from our kitchen when you need it and call the cops if we're having too much fun?"

And then he blurted it out. "Do you want to get married? We can live next door to Miss Gloria and you can keep an eye on her and have coffee on her deck every morning. She can come to dinner every night if you want. And I can stay awake all night because of the incessant rocking of the damn boat and the yakking of your oddball neighbors." He crooked a heartbreaking smile.

I leaned back, flabbergasted, trying to process the words. I certainly hadn't guessed this when he'd asked me out for drinks and dinner. I was almost embarrassed to admit—even to myself—that I'd thought maybe he needed me to go under-cover in one of his pending cases.

Robert Albury rumbled into his microphone, "I believe this fellow asked you a question. Something about getting married."

"Married?" I started to giggle hysterically as it sunk in. "You and me?"

Nathan's face got very stern. "You and me. Though we should probably talk about the fact that I'm a cop, and what that might mean for you, as my wife."

His *wife*? My head said, *Slow down and think about it*, but my heart said something altogether different. "Absolutely!" I threw my arms around Nathan and gave him a big kiss. The crowd around us cheered and clapped.

He let me go and glanced at his watch. "I've got to get to the station for the SWAT training. I can't skip it because I'm in charge. How about you talk to your ladies and get back to me with the details? No monkey suit, remember? That one's nonnegotiable."

I could feel myself grinning from ear to ear. "No monkey suit; it's a deal! Can we walk out through Mallory Square so I can tell Lorenzo?"

We forded the crowd, which had diminished since the sun set, leaving behind the harder-core party people and the buskers and vendors. We passed a man juggling fiery pins and a man preaching doom and damnation from a worn Bible. Lorenzo's table was set up on the small alley perpendicular to those lined up along the water. I remembered that spaces were assigned according to seniority and who showed up when on a particular night. Maybe he'd arrived late, or maybe he preferred the modicum of privacy this allowed his customers. His current customer was getting up from the table, wringing Lorenzo's hand and thanking him profusely. I waited until he was gone, then stepped in to hug my friend.

"We won't keep you," I said, "but wanted to let you know that we're getting married." Wow, those words sounded weird coming out of my mouth.

Nathan flashed a shy smile and Lorenzo clapped and then blew him a kiss. "Seems to me you drew a two of cups in your last reading. I may have even asked if something was up."

Eyes twinkling, he came out from behind the card table to hug me again. I watched as he then hugged Nathan and planted a big kiss on his cheek, which was absolutely crimson.

"You're always a step ahead," I said to my friend. "More to come on plans later. I have to go tell Mom and Miss Gloria." I paused, glancing between the two men. "Hey, what about tarot readings at our wedding reception?"

Nathan winced and Lorenzo and I burst out laughing.

Nathan dropped me off in the Tarpon Pier parking lot, then got out of the car to give me a sweet kiss.

I felt another huge grin nearly splitting my face in two. "Are you sure you don't want to come to the boat with me and make the announcement?"

"I'd love to, but I'm already late." He quirked a little Nathan smile, pointing at his watch. Then he wheeled around to his cruiser, which he'd left running.

And I went skipping up the finger to our houseboat, squealing like Snorkel the Pig, another of my favorite acts on Mallory Square.

"Guess what?" I flung my arms around my mother, and then Connie, and Sam, and finally my octogenarian roommate, Miss Gloria, nearly knocking the glass of wine out of her hand. "I'm getting married."

"To whom?" Miss Gloria asked with a poker-straight face.

Then she burst into cackles of laughter and leapt up to join Connie and my mother in a group hug.

"So he finally popped the question," said my mother. But then a worried look flitted across her face. "Don't tell me you asked him."

"Not to worry." My mother had a major superstition about asking men for their hand in marriage. According to an informal survey of her friends and their daughters, all the marriages that started that way had ended in divorce within the first year.

So I described how Nathan had set up the night with the singer and the dinner and how two people had vacated their seats at just the right moment. "I think I recognized one of them. He must have arranged for them to hold those stools until we arrived and then get up and leave."

"Who knew he was a romantic deep down inside?" Connie asked. "Where is he, anyway?"

I explained about the emergency SWAT training.

"Is there a ring?" Miss Gloria asked. "Don't mean to be greedy, but we'd love to see if he delivered the goods. And I'm aware it's not fair that men are judged on the quality of their proposal and engagement ring. By the way, Nathan gets an A, maybe A minus, for his. I would have liked to see a ring on your finger."

"We're going to pick that out later. He was afraid to choose something I wouldn't like. And he didn't ask you, because he suspected that none of you would be able to keep a secret."

My mother and Miss Gloria immediately began to protest.

"Don't take it personally. Remember, he's a cop. That job would make anyone suspicious about leaks. But in the meantime, he gave me something even better." I pulled the box out of my pocket and handed it to Miss Gloria. She held it to her ear and shook it, and the key inside rattled against the cardboard. She took the lid off.

"What's this?"

"It's a key to our neighbor's houseboat." I pointed next door, where the dreaded SOLD! sign hung, flapping in the little breeze that had kicked up. "He bought it so we could move in and live next door to you, forever."

Her eyes filled with tears. "He hates Houseboat Row."

"I know, but he loves me and he knows that I love you." I tucked her into a full-body squeeze.

"I'm impressed with that man. That's the sweetest proposal I've ever heard," said Connie.

"Ditto," said Mom, passing her phone off to Sam and taking her turn with a hug. "Will you call Eric and Bill right now and ask them to bring over some champagne? This is so exciting! Where and when will you get married and who will officiate?"

"We haven't gotten that far," I said. "I don't mean any offense, but not during the hurricane season." I winked at Sam. "But definitely Reverend Steve Torrence."

"Hadn't you better call him right away?" my mother asked.

I thought we probably had time, but on the other hand, it was so much fun to tell this news. So I dialed him up. "Nathan proposed and I said yes! Did you know about this? Did you coach him on how to do this? Because it was very, very romantic. And of course, I want you to do the ceremony."

He sputtered with laughter and assured me he'd had nothing to do with it. "Of course I'll do your wedding. I'll make sure to be available. Congratulations. I hope you'll be very happy!"

Bill and Eric arrived at our place shortly after with a couple of bottles of prosecco. After another round of hugging, Bill said, "I'm sure I could get you a discount on a wedding at the Little White House. Bob couldn't be more grateful. Two of the attendees at the opening party came through with surprise donations. Massive donations that could fund our future for decades. Instead of getting canned, he's receiving a special letter of commendation from the board. And they've asked the mayor to read a similar proclamation."

"But take your time," Eric said. "Hopefully you'll have only one wedding, and you should enjoy the process."

"You're so smart," I said to Eric. And then I reached for the hands of Miss Gloria and my mother. "I can't wait for one more second to see what Nathan bought."

"Let the ladies go first," Sam suggested. "It doesn't look big enough to hold all of us."

I hopped off the deck, with Miss Gloria and my mother and Connie and the two cats behind me, and then onto the deck of the boat next door. My hands were shaking as I inserted the key into the lock and pushed open the door.

A living area lay just inside, separated from the kitchen by a short bar. The walls were paneled with the kind of old-fashioned faux-wood that people used to plaster over the cement walls in their basements, and the floor was covered with orange honest-to-god shag carpet. It smelled like someone's cellar, too. And the prior owners had clearly never turned on an exhaust fan while frying.

"Wow," I said, my heart sinking like a grease-saturated fritter. "This place is a dump."

"It needs lots of work—lots of things need to be ripped right out and replaced, and you'll need some decorating advice from your mother," said my mom.

After a quick tour of the two bedrooms in back and the small bath, all of which my mother and Miss Gloria insisted could be fixed, we headed back home.

"It's a dog, but we'll renovate and send the bills to the fiancé. Quickly, before he changes his mind," said Miss Gloria, giggling. "But as my Frank would have said, it's got excellent bones. Imagine cedar or reclaimed Dade County pine on the walls and floors. Built-ins everywhere. And a whole new kitchen with a double oven. Not a Kidcraft mini-kitchen like you have at my place."

"I love your place," I said. "It's home to me."

"This will become home," she said, beaming. "And people say you've got the best neighbors!"

Recipes

Mojito

Before I began spending half the year in Key West, I had never tasted a mojito, never mind made one. But now it's my new favorite drink. What spells tropical paradise better than the combination of lemons, limes, mint, and rum? Add a splash of bitters and a Key West mystery and you're on vacation—but without the hassle of airports, freeways, and bank-busting expenses! Janet Snow and her gang served these at the opening party . . .

1 lime, sliced
1 lemon, sliced
4 to 5 sprigs fresh mint
2 teaspoons sugar
1 to 2 ounces rum, depending on how strong you want the
    drink

Lucy Burdette

Club soda
Ice
Bitters

Start by crushing several slices of lime, several slices of lemon, the mint, and the sugar in the bottom of an old-fashioned glass. Add the rum and stir. Fill the glass with ice. Cover the ice with club soda. Mix all that together and add a splash of bitters on top.

Ropa Vieja (Old Clothes)

Some people consider this to be the national dish of Cuba. I made it for friends, one of whose family came from Cuba. I felt honored and relieved when he announced that it tasted like the dish his mother used to make.

3 pounds flank steak, cut into chunks
Salt and black pepper to taste
Olive oil
1 medium yellow onion, thinly sliced
2 bell peppers, thinly sliced
6 ounces tomato paste
1 tablespoon cumin
1 tablespoon dried oregano
5 cloves garlic, finely chopped
1 bay leaf
½ cup dry white wine
2 cups beef stock
1 (28-ounce) can crushed tomatoes
½ cup halved, pitted green olives
⅓ cup sliced jarred pimiento peppers
3 tablespoons capers, rinsed and drained
1 tablespoon white wine vinegar
¼ cup roughly chopped cilantro

Season the steak with a little salt and pepper. Working in batches, cook the meat in hot olive oil in a frying pan until browned on both sides, about 6 minutes. Remove the meat to a stockpot. Add onion and peppers to the pan; sauté until soft, about 4 minutes. Add tomato paste, cumin, oregano, garlic, and bay leaf; cook until lightly caramelized, about 3 minutes. Add wine; cook, scraping bottom of pot, for 1 minute. Add this mixture to stockpot along with stock and tomatoes. After bringing the liquid to a boil, reduce heat to medium-low; cook, covered, until steak is very tender, 2 to 3 hours.

Refrigerate overnight. Skim the fat, then remove the steak. Shred the meat using two forks. Add this back to the pot with the olives, pimientos, capers, and vinegar. Cook until sauce is slightly thickened, about 30 minutes. Stir in cilantro before serving with white rice and black beans.

Aunt Estela's Flan

Homemade flan is an incredible treat. Analise Smith (Key West Food Tours) told me that she plans to serve her aunt's flan at her wedding reception (instead of cake) when that day comes. This is her Aunt Estela's actual recipe. It makes a lot!

8 (8-ounce) cans sweetened condensed milk
8 (8-ounce) cans evaporated milk
16 eggs
1 (16 Oz) large bottle imitation vanilla extract
2 pounds sugar
2 large cafeteria-sized baking pans, one bigger than the other

Preheat oven to 350 degrees. Fill the larger baking pan with enough water so that the smaller pan fits inside it without the water spilling out. Place the smaller pan on two burners so that the pan can get warm. In a pot, whisk the condensed milk, evaporated milk, eggs, and vanilla and set aside. In another pot, melt the sugar over low heat until it turns into a caramel mixture. (Do not burn.) Pour into the top baking pan and spread around to cover the bottom and sides of the pan. Place top pan in the larger baking pan, then pour the egg-milk mixture on top of the melted sugar. Bake for 1 hour, then start checking every 15 minutes until a knife inserted in the center of the custard comes out clean. Remove from the oven and let it cool. Cover and place overnight in the fridge. To serve, take a butter knife around the edge to loosen the flan from the pan; place a serving tray over the pan and flip it over. Pour any excess caramel sugar over the flan. Cut, serve, and enjoy!

Cuban Mix Sandwiches

As Hayley herself says, you could eat Cuban sandwiches (aka Cuban mix, aka Cubanos) every day for a year in Key West and still not scratch the surface of all the varieties. You might try a sandwich at each establishment, as Hayley and Miss Gloria do. Or, you can try making them yourself. This recipe is based on one found in *Cuba! Recipes and Stories From the Cuban Kitchen* by Dan Goldberg, Andrea Kuhn, and Jody Eddy (Ten Speed Press, 2016).

One large loaf Cuban bread (use Italian if you can't find Cuban)
Slices of leftover Cuban pork, mojo style
About ½ pound Swiss cheese
About ½ pound sliced ham
Finely sliced dill pickles
Yellow mustard

Slice the entire loaf of bread open lengthwise. Spread mustard on both sides. Layer the Swiss cheese on the bottom, followed by pickles, followed by pork, followed by ham, followed by the rest of the cheese. Press the sandwich together. Either cut in half to cook in a press, or wrap in foil and grill until the cheese is melted and the bread toasty.

Black Bean Soup

All the most authentic Cuban black bean soup recipes I came across shared two instructions: First, soak the beans in a pot the day before you plan to cook, along with an onion and a green pepper. Second, cook these vegetables along with the beans, and then puree them and add them back into the soup. I was dubious, but I followed these instructions and was very happy with the results.

1 pound dried black beans
2 onions, peeled, one halved, one diced
2 green peppers, one halved, one diced
2 bay leaves
¼ to ½ teaspoon salt
2 jalapeño peppers, diced
4 cloves garlic, diced
2 tablespoons olive oil
2 cups good beef stock
1 teaspoon oregano
1 teaspoon ground cumin
1 tablespoon sugar
1 tablespoon red wine vinegar

Cover the beans, the halved onion, and the halved pepper with water in a pot and refrigerate overnight. The next day, simmer with the bay leaves until tender, up to an hour. Stir in salt.

Make the sofrito:

Sauté the diced onion, diced green pepper, jalapeños, and garlic in olive oil until soft. Stir this mixture into the beans.

Remove the bay leaves. Take the mushy onion and green pepper along with 2 cups of beans and process them in a blender until smooth. Add this back into the pot along with the beef stock. Stir in oregano, cumin, sugar, and red wine vinegar. Simmer at least another 30 minutes, though the dish can go longer.

Serve with white rice, sour cream, and a sprinkle of fresh cilantro.

Baked Bananas with a Cuban Flair

Often in Cuba and in Cuban restaurants, fried plantains are found on the side of meat and rice dishes. (Confession: I don't love plantains.) I discovered a version of this banana recipe in the *Nantucket Open-House Cookbook* by Sarah Leah Chase and loved it. It's easier than frying individual slices of plantain, which is important if you're working on a lot of other dishes. These were delicious with the pork roast I made, but I could see them pairing well with a lot of other main dishes. They look as if you've gone to a lot of trouble when they're really easy as pie.

5 to 6 bananas, halved lengthwise
½ stick butter
1 tablespoon fresh lime juice, or squeeze half a lime
1/3 cup brown sugar
2 tablespoons rum
Cinnamon, optional

Lay out bananas in an 11 × 13 pan. Heat the butter and other ingredients in a small saucepan. Pour over the bananas. Bake at 375 degrees for 12 to 15 minutes or until the butter is bubbling and the bananas are just beginning to brown. Sprinkle with cinnamon if desired. That's it!

Mojito Cake

In this eighth Key West mystery, Hayley and her mother Janet are catering a Key West/Havana conference at the Truman Little White House. This is the dessert they serve for the final dinner. The basis of this recipe again came from *Cuba! Recipes and Stories From the Cuban Kitchen*. I love lime cake and yellow cake and whipped cream, so you can imagine that this recipe was irresistible. I know mojitos require rum, and yet I'm not a big fan of alcohol-flavored desserts. So I chose to leave the rum extract out of the cake and instead add a teaspoon of rum. This gives it a little soupçon of flavor without overwhelming the cake. I also reduced the salt in the batter and the rum in the frosting. You can adjust the rum upward to a tablespoon if you choose.

For the cake

3 cups all-purpose flour
3 teaspoons baking powder (low-sodium works fine)
½ teaspoon salt
2 sticks unsalted butter, room temperature
2 cups sugar
4 eggs, room temperature
2 teaspoons vanilla extract
2 teaspoons lime zest
2 tablespoons freshly squeezed lime juice

1 teaspoon rum
½ cup whole milk

For the lime-mint syrup

¼ cup water
¼ cup brown sugar
¼ cup fresh mint leaves, tightly packed
¼ cup freshly squeezed lime juice
2 cups heavy whipping cream
2 tablespoons powdered sugar
1 teaspoon dark rum

For decoration:

Thin slices of lime, lime zest, or mint leaves

Prepare two 9-inch cake pans by buttering them and lining them with parchment paper. Butter the paper too. Preheat the oven to 350 degrees. Mix the dry ingredients for the cake (except the sugar) together and set aside. In your KitchenAid or food processor or with an electric beater, beat the butter well with the sugar until light and fluffy. Beat in the eggs one at a time. Mix in the vanilla extract, lime zest, lime juice, and rum. Fold in the dry ingredients; don't overmix. Stir in the milk.

Divide the batter into the two prepared pans and bake about 30 minutes, or until the cakes spring back when touched. Cool for 10 minutes in the pans, and then remove from the pans and cool completely.

For the lime-mint syrup, heat the water and brown sugar in a small pan until the sugar is dissolved. Turn off the heat and stir in the mint leaves. Let them steep for 10 minutes, then strain them out and stir in the lime juice. Paint this glaze onto each layer of cake with a pastry brush.

Whip the cream and powdered sugar until stiff, then stir in the rum. Dollop half of the whipped cream onto the first layer. Place the second layer on top and spread the remainder of the cream over that. Decorate with thin slices of lime, lime zest, or mint leaves as desired.

Acknowledgments

While I was finishing this book, my beloved Florida Keys sat right in the crosshairs of Hurricane Irma. Honestly, I wondered if I'd ever feel like writing again if the storm wiped out the island and the community of people I've grown to know and love. This experience made me feel all the more grateful about my time on this magical spray of keys . . . and reminded me of something my friend Mark Hedden wrote several years ago: "The thing about Key West is that it is ultimately a fragile place. Low and small and flat and just sitting there, unprotected, in the middle of all that ocean. One big hurricane, a foot or two of sea level rise, and we could be wiped off the map. Every day you live here, there's a sense that you're getting away with something."

As always, so many people helped me as I wrote this book. Thanks to Ranier and the folks at the Florida Keys Tree Institute, who gave us a wonderful window into the people and history of Cuba; Richard from Gourmet Nibbles and Baskets for the fabulous idea about the *Pilar* flower arrangement; John Hernandez and Margaret Clark for checking my Spanish; Edgardo for the Spanish lessons; and Steve Torrence for helping to correct my fictional police procedure—I am so lucky to

Acknowledgments

be able to text him at a moment's notice! Fact-checking aside, he is a dear friend and an island treasure. Thanks to Ron Augustine for helping me with Lorenzo's insights; Leigh Pujado for cracking the whip so I stay strong, and making me laugh while I work; Chris Fogarty for providing building details and his wife, Renee, for the s'mores; Bud and Darlene for the mango honey, which was absolutely the best I've ever tasted; Marius Venter for the loan of the Cuban Coffee Queen poem; Stephanie Jones and Tersi Bendiburg for epigraph suggestions; Rusty Hodgdon for a tour of the Hemingway Home and for leading the Key West Writers Guild—to my knowledge, he has never written any copycat Hemingway stories; Jane Newhagen for help with the cemetery; Nancy Klingener for her work at NPR in Key West; and Dana and Joe Sebek for their friendship and support—they are lovely people and true Parrot Heads. Analise Smith from Key West Food Tours is also a real person—and her tours are a wonderful way to get a taste of the island. Thanks to her for insider Key West history, tastes of delicious food and rum, and for persuading her Aunt Estela to loan me the flan recipe. Thanks to my amazing friends at Jungle Red Writers, who are always there to brainstorm an idea, to celebrate, or to commiserate: Hallie Ephron, Hank Phillippi Ryan, Rhys Bowen, Deborah Crombie, Julia Spencer-Fleming, Jenn McKinlay, Ingrid Thoft. Love you guys!

Thank you to my fabulous agent, Paige Wheeler, who brought this series to Crooked Lane Books and persuaded them to continue it. And more thanks to the folks at Crooked Lane, including Matt Martz, Jenny Chen, Ashley Di Dio, and Sarah Poppe, who shepherded the book to life. Special thanks also to

Acknowledgments

their excellent independent editor, Jen Donovan, and the best cover artists ever, the team of Griesbach and Martucci.

The real Bill Averyt took me on multiple tours of the Little White House, drew a map of the home's layout, and generated plot ideas—I'm so grateful for his friendship! The real Bob Wolz is the keeper of the Truman Little White House, which is not in financial trouble and in no danger of being usurped by a developer, shady or otherwise. Bob is devoted to this old house and its history and takes exquisite care of it. You must put this on your Key West bucket list—go for a tour. Maybe you'll get lucky and score Bill as your guide.

While I use some names of real people who live in Key West, please remember that the characters are fictional, so the real people should not be held responsible for their actions or thoughts on these pages. I have the greatest admiration and respect for our city commissioners, employees, and police department. Their love for our town is evident always, but was especially clear in the days and weeks after Hurricane Irma blew through. They would never behave like the people in this book!

I am endlessly grateful to Ang Pompano and Chris Falcone, who read every word carefully—often more than once. Chris was also the creator of the faux-Hemingway title "A Farewell to Harm." And I'm so lucky to have John, the best life partner ever. And to my readers, my deepest gratitude and affection. Thank you for sharing my love of this magical island and believing in my characters.

Lucy Burdette
December 2017